Unraveling Intent

Luna Hope

Published by Luna Hope, 2024.

This is a work of fiction. Similarities to real people, places, or events are entirely coincidental.

UNRAVELING INTENT

First edition. October 28, 2024.

Copyright © 2024 Luna Hope.

ISBN: 979-8227377975

Written by Luna Hope.

Chapter 1: A Stormy Encounter

The inn's heavy oak door groaned as I pushed it open, a gust of wind howling at my back like a discontented spirit, eager to escape the tempest outside. Rain lashed against the windows, turning the world into a watercolor painting smeared with gray. I stepped over the threshold, letting the warmth of the hearth draw me in like a moth to a flame, my coat dripping with the storm's rage. The crackle of the fire mingled with the soft murmur of conversation, creating a cocoon of comfort that felt worlds away from the chaos I had left behind.

Taking a deep breath, I surveyed the room, the flickering candlelight casting playful shadows across the wooden beams overhead. This place was a treasure trove of character—stone walls adorned with vintage photographs, a bar stocked with an assortment of spirits that seemed to beckon. It felt like a refuge, a cocoon from the relentless demands of the world outside, and for a moment, I let the tension in my shoulders ease. But that serenity shattered the instant my eyes locked onto his.

He sat at a small table near the fire, the flames reflecting in the striking blue of his eyes. His dark hair, tousled and damp from the rain, framed a face that was chiseled and brooding, as if he had stepped out of a novel. My heart skipped a beat, caught in a sudden wave of irritation and unexpected attraction. What was it about him that made my pulse quicken? Perhaps it was the way he appeared so perfectly at ease amid the chaos, his presence both magnetic and intimidating.

With an imperceptible tilt of his head, he regarded me, an amused smirk tugging at the corners of his lips. I felt an unwelcome heat rise to my cheeks, a sensation that was far too familiar lately. A cocktail of annoyance and intrigue brewed within me, as if I had just bitten into a lemon meringue pie, all sweet promises overshadowed by a tart aftertaste. I returned my gaze to the bar, determined not to let him ruffle my composure. After all, I had come here to escape—not to get entangled in the complexities of romantic tension.

Yet the tension crackled between us, thick enough to cut with a knife. I could feel the weight of his gaze, a tangible force that pulled at my resolve. I turned to the bartender, a wiry man with a weathered face who seemed to know everyone by name. "What do you recommend?" I asked, feigning disinterest while sneaking glances at my enigmatic counterpart.

"Depends on what you're looking for, love," he replied with a cheeky grin, wiping down the bar with a stained cloth. "You want something to warm your bones or something to help you forget?"

"Let's go with warm," I decided, glancing back at the stranger just in time to catch him rolling his eyes, as if he could read my thoughts. "A hot toddy, please."

As the bartender busied himself, I felt the weight of the stranger's stare intensify. It was as if he was peeling back the layers of my facade, seeing right through the carefully constructed walls I had built. Frustration bubbled up inside me, fighting against the burgeoning curiosity that swirled like autumn leaves caught in a gust of wind.

"Are you always this grumpy when it rains?" His voice cut through the haze of my thoughts, rich and smooth, laced with a playful challenge.

"Grumpy?" I echoed, my eyebrows arching in disbelief. "I prefer to think of it as... pragmatic."

"Pragmatic?" He chuckled, the sound low and rich. "Is that what you call it when you glare at the world as if it owes you something?"

I turned to him fully, narrowing my eyes, an involuntary smile threatening to betray my irritation. "And what do you call it when you sit there looking like you've just won a staring contest with the sun? What's your secret, sunshine?"

"Ah, so you noticed," he said, a hint of mischief dancing in his eyes. "It's all in the technique. You just have to squint a little, let the light reflect off your charm."

"Is that how you win over all the innocent bystanders? With your dazzling charm?" I shot back, my heart racing at the unexpected banter. The room buzzed with life around us, but in that moment, it felt as if we were the only two people in existence.

He leaned back, an easy confidence radiating from him. "You have no idea how effective it is. But it seems you're immune."

"Consider it a blessing," I replied, unable to suppress a smirk. "Some of us prefer to think for ourselves."

"Touché." He nodded, the corners of his mouth lifting in appreciation. "But isn't it exhausting? Wading through life with your guard up?"

There was something in his gaze, a flicker of understanding that sent a shiver down my spine. My defenses rose instinctively, as if he were a cat poised to pounce on a mouse that had wandered too close. "I can assure you, I'm perfectly capable of handling myself," I said, though my voice wavered slightly.

"Then why come to a place like this, stranded in a storm, if you didn't want a little excitement?" His eyes sparkled with mischief, the firelight dancing across his features, making him appear almost ethereal.

"Excitement? I came for solitude," I replied, struggling to keep my composure. The storm outside raged, but it was the storm brewing between us that truly unsettled me.

"Solitude is overrated," he countered, a playful glint in his eye. "Besides, I don't believe for a moment that you could stand the silence. Not with that fire in your spirit."

There was something unsettlingly disarming about him. With every word, I felt the layers of my carefully curated shell begin to crack, revealing a vulnerability I had fought so hard to conceal. I searched for something to say, but the right words eluded me, slipping through my fingers like grains of sand.

As the bartender slid my hot toddy across the bar, I wrapped my fingers around the warm mug, seeking solace in its heat. Perhaps solitude wasn't what I truly desired; perhaps, in the heart of this storm, what I sought was connection, even if it came wrapped in irritation and unexpected attraction.

The heat of the mug seeped into my palms, a welcome contrast to the chill still clinging to my skin. As I took a cautious sip of the hot toddy, the warmth cascaded down my throat, easing the tightness in my chest, if only for a moment. I set the mug down and turned my full attention to the enigmatic stranger across the bar. His presence filled the space around him, a magnetic pull that made it impossible to ignore him for long.

"Tell me," he said, his voice smooth like the whiskey he was undoubtedly nursing, "are you always this standoffish, or am I just lucky to catch you on a particularly prickly day?"

"Prickly?" I raised an eyebrow, savoring the challenge in his tone. "I'd call it cautious. There's a difference."

"Cautious is what you say when you're trying to be polite about being closed off." He leaned in slightly, an air of playful defiance lighting up his eyes. "It's okay, really. Some people have trouble with connection. It's a common ailment in this digital age."

"Ailment?" I scoffed, swishing the warm liquid in my mug as if it could somehow fortify my argument. "How dramatic of you. I prefer to think of it as a protective measure. Connections lead to complications."

"Ah, so you've been burned before," he said, his tone shifting to something softer, almost empathetic. "Can't say I blame you. Trust is a fragile thing, easily shattered."

I didn't like where this conversation was heading. "Why are you so interested in my trust issues? Do you have a degree in psychology or something?"

"Not quite," he chuckled, a low, throaty sound that sent an involuntary shiver down my spine. "But I've learned a thing or two about human nature. And right now, you're practically a locked vault, but I'm a sucker for a challenge."

"Or perhaps you're just bored," I shot back, a defensive wall creeping back into place. "I can't imagine how difficult it must be to find something stimulating in a place like this."

"Touché again," he said, raising his glass in mock salute. "But you seem like the kind of person who has an interesting story to tell. I'm merely trying to unlock it."

There it was again, that disarming candor that made me want to spill my secrets like confetti, yet I couldn't shake the sensation that revealing too much would open the floodgates to even more vulnerability. The last thing I wanted was to divulge the burdens I carried, especially to a stranger with an unnervingly charming demeanor.

As if sensing my hesitance, he leaned back, a flicker of understanding flashing across his face. "Okay, fair enough. Let's talk about something else then. You're not from around here, are you?"

"No, just passing through." The truth slipped out before I could think better of it. I was in town for a business meeting that had been postponed due to the storm, but that felt too mundane to share. "Just needed a break from... life."

"Ah, the age-old desire to escape the grind. I can relate." He glanced outside at the torrential downpour, his expression softening as he added, "The weather doesn't exactly scream vacation, though."

"No, it really doesn't. But sometimes, a little chaos can provide clarity." I found myself drawn into his gaze, the storm outside becoming a mere backdrop to our conversation. There was something refreshing about his candor, as if I could trust him to hold my thoughts without judgment, even if just for a moment.

"Clarity is overrated," he said, smirking. "Most of the time, it just leads to the realization that you're stuck in a situation you've created for yourself."

"That's rather cynical of you," I replied, feigning offense while allowing myself a smile. "What happened to the idealistic views of life's possibilities?"

"They got rained out, like your vacation plans." He grinned, the mischief in his eyes making my heart race against my better judgment.

"So you're saying I should just embrace the chaos?" I challenged, swiping a strand of hair behind my ear as I leaned in slightly, curiosity bubbling beneath the surface.

"Why not?" He shrugged, an easy confidence radiating from him. "I mean, look at us. We're both here, strangers thrown together by a storm, having what could possibly be the most interesting conversation of our lives."

I couldn't deny the thrill coursing through me. There was a spark of connection, an electric energy I hadn't felt in ages. But lurking beneath that excitement was an unease, a reminder of the walls I had built over the years, brick by painstaking brick. "And what if I don't want to be interesting? What if I prefer my life to be ordinary?"

"Ordinary can be delightful, I suppose," he mused, his gaze thoughtful. "But I suspect you're anything but ordinary. There's a fire in you waiting to ignite."

"Careful," I warned, feigning a serious demeanor. "If you keep pushing, I might just reveal my secret plan for world domination."

"Now that sounds intriguing!" His laughter rang through the inn, drawing the attention of a few nearby patrons. "So what's the first step? I assume it involves a lot of hot toddies and strategic planning?"

"Exactly. Step one: get everyone pleasantly intoxicated. Step two: unveil my manifesto." I couldn't help but chuckle, the playful banter making the air around us feel lighter.

"Sounds like a foolproof plan. I'd love to be a part of it." His tone shifted, an earnestness creeping in that sent a flurry of emotions tumbling through me.

"What's your angle, then?" I quipped, although my heart raced at the thought of him becoming a partner in this ridiculous scheme. "Are you looking for power? Wealth? An empire built on the finest hot beverages?"

"Honestly? I'm just looking for a reason to stick around." The earnestness in his voice caught me off guard, my breath hitching at the vulnerability of his admission. "I've been doing the whole heir-to-the-throne thing for too long, and it's just... exhausting. I'd trade it all for a moment of genuine connection."

His words hung in the air like a delicate thread, weaving our fates together in an unexpected tapestry. I was struck by the honesty, the quiet desperation that lay beneath his bravado. "And what do you think this is? A genuine connection?"

"Maybe." He shrugged, his casual demeanor belying the intensity of the moment. "Maybe it's the storm talking, or the hot toddy, but I feel like we're kindred spirits. Two people seeking refuge from their own storms."

"Or two people foolishly ignoring the real world," I countered, but my voice lacked conviction. The truth was, I didn't want to ignore this moment. I didn't want to let it slip away like so many had before.

"Perhaps," he agreed, the corner of his mouth curving upward as if he knew exactly what I was thinking. "But the real question is, are you brave enough to step out into the chaos with me? After all, nothing worth having ever came from playing it safe."

His challenge hung in the air, tantalizing and terrifying all at once. As I gazed into those mesmerizing blue eyes, I felt the urge to leap, to abandon the careful constraints of my life for something—anything—more exhilarating. The storm outside raged on, but within the walls of this quaint inn, a different kind of tempest brewed, one filled with laughter, potential, and the uncharted territory of human connection.

The fire crackled, punctuating the tension that hung between us like an uninvited guest, lingering in the air with an undeniable weight. I took another sip of my hot toddy, relishing the warmth spreading through my chest. It was a bold move to let my guard down, even slightly, and I couldn't shake the feeling that I was treading on dangerous ground.

"Tell me," he began, his voice smooth and inviting, "what kind of chaos are you running from? A disgruntled ex? A botched business deal? Or maybe just the horror of having to socialize during a storm?"

I glanced away, pretending to inspect the vintage wallpaper, its muted floral pattern somewhat comforting in its familiarity. "It's just... life, I suppose. The usual family drama, work nonsense, and all that jazz. But it's not nearly as intriguing as your reasons for being here." I shot him a playful smile, hoping to deflect the conversation back onto him.

He chuckled, a low rumble that sent shivers through me. "Fair enough. But you'd be surprised—sometimes, the most mundane dramas can be the most fascinating."

"Sure, if you're a bored heir looking for amusement." I couldn't resist, my sarcasm sliding out like a well-rehearsed line. "But for the rest of us, mundane is a real thing. It's the fine print of life, the stuff that keeps us up at night."

"Is it really so bad?" He leaned closer, the warm scent of cedar and rain mingling with the spiced aroma of my drink. "I mean, look at where we are. A cozy inn, a storm raging outside, two strangers sharing drinks. It's practically a scene from a rom-com."

"Rom-com?" I echoed, my laughter bubbling up before I could hold it back. "Let's not kid ourselves. This is more like a dramatic thriller, with both our families poised to make a dramatic entrance any moment now."

"Ah, but that's where the plot thickens," he replied, his eyes glinting with mischief. "What if, instead of a family feud, we concoct a scandalous romance that leaves them all gasping? It could be the most entertaining story of the season."

"Now that sounds like a plan." I feigned serious contemplation, resting my chin on my hand. "But then we'd have to keep up appearances, maybe even go so far as to hold hands in public. That's a whole lot of pressure."

"Pressure builds character," he shot back, a teasing smile dancing on his lips. "Or, you know, it just makes you really good at hiding your true self."

"Or creates a breeding ground for resentment," I countered, enjoying the back-and-forth as the room filled with the buzz of other patrons, their conversations blending into a warm hum around us. "What's your angle, really? Are you just looking for a fun story to tell your friends?"

He paused, his expression growing serious. "I'm just looking for something real. This life, the expectations—it can be suffocating. Sometimes, you want to be anyone but yourself, if only for a moment."

His words hung in the air, and for a brief second, the lighthearted banter faded, revealing a raw truth that resonated deeply within me. "And you think I'm the answer to that? A stranger with my own set of baggage?"

"Maybe not the answer, but definitely part of the adventure." He leaned back, the confident smirk returning to his face. "What if we decided to be spontaneous? Just for tonight?"

Spontaneous? The word rolled around in my mind, tinged with excitement and trepidation. A part of me wanted to say yes, to step into the storm of uncertainty with him, while another part warned me to hold back. Life had taught me to tread carefully, to consider every move before making it.

But what if tonight was different? What if this moment, this strange connection we shared, could be the spark I needed to ignite a change in my life? Before I could overthink it, I found myself nodding. "Fine. I'm in. What do you have in mind?"

His grin widened, revealing a dimple I hadn't noticed before, a charming imperfection that made my heart race. "Let's explore this inn. They say it's haunted."

"Haunted?" I raised an eyebrow, half-amused and half-convinced he was pulling my leg. "Please tell me you're joking."

"Not at all." He gestured toward the dimly lit hallway leading deeper into the inn. "There are whispers of ghostly residents who have unfinished business. Think of it as our very own spooky adventure."

"Great. Nothing like a little ghost hunting to lighten the mood," I retorted, my pulse quickening at the idea. A strange thrill shot through me at the thought of roaming the inn with him, just the two of us, laughing at the absurdity of it all. "Lead the way, brave ghost hunter."

With a flourish, he stood and extended a hand toward me, his eyes sparkling with delight. I hesitated for just a heartbeat before slipping my hand into his. His grip was warm and steady, anchoring me in a way that felt oddly comforting, even amidst the storm raging outside.

We wandered through the dimly lit corridors, the floorboards creaking under our weight as if the inn itself was awakening to our presence. "I wonder if the ghosts are friendly," I mused, looking around with mock seriousness. "Or if they're the type to demand ransom for their secrets."

"Let's hope they don't ask for too much. I'm not exactly loaded," he replied, laughter lacing his words. "But if they did, I suppose I could offer them the first chapters of my terrible novel."

"Now that sounds like a fate worse than death," I said, feigning horror. "I'd rather take my chances with the ghosts."

We rounded a corner and stepped into a small sitting room, decorated with mismatched furniture that seemed to tell its own stories. Dust motes danced in the flickering light, and the air felt thick with history. I glanced back at him, half-expecting him to make a ghostly noise, but instead, he simply studied the room with a thoughtful expression.

"What do you think? Should we take a seat and invite our ethereal friends to join?" he asked, his tone light, but there was a seriousness in his gaze that made my heart flutter.

"Why not?" I replied, a sense of adventure welling up inside me. "After all, I'm here to embrace the chaos, remember?"

We settled onto a faded couch, the fabric worn but oddly cozy. The fire crackled faintly from the other room, a comforting backdrop to our daring escapade. I leaned back, glancing at him sideways, the warmth of the moment washing over me like a soft blanket.

"Tell me about your terrible novel," I urged, eager to keep the conversation flowing, to draw him out.

"Well," he began, his eyes sparkling with mischief, "it's a story about two people who meet in a storm and get swept away into a whirlwind of chaos."

I laughed, the sound bright and genuine. "How original. I'm sure that plot hasn't been used before."

"Right?" He grinned, and for a moment, it felt as if we were weaving our own narrative, one filled with laughter and intrigue. "But I think the twist is that they realize they've been rivals their entire lives—"

Before he could finish, the lights flickered ominously, plunging us into darkness for a heartbeat before the emergency lights kicked on, casting eerie shadows across the room. My heart raced, the sudden change heightening my senses. "Okay, that's not creepy at all," I said, attempting to inject levity into the tension.

"Just a little atmospheric effect," he quipped, though his smile faltered as he scanned the room, his gaze darting toward the door.

The distant sound of thunder rumbled through the walls, echoing the unease building between us. I leaned forward, straining to hear the whispers of the storm outside, suddenly feeling as if the walls were closing in. "Do you hear that?"

"What?" He paused, his expression shifting from playful to serious.

"There's something... else," I whispered, barely able to make sense of the sudden chill that danced along my spine.

Before I could finish my thought, the heavy wooden door creaked open with a sudden gust, revealing an inky darkness beyond. The wind howled, sounding almost like a wailing ghost, and I instinctively shifted closer to him.

"Okay, that's definitely creepy," he murmured, his eyes wide with a mix of excitement and concern. "Maybe we should—"

Suddenly, the lights flickered again, plunging us into darkness, and a shadow swept through the doorway. It moved so quickly, I could barely make it out, but I felt an icy chill seep into the air around us.

"Did you see that?" I gasped, my heart pounding in my chest.

"Yeah," he said, his voice low, barely above a whisper. "We should probably—"

But before he could finish, the shadow lunged forward, and the last flicker of light illuminated a familiar face. My breath caught in my throat as I recognized him—a face I had hoped to never see again.

Chapter 2: Rivals in the Rain

The incessant rain drummed against the inn's windows like a disapproving audience, a cacophony of nature that felt oddly fitting for the mood swirling within these four walls. I stood at the lobby's weathered counter, my fingers tracing the rough grain of the wood, grounding myself as the air crackled with tension. The scent of damp earth wafted through the open window, mingling with the musty aroma of old books that lined the shelves, remnants of a bygone era when this place had seen more laughter than storms. Now, however, it felt like a battlefield, and my opponent stood just a few paces away.

"Did you really think that selling off your family's estate was a good idea?" he challenged, his voice smooth yet sharp enough to cut through the heavy atmosphere. Declan Thompson, with his tousled hair and an all-too-sure smirk, leaned against the wall as if he owned the very air I breathed. I bristled, my heart racing, though not entirely from anger. It was infuriatingly clear that he reveled in this tête-à-tête, and I had to remind myself that his attempts to undermine my family's legacy were personal, not just business.

"Better to sell it than watch it rot," I shot back, crossing my arms as if that could shield me from his penetrating gaze. "Besides, unlike you, I have real plans for the future." The storm outside intensified, sending sheets of rain tumbling against the glass, a reminder that we were both stuck here together, like two raindrops caught in a relentless downpour, destined to collide.

He chuckled, a low, rolling sound that made my skin prickle. "Plans? Or fantasies? You can't just will your family's reputation back into existence with wishful thinking, Clara." His green eyes sparkled with a mix of challenge and mischief, and I wondered for a fleeting moment if I could bring myself to like him—if I could overlook the barbs he flung my way. But those thoughts evaporated the moment

I recalled the stakes: our families had been rivals for generations, the history stained with jealousy and bitterness.

"I'm doing the best I can," I said, my voice rising, drowning in the sound of thunder rumbling overhead. "Not that you'd know what that means." I didn't mean to poke the bear, but there was something thrilling about our exchanges, like the moment before lightning struck, charged with anticipation.

He took a step closer, his presence overwhelming in the dim light. "And what exactly are you doing, Clara? Rebranding your family's failures as a 'refreshing new perspective'? Because that's quite the reimagining you've got going on there."

"Better than living off your parents' name," I shot back, my heart racing. The competitive spark ignited more than just anger; it lit a fire within me that I could not afford to extinguish. I was determined to prove that the Millers still had merit, that we could rise from the ashes of our tarnished legacy while the Thompsons continued their reign of arrogance.

A gust of wind howled outside, rattling the windows as I turned my back to him, desperately trying to compose myself. I could feel his gaze lingering on me, and it ignited an uninvited warmth in my cheeks. Shaking my head, I focused on the clutter of paperwork strewn across the counter. The dull ache of determination pushed me forward; my family's survival depended on these deals. The storm outside mirrored the tumult in my heart, a chaotic dance of conflict and unresolved tension.

Hours slipped by in a blur of half-hearted business calls and the persistent downpour that kept us both inside the inn. Declan remained an unwelcome shadow, drifting through the lobby, seemingly at ease while I fumbled through my notes and schematics. His laughter occasionally broke through my concentration, a mocking soundtrack to my struggles. Each chuckle felt like a dagger, but I couldn't let him see the effect he had on me. I was here to reclaim my family's honor, not to become another pawn in his game.

Eventually, the storm unleashed its fury, the wind howling like a banshee, creating a deafening backdrop. I sighed, leaning against the wall, grappling with the impending sense of doom that settled in my stomach. The power flickered momentarily, the room momentarily plunged into darkness before the generator kicked in, casting a warm glow that illuminated Declan's features, sharp and striking against the shadows.

"Looks like we're in for the long haul," he said, his voice low and oddly sincere. "You know, Clara, there's a fine line between stubbornness and resilience. You might want to rethink your strategy."

The suggestion caught me off guard, and for a moment, I wondered if he was genuinely trying to help—or if this was yet another layer to his relentless pursuit to undermine me. "And what would you know about strategy?" I challenged, my defenses still bristling. "You've made a career out of smirking and stepping on others' toes."

He stepped forward, the distance between us shrinking, a tension crackling like electricity in the air. "And you've made a career out of playing the martyr. If you want to win, you need to stop letting your emotions cloud your judgment."

The boldness of his words struck me harder than the thunder outside, and I opened my mouth to retort, but found myself momentarily speechless. There was a sincerity in his gaze that made me question everything I thought I knew about him. The inn felt smaller, our differences suddenly insignificant in the face of the storm outside.

For the first time, I considered that perhaps he wasn't just a rival. Perhaps he was a mirror, reflecting my own doubts and insecurities, and maybe, just maybe, he was right. As the rain continued to pour, the boundaries between us seemed to blur, the relentless bickering shifting into something deeper, something that could redefine our legacies forever.

The rain lashed against the windows with renewed vigor, a relentless symphony that provided the perfect backdrop for our escalating conflict. I found myself trapped in this charming, old inn, with its creaking wooden beams and a faint smell of mildew that seemed to cling to everything, including the very air I breathed. It was supposed to be a sanctuary, but with Declan loitering nearby, it felt more like a prison. I busied myself at the small table in the corner, scattered with blueprints and contract proposals, as if somehow burying myself in paperwork would shield me from his piercing gaze.

"Do you always work in solitude, or is today a special occasion?" Declan leaned against the doorframe, arms crossed, that infuriating smirk plastered across his face. The way the light caught his tousled hair made him look almost boyish, but there was nothing innocent about him. I shot him a glare, the type that could freeze a thousand suns.

"Some of us prefer to focus rather than indulge in idle banter," I replied, my tone sharper than I intended. The truth was, I craved his presence, yet it irked me that I felt that way. He had this knack for turning mundane moments into something electric, and it both thrilled and frustrated me.

"Interesting choice of words," he said, pushing off the door and taking a step closer. "But tell me, how's that focusing working out for you? From what I hear, your family's financial situation is as stormy as the weather outside." His words dripped with honeyed sarcasm, designed to provoke.

I forced myself to look back at the scattered papers, willing my racing heart to calm. "It's a work in progress. Some people actually believe in hard work and resilience," I muttered, not looking up.

It was hard to concentrate when the weight of his gaze felt like a physical force, pinning me in place.

"Is that what you call it? Because it looks a lot like wishful thinking from here." He chuckled, and I couldn't decide whether I wanted to laugh with him or throw something heavy at his head.

I lifted my chin, refusing to show any weakness. "Well, if you're so confident in your own success, why don't you stop lurking around and actually work on your own deals? Or are you just here to sabotage mine?"

"Sabotage? No, no. I'm merely an interested observer." His voice was smooth, almost playful, as if we were playing a game of chess and he had just moved his knight into a vulnerable position. "Besides, I find your attempts at negotiation utterly fascinating."

I finally met his gaze, and for a moment, the world narrowed down to just us two, surrounded by the muffled sounds of the storm. "You don't know anything about my deals," I snapped, though doubt crept in. Perhaps he did know more than I wanted to admit. "You're just trying to get under my skin."

He tilted his head slightly, a glimmer of genuine curiosity in his eyes. "And what if I am? You've got to admit, it's entertaining watching you pretend you're not on the brink of disaster."

As he spoke, the lightning outside illuminated his features, casting dramatic shadows across the room. I hated how effortlessly he could pull me into his orbit, making me feel like I was floating in some chaotic storm rather than standing my ground. "You think this is funny?" I countered, a mix of irritation and intrigue bubbling within me.

"Only when you respond like that," he said, crossing his arms with a feigned air of innocence. "You could take a lesson from the storm outside. It doesn't hide; it embraces its power, unapologetic."

"That's rich coming from someone who hides behind sarcasm," I shot back, but there was a part of me that wondered if I could take his advice to heart. Could I be as fierce and unapologetic as the rain pounding against the roof? The thought was both intoxicating and terrifying.

Our repartee was interrupted by a loud crash of thunder, reverberating through the inn like the sound of an angry beast. I jumped slightly, the noise echoing in my chest. "Perhaps we should find a safer topic," I suggested, attempting to steer the conversation away from the awkward edges it had just teetered on.

"Safer? Where's the fun in that?" he said, a mischievous glint in his eye. "You know, I hear that arguing can be a sign of deeper feelings. What if beneath all this rivalry, there's something more... compelling?"

My breath caught at the implication, and I had to blink away the sudden surge of heat that rose to my cheeks. "You've got it all wrong," I managed to retort, but my voice lacked conviction. "This is business, nothing more."

"Is it?" His tone was teasing, yet his eyes held a glimmer of seriousness. "It could be something else entirely if you'd just admit it."

"You're insufferable," I huffed, trying to mask the disconcerting effect he had on me. Yet, there was a flicker of truth in his words that I couldn't shake. "Why do you always have to twist everything? Can't you just take a conversation at face value?"

"Where's the fun in that?" he repeated, and this time, his laughter echoed in the air, brightening the gloom that had settled in the room.

As the rain continued to pour, I felt the walls of the inn close in, creating a world that was just ours. The noise of the storm faded into the background, leaving only the sound of our banter. It was intoxicating, and despite my best efforts to resist it, I found myself leaning into the dialogue, the challenge of it.

"Fine," I said, folding my arms defiantly. "If you want to play this game, let's see who can make the better deal first. Winner gets to gloat."

His eyes sparkled with delight, as if I had just handed him the most glorious prize. "You're on, Clara. But prepare yourself; I don't intend to lose."

And just like that, the competitive spark ignited again, racing through my veins as the storm outside raged on, a fitting companion to the brewing tempest between us. With each exchanged word, we both delved deeper into the intricacies of our rivalry, a duality that thrummed with potential, leaving me wondering if we might yet find common ground in this relentless rain.

The storm outside raged on, relentless and unforgiving, as though nature itself had decided to join our battle of wills. With each clash of thunder, I could feel the air crackle with energy, reflecting the tension that hung between Declan and me like a taut string, ready to snap. I sat at a small table near the inn's fireplace, the flickering flames casting dancing shadows on the wall, while I fiddled with my laptop, attempting to refocus on my pitch. Yet, the very presence of Declan, now seated at the bar nursing a cup of coffee, proved to be a significant distraction.

"You look like you're about to conquer the world," he called over, a mocking edge to his tone. "Or at least the coffee machine."

I glanced up, arching an eyebrow. "Conquering the coffee machine seems far more likely with your dubious skills in play."

"Oh, please. If I wanted to make coffee, I could brew a pot that would knock your socks off," he retorted, a grin spreading across his face that made my insides flip.

"Is that a challenge?" I shot back, unable to resist the bait. "Maybe your talents extend only to charmingly poor behavior."

"Charmingly poor? That's quite a compliment coming from you." His eyes sparkled, and in that moment, the competitive edge that had driven us both felt strangely inviting.

I tried to shake off the warmth creeping into my cheeks. "Do you always have to be so insufferable? Can't you just let me work in peace?"

"I thrive on chaos, Clara. You should know that by now." He leaned back, folding his arms behind his head as if the world were his oyster, and for a moment, I envied his nonchalance.

"Maybe that's your problem," I replied, biting back a smile. "You confuse chaos with charm. There's a fine line between the two."

"Ah, but that's where you're mistaken. Chaos can be very charming, especially when it's used strategically." He glanced at my screen, the flickering light illuminating his features. "Speaking of strategy, how's the pitch coming along?"

"None of your business," I snapped, quickly closing my laptop, as if hiding my work from him could somehow safeguard my plans.

"Suit yourself, but you might want to keep an eye on that deadline," he said, his voice smooth like honey, dripping with a confidence that made me want to throw my coffee at him. "Or is that part of your grand strategy?"

The playful jabs turned into something more meaningful, a peculiar game of chicken where neither of us wanted to blink first. The tension in the air felt almost palpable, thickening as the wind howled outside. I looked out the window, watching the rain streak down like liquid glass, but my thoughts were far from the storm.

"What's it like?" I blurted, surprising even myself with the question.

"What's what like?" He leaned forward, intrigued.

"Living up to the Thompson name. Do you feel like you're constantly competing against a ghost?"

His expression shifted, amusement fading slightly as he considered my words. "You think it's easy, being the heir to a legacy that feels like a straitjacket? Every decision comes with a shadow, Clara."

"I wouldn't know. I'm just trying to keep mine from crumbling," I admitted, my tone softer. The admission hung in the air, charged with a vulnerability that felt foreign.

"Maybe we're not so different, you and I," he replied, his voice low and earnest. "Both of us shackled to the past, trying to carve out a future."

"Then why can't you stop being such a jerk about it?" I shot back, though the question felt more like a challenge than an accusation.

"Because being a jerk is far more fun than being boring." His grin returned, and I found myself unable to resist the pull of laughter bubbling up, despite the seriousness of the moment.

Just then, the lights flickered again, plunging us momentarily into darkness before the generator kicked in, casting a warm glow over our faces. I looked around, feeling a strange camaraderie in this dimly lit room, a shared moment amidst the chaos.

"You know," I said, allowing the walls to come down just a fraction, "if you weren't so infuriating, I might even consider you a worthy opponent."

"Only a worthy opponent?" he teased, leaning closer. "I was hoping for something more like a partner in crime."

"Only in your dreams," I replied, trying to keep the banter light while my heart raced at the implications of his words. I glanced at the window again, where rain lashed against the glass like an angry lover.

The atmosphere shifted, the air between us thickening with unspoken words. Just as I was about to respond, a loud crash echoed from outside, shaking the inn's very foundation. We both jumped to our feet, the playful banter replaced by a sudden urgency.

"What was that?" I asked, my pulse quickening.

"Maybe a tree fell?" Declan suggested, moving toward the door. "We should check."

"Are you out of your mind? It's a storm out there!" I protested, grabbing his arm to stop him. His warmth seeped through my fingers, and a spark of electricity coursed between us, catching me off guard.

"Better to know what we're up against than to sit here waiting for it to come crashing in," he argued, his voice steady despite the rising storm.

With my heart racing, I hesitated for a moment. I couldn't let fear dictate my actions. "Fine, let's go see what kind of disaster you've invited into our lives," I said, steeling myself as I followed him out into the storm.

The inn's door creaked open, revealing a world transformed by the tempest. Rain battered my skin, drenching my clothes in seconds as we stepped outside. The wind howled, sending chills down my spine, but I followed Declan into the fray.

The scene was chaotic. Trees swayed dangerously, and debris littered the ground like remnants of a battle. "Over here!" Declan shouted, pointing toward a fallen branch that had landed perilously close to a nearby car.

My eyes widened as I approached, the reality of the situation dawning on me. "This is bad," I muttered, glancing back at him. "We need to call someone."

But before I could reach for my phone, a low rumble of thunder sounded, closer this time, vibrating through the ground beneath us. "Look!" Declan shouted, and I turned just in time to see another tree, larger and more menacing, beginning to topple.

"Declan!" I screamed, adrenaline surging as I grabbed his arm and yanked him back, pulling him away from the impending disaster.

The tree crashed down with a deafening roar, splintering and cracking as it hit the ground mere feet from where we stood.

Panting, I glanced up at him, heart racing. The moment hung heavy between us, charged with the closeness of our bodies and the realization of how fragile life was. Just as we both took a breath, ready to process what had just happened, a figure emerged from the shadows, drenched and panting, eyes wide with urgency.

"Help!" the stranger called, stumbling toward us, and the sense of calm we'd shared shattered like glass, leaving us standing at the edge of an unexpected storm, unprepared for what would come next.

Chapter 3: Secrets in the Shadows

The night air wrapped around me like a velvet cloak, thick with the scent of rain-soaked earth and the distant, tantalizing aroma of woodsmoke. I had been restless, the stillness in the house amplifying the tension thrumming through my veins. The flickering candlelight danced against the walls, casting shadows that seemed to whisper secrets of their own. Outside, the storm brewed, the wind howling as if it were a herald announcing the chaos soon to come.

It was a mere coincidence that led me to my window, drawn by the crack of lightning that momentarily illuminated the darkness. As I peered into the inky blackness, my eyes caught sight of a figure moving stealthily across the yard. It was Elias, the enigmatic owner of Ardent Enterprises, known as much for his striking blue eyes as for the rumors that clung to him like ivy. He had become a fixture in my thoughts, an intriguing puzzle that defied easy comprehension. What was he doing here, at this hour, in the storm? The questions buzzed in my mind like bees in a wildflower meadow, relentless and eager for answers.

My heart quickened as I watched him pause, glancing around as if he were checking for unseen observers. There was something almost feral in the way he moved, a predator alert to the slightest sound. I couldn't help but admire the way he commanded the shadows, his presence both alluring and unnerving. Against my better judgment, I slipped on my coat and stepped out into the cool embrace of the night, drawn to him like a moth to a flame.

The wind whipped around me, and raindrops began to patter softly on the leaves overhead. As I approached, I noticed the faint glow of a lantern flickering in the distance. It flickered like a heart that had yet to learn to beat steadily, and for a moment, I hesitated. But the pull of curiosity was stronger than my apprehension, urging me forward.

"Elias?" I called, my voice breaking the fragile silence. The sound felt foreign in the weighty air, as if the world itself held its breath.

He turned sharply, the lantern casting a golden halo around his figure. "What are you doing out here?" His voice was low, edged with surprise and something darker that sent a shiver down my spine.

"Wondering what secrets you're hiding," I replied, my tone flippant, masking the tension building within me. I couldn't help but admire his rugged appearance, the way the rain slicked his hair back from his forehead, accentuating the sharp lines of his jaw.

He stepped closer, the lantern swinging slightly, creating a dance of light and shadow. "This isn't a place for you," he said, his gaze intense, almost possessive.

"Neither is it for you, lurking like a ghost in the night," I shot back, my pulse quickening.

The tension hung between us like a taut string, ready to snap. But before he could respond, the lights flickered and then—darkness. An unsettling silence enveloped us, punctuated only by the sound of the rain pouring down, its rhythm like a heartbeat. The storm intensified, creating a cacophony that drowned out the world outside.

My heart pounded in the silence, the darkness suddenly overwhelming. I felt lost in the inky void, with only the sound of Elias's breathing to anchor me. It was then that I heard something else, a muffled conversation drifting through the air.

"...not just competition anymore. It's more than that," a voice said, the words edged with a sharpness that made my stomach drop.

Curiosity tugged at me, and I leaned in closer, hoping to catch more of the clandestine exchange. "You have to make it disappear. If anyone finds out, it will destroy everything," came another voice, laced with panic.

A chill slithered down my spine as I strained to hear more. What were they discussing? It felt as if I had stumbled into the middle of a treacherous game, one I wasn't prepared to play. My mind raced through the implications, connecting the dots between Elias's family and the shadows swirling around my own.

I turned to Elias, my voice barely above a whisper, "What's going on?"

He seemed to snap back to reality, his expression shifting from surprise to a steely resolve. "You shouldn't be here. You don't know what you're getting into."

The sharpness of his tone stung, igniting a flame of defiance within me. "Then tell me!" I demanded, stepping closer, the rain plastering my hair against my forehead. "What's at stake? Who are you really?"

"Stop asking questions that could get you hurt," he replied, his voice low and warning, yet there was an undeniable intensity in his gaze that set my heart racing for reasons I didn't fully understand.

"Too late for that," I replied, crossing my arms defiantly, refusing to back down. "You dragged me into this when you walked into my life, Elias."

He moved closer, the air between us crackling with an energy that was both electrifying and dangerous. "You have no idea what you're playing with," he said, his breath warm against my cheek, a mix of concern and something deeper that sent a thrill of adrenaline coursing through me.

"Try me," I challenged, my voice steady despite the chaos swirling around us.

Just as he opened his mouth to respond, a flash of lightning illuminated the night, revealing a look of fierce determination on his face. The storm raged, and in that moment, I realized that we were caught in something far more complicated than mere competition. Secrets thrummed beneath the surface, and lives hung in the balance—my life, his, and the web of families entwined in this dark tapestry of deceit.

It was then that I understood the stakes had escalated. This wasn't just about me or Elias; this was about a dangerous truth that had the potential to unravel everything we knew, everything we loved. And as the wind howled and the storm raged on, I felt a spark ignite between us, a fire fueled by the tension of unspoken words and buried desires.

"Then let's uncover those secrets together," I proposed, the conviction in my voice surprising even myself.

For a heartbeat, he seemed taken aback, as if my words pierced through the fog of uncertainty surrounding us. Then, a flicker of something—perhaps hope, perhaps fear—danced in his eyes. "Together?"

"Yes," I affirmed, my heart pounding with an intoxicating mix of dread and exhilaration. "Together."

The tension between us crackled like static electricity, a palpable force that felt both exhilarating and terrifying. The rain fell in relentless sheets, drumming against the ground, but it was as if the world had narrowed down to just Elias and me, caught in a storm of secrets and unspoken desires.

"Together," I echoed, the weight of the word settling heavily in the air, drawing us closer. My heart raced, fueled by a mixture of dread and anticipation. What had begun as a mere curiosity now spiraled into something much larger, something that felt as significant as the storm that raged around us.

Elias's expression shifted, shadows playing across his features. He seemed to wrestle with something deep inside him, a battle of wills between the man I'd come to know and the hidden truths that lay buried beneath his surface. "You don't understand what you're asking for," he said finally, his voice a low rumble, edged with an urgency that sent shivers down my spine.

"Try me," I challenged, folding my arms defiantly. "I've come this far; I deserve to know."

With a resigned sigh, he turned away for a moment, staring into the dark void beyond the flickering lantern. The tension in his shoulders hinted at burdens he carried alone, burdens that threatened to consume him. I could almost feel the weight of his secrets pressing against my chest, and I longed to ease that pressure, to find a way through the fog that surrounded him.

"Fine," he said, his tone softening. "But you have to promise me one thing. No matter what you hear, no matter what we discover, you have to trust me."

Trust. The word hung in the air like a fragile promise. "Trust is earned, Elias," I replied, my voice steady but my heart racing. "I can't just hand it over."

He nodded, accepting the challenge as a flicker of determination sparked in his eyes. "Let's start with the rumors. There's more to my company than what you see. It's not just about business; it's a tangled web of alliances and betrayals."

As he spoke, I felt my resolve strengthen. "So, what's the first step? Where do we start?"

"Follow me," he said, his voice low and commanding, and I fell into step beside him, our paths converging into the unknown. The rain continued to pelt down, but the storm felt more like a backdrop to the charged atmosphere surrounding us.

We navigated through the labyrinthine grounds of his estate, my heart pounding as we ventured deeper into the shadows. The world felt alive, the air thick with tension and the heady scent of wet earth mingling with the unmistakable aroma of impending revelations.

Finally, we arrived at a small, ivy-clad building tucked away from the main house. Its façade, worn and unassuming, held a promise of secrets waiting to be unearthed. "This is where I keep the records," Elias said, gesturing to the heavy wooden door, his expression serious. "What we find inside might change everything."

I nodded, unable to shake the feeling that I was stepping into a world far removed from my own, one where danger lurked behind every corner. With a deep breath, Elias pushed the door open, the hinges creaking in protest. Inside, the air was cool and musty, filled with the scent of aged paper and something else—something ominous that seemed to whisper warnings as I crossed the threshold.

Rows of shelves stretched before us, cluttered with files and dusty ledgers, the remnants of countless stories waiting to be uncovered. "We need to find the records from the last five years," he instructed, moving swiftly through the room, his hands expertly skimming over the spines of the books as if he were searching for a long-lost treasure.

I followed closely, the silence thickening as we delved into the depths of his secrets. "Why hide all of this?" I asked, breaking the silence that enveloped us. "If your company is above board, why the need for secrecy?"

His gaze flickered to mine, a storm brewing in those vivid blue depths. "Not everything is black and white, you know. Some truths are better left hidden to protect those we care about."

"And what about the people you're protecting?" I countered, frustration rising within me. "What if the lies put them in even more danger?"

He opened his mouth to respond but stopped, his expression shifting as he pulled a battered file from the shelf. "Here. This might help." He handed it to me, his fingers brushing against mine, a fleeting contact that sent a jolt of awareness coursing through my veins.

I opened the file, my heart racing as I scanned the contents. Inside were names and dates, connections I hadn't anticipated. "These are... my family's connections," I murmured, my brow furrowing as I pieced together the tangled web laid out before me. "Why would you have these?"

"They intersected with my father's dealings," he replied, his voice thick with tension. "But it goes deeper than that. This isn't just about competition; it's about old debts and unfinished business."

I felt the weight of his words sink in, the realization crashing over me like the rain outside. The stakes were higher than I had imagined, the consequences of our investigation potentially catastrophic. "What kind of business?"

"Business that has ties to my family's past," he said, his expression clouded with something akin to regret. "There are factions within my company that would rather keep these ties hidden. If they find out we're digging around…"

The implications loomed over us, and I could feel the ground shifting beneath my feet. "Then we need to be careful," I said, closing the file and meeting his gaze with newfound determination. "We can't let them see us coming."

Elias nodded, his eyes narrowing in focus. "We'll need to work in secret. Meet me here after dark. We can go through the records and piece together the connections."

As I turned to leave, a sudden crash of thunder shook the building, rattling the windows. "Are you okay?" I asked, glancing back at him.

He chuckled, but there was an edge to it. "It's just the storm. Nothing to worry about."

"Just a storm, huh?" I said with a smirk, trying to lighten the mood. "Next thing you know, we'll be dealing with a tornado."

"Let's not tempt fate," he replied, his tone half-serious, half-playful.

As I stepped back into the night, the rain drenching me, I couldn't shake the feeling that we were venturing into uncharted territory, a path laden with danger and discovery. The secrets of our families intertwined like vines, threatening to choke the life from everything I thought I knew. Yet the thrill of uncovering those secrets propelled me forward, igniting a fire within me that I could no longer ignore.

With each step, I felt the weight of the world pressing down, but alongside that weight was the exhilarating possibility of truth. And as I made my way back home, I knew one thing for certain: I was no longer just a curious bystander. I was a player in a game far more complex than I could have ever anticipated, and I was ready to uncover the truth, no matter the cost.

The air crackled with an electric tension as I retraced my steps back to my home, the rain easing but the weight of secrets pressing heavily on my mind. Each puddle I passed reflected the dim glow of streetlights, dancing with potential as they rippled underfoot. The night felt charged, filled with whispers of what lay beneath the surface, and I was determined to unearth every last one.

When I finally stepped inside, the warmth of the house wrapped around me like a familiar blanket, but it did little to dispel the chill that settled deep within my bones. I was far from safe. I glanced around the quiet rooms, half-expecting shadows to leap from the corners, eager to reveal the truths I had yet to confront. My parents' voices echoed in my mind, memories of countless warnings about the power of connections, the dangers of unearthing past grievances. They had always insisted that the world was a place where alliances could turn to ash in an instant, and yet here I was, choosing to dive into the fire.

With a resolute sigh, I gathered a few supplies—a notebook, a pen, and a flashlight—before sinking into the familiar comfort of the kitchen table. The silence felt almost conspiratorial as I opened the file Elias had handed me. My heart raced with the promise of secrets lying in wait, the thrill of knowledge tinged with an anxiety that coiled tightly around my chest.

As I flipped through the papers, the names danced before my eyes, some familiar, others long forgotten. Each name was a thread woven into the tapestry of our families, a reminder of old ties and unresolved conflicts. The more I read, the more the pieces began to connect. I found mentions of clandestine meetings, debts that had never been settled, and alliances formed in the shadows, all too close to home.

A knock on the door jolted me from my thoughts, my heart skipping a beat. I glanced at the clock—late enough to suggest that whoever stood outside had a purpose. I padded silently to the door, heart pounding with a mix of curiosity and trepidation. Peering through the peephole, I caught sight of Elias, his silhouette framed by the dim porch light.

I hesitated only a moment before opening the door, adrenaline surging through my veins. "What are you doing here?" I asked, a feigned bravado slipping through my lips.

"I needed to talk," he said, his voice low, eyes scanning the darkness as if to ensure we were alone. "It's about the records."

I stepped aside, letting him in, feeling the weight of the storm still hanging in the air, the tension thick enough to cut with a knife. "What's wrong? Did you find something?"

He shook his head, his expression grave. "Worse. There are people who know we're looking. They've been watching."

My stomach dropped, dread pooling inside me. "How do you know?"

"I received a warning," he said, running a hand through his damp hair, his expression a blend of frustration and concern. "Someone doesn't want us poking around."

"Great. Just what I needed," I replied, attempting to mask my fear with sarcasm. "A sinister shadow organization on my first night of sleuthing."

"Don't joke about this," he said, his voice sharp. "You don't understand what they're capable of."

"Then enlighten me," I shot back, the tension igniting a fierce determination within me. "What are we dealing with?"

Elias sighed, his shoulders slumping slightly. "My family has made enemies. Powerful ones. If they catch wind of our investigation, we could both be in serious danger."

"Duly noted," I replied, crossing my arms defensively. "But we can't back down now. There's too much at stake."

His gaze softened, a flicker of admiration mixing with the concern etched across his face. "You're brave. That's admirable, but this is dangerous territory."

"Bravery is just stupidity with a pretty bow," I countered, unwilling to let him underestimate me. "Besides, I'm in this now. What's the plan?"

"I've been thinking we need to be more cautious, maybe even disguise our inquiries," he suggested, pacing the small space as he considered our options. "We should focus on gathering information discreetly, making sure we're not being watched."

"Great idea," I replied, leaning against the counter, my mind racing. "But how do we do that? If they're already aware of our digging, what's to stop them from pulling more strings to keep us in the dark?"

He paused, the air thick with contemplation. "We might need a different angle, a way to gain insight without drawing attention. I have an old contact who might know something—someone who's on the fringes but has his ear to the ground. We could pay him a visit."

"Are you sure he can be trusted?" I asked, eyebrows raised.

Elias gave a half-hearted shrug. "In this world, trust is a luxury we can't afford. But he's the best shot we have."

With the weight of the decision settling over us, I nodded. "Let's do it. The sooner we uncover what's happening, the better."

Elias opened his mouth to respond, but a sharp rapping at the door interrupted us. My heart leaped into my throat as we exchanged a glance, the unease palpable.

"Did you invite anyone else?" he asked, his voice a mere whisper, eyes narrowing.

"No," I replied, panic bubbling just beneath the surface. I moved cautiously toward the door, peering through the peephole once again.

"Who is it?" he pressed, stepping closer, his presence warm and grounding, yet charged with tension.

"It's... it's my father," I whispered, dread pooling in my stomach.

Elias's expression darkened, his jaw tightening. "What's he doing here?"

"I have no idea," I said, feeling the weight of uncertainty settle heavily between us. "He shouldn't be here, not at this hour."

"Then we need to act fast. He can't know we're involved in this," Elias urged, urgency lacing his tone.

"I'll keep him distracted," I said, my mind racing. "You find a way to slip out the back."

He nodded, a flicker of admiration flashing in his eyes, but also a tinge of worry. "Just be careful."

I opened the door, forcing a smile to mask my rising anxiety. "Dad! What are you doing here?"

My father stood there, rain-drenched and frowning, his eyes scanning the room behind me. "I was worried. You disappeared into the night. Are you alright?"

"Of course, I'm fine!" I said, the feigned cheerfulness clashing with the tension in my stomach. "Just... working on a project. Nothing to worry about."

His gaze shifted, sharp and searching, as if he could see through the thin veneer I was attempting to present. "A project at this hour? What kind of project?"

Before I could respond, I caught a glimpse of Elias slipping out the back door, the shadows swallowing him whole. My heart raced as I turned my attention back to my father, his expression darkening with suspicion.

"Just a school project," I stammered, forcing a laugh that felt too tight in my throat. "You know how it is."

But his gaze hardened, a steely resolve settling over his features. "You're hiding something, aren't you?"

The words hung between us like a blade poised to drop, and I knew in that moment that everything had changed. My father's instincts were as sharp as his demeanor, and I could feel the walls closing in around me. "I—"

Before I could finish, a loud crash resonated from outside, sending a jolt of adrenaline through me. My heart raced as I exchanged a look with my father, and in that split second, we both realized that the game was no longer just about secrets; it had escalated into something much more dangerous.

"Stay here," my father commanded, his voice low and urgent, as he moved toward the door, determination etched into his features.

But something inside me screamed for action. "No! Dad, wait!"

But it was too late. He swung the door open, and in that moment, I knew that our lives were about to change forever. The storm outside mirrored the chaos brewing within, and as my father stepped out into the unknown, the shadows shifted around us, ready to reveal their darkest secrets.

Chapter 4: Dangerous Alliances

The rain drummed steadily against the window, creating a soothing backdrop to the tension swirling in the room. I leaned against the cool glass, peering out at the darkened streets of our small town, the world cloaked in shadows and uncertainty. My heart raced, not from fear, but from the looming threat that had quietly wrapped itself around my family like a vine, tightening with each day. The air was thick with a mix of anxiety and something else—something I could only attribute to the presence of Jace, who sat across the room, his gaze locked on me with an intensity that made my pulse quicken.

"I can't believe we're doing this," I muttered, pulling away from the window, my voice barely above a whisper. "Working together, I mean."

Jace leaned back in his chair, a hint of a smirk dancing on his lips. "Believe it. The enemy of my enemy and all that." His eyes twinkled with mischief, a spark that had me fighting the urge to smile back despite the gravity of our situation. His confidence was infectious, and it was hard to ignore the way the room seemed to hum with unspoken possibilities.

"I just didn't think our families would ever force us into such a… cooperative arrangement." I picked up the stack of papers we'd been poring over for the last few hours. They were filled with handwritten notes, sketches of what we assumed were our foes, and snippets of overheard conversations, all pieced together like a jigsaw puzzle.

Jace leaned forward, the playful glint in his eyes replaced with a serious glimmer that drew me in. "Look, I know this isn't ideal. But if we don't figure out who's behind these threats, we're both going to lose everything. My family… they've sacrificed too much already."

There was an honesty in his voice that cut through my skepticism. Jace was known for his bravado, the swagger that made him the object of many a crush at school, myself included. Yet here he was, stripped of that veneer, revealing a vulnerability that surprised me. It was in these moments, when he spoke of loyalty and family, that I began to see him not as a rival but as an ally—perhaps even a friend.

"Fine," I said, crossing my arms defiantly, though the fluttering in my stomach contradicted my bravado. "But I'm not going to take any unnecessary risks. We'll stick to the plan."

"Agreed. But you have to promise me something." He leaned closer, the faint scent of cedarwood and something sweet wrapping around me like a warm blanket. "If you ever think I'm going too far, you need to call me out. No holding back."

I raised an eyebrow, intrigued. "You really think I'll let you run wild?"

His grin widened. "I expect nothing less than a full-blown protest when I suggest something reckless. It's part of the deal."

We shared a laugh, the sound cutting through the tension like a warm breeze on a chilly day. It felt good—almost liberating—to share this moment with him, a moment that hinted at an uncharted territory between us, one filled with camaraderie and maybe even a touch of something more.

As we dove deeper into the night, pouring over every scrap of information we had, the room began to transform. The shadows cast by the flickering candlelight danced along the walls, bringing an almost magical quality to our surroundings. With each passing hour, we found ourselves slipping into a rhythm—his voice becoming the melody that guided my thoughts, my laughter punctuating his serious demeanor with unexpected levity.

"Okay, so if I were the one pulling the strings," Jace mused, tapping his chin thoughtfully, "I'd make my first move at the charity gala next month. It's the perfect opportunity for chaos."

"The gala?" I echoed, the thought sending a shiver of both excitement and dread down my spine. "You think they'd actually strike there?"

"Why not?" he shrugged, a boyish grin on his face. "It's high profile, and everyone will be watching. Perfect distraction."

"Not to mention it's a perfect chance for our families to be caught in the crossfire," I added, biting my lip as I considered the implications.

Jace leaned closer, our shoulders brushing together, sending a jolt of electricity through me. "That's why we need to be ready. We can't let them outsmart us. We have to stay one step ahead."

His determination ignited something within me—a sense of purpose that I hadn't expected. I found myself leaning into him, buoyed by the thrill of our plan and the chemistry crackling in the air between us. "Alright, let's make a plan. We'll need to gather intel discreetly."

As the night stretched on, we plotted and schemed, weaving together ideas and strategies with the ease of old friends. With every passing moment, the line between rivalry and camaraderie blurred, and I began to realize that beneath the bravado, Jace was fiercely loyal and protective. The way he spoke of his family, his desire to shield them from the darkness creeping into our lives, struck a chord deep within me.

And just like that, the delicate dance between us shifted. What had started as a reluctant alliance became a partnership filled with laughter and late-night revelations. I found myself laughing more than I had in months, the kind of laughter that bubbled up from deep inside and reminded me that even in chaos, there could be moments of joy.

Yet, beneath the lightness, a shadow loomed—a reminder that our world was fragile. Each laugh shared and each secret uncovered felt like stepping closer to a cliff's edge, the ground beneath us ready to crumble at any moment. Trust was a precarious thing, and I couldn't shake the feeling that with every alliance forged, we were treading a fine line between safety and betrayal. The stakes had never felt higher, and as Jace's laughter filled the room, I couldn't help but wonder: how long could we dance in the light before being consumed by the darkness?

The days that followed our late-night strategizing transformed into a peculiar rhythm, an unexpected harmony that had both of us dancing around our evolving partnership. Each afternoon, I found myself anticipating Jace's arrival, the way the sun crept into my room, casting warm light on the worn wooden floor. We'd meet in the library, a place that had long been a refuge for me, with its high ceilings and shelves brimming with books, their spines whispering stories of adventure and romance. It was the perfect backdrop for plotting our next moves, even as our laughter often drowned out the gravity of our mission.

"Okay, so let's recap," Jace said one afternoon, lounging comfortably on the oversized leather couch, his feet kicked up on the coffee table. "We've got the gala, the intel from your dad's sources, and my uncle's questionable business dealings. What else do we need to stir the pot?"

I leaned forward, propping my chin on my hand, watching him with a mixture of admiration and annoyance. "You make it sound so easy, but these are people who won't hesitate to play dirty. We can't underestimate them."

His smirk was infuriatingly charming. "That's why we're here. To outsmart them. Think of it as a game of chess, where the stakes are a bit higher than just losing a piece."

"A game of chess? Is that your idea of a fun afternoon?" I shot back, unable to hide my grin. "I didn't know you were such a strategist."

"I've been known to play a mean game of Monopoly, too," he quipped, his eyes sparkling with mischief. "But seriously, we need to think a few moves ahead. If they're planning something at the gala, we can't just show up with party hats and streamers."

His earnestness tugged at something deep within me, a sense of camaraderie that felt both exhilarating and terrifying. I had spent so long guarding my heart and my family's secrets, and here I was, opening up to someone I once viewed as an adversary.

"Alright, Mr. Chess Master, what's your next move?" I leaned back, crossing my arms and forcing myself to focus. "We need a way to gather information without drawing attention."

"What if we use the gala to our advantage?" he suggested, his voice steady as he spun ideas like a well-practiced magician. "We can blend in, but also make connections. You know those rich socialites will spill secrets over a glass of champagne."

"And what makes you think they'll trust us?" I shot back, a brow raised. "I mean, look at us—two kids caught in the middle of a family feud."

He shrugged, that infuriatingly confident smile never wavering. "We're not just 'two kids.' We're the perfect distraction. Besides, everyone loves a good story. We'll just have to play the part."

As he spoke, I imagined us gliding through the elegantly adorned ballroom, our movements choreographed in the delicate dance of subterfuge. There was something undeniably thrilling about the idea, the possibility of slipping beneath the surface of our lives and becoming part of something larger. Yet the thought of being so close to the danger sent a chill down my spine.

"We should probably get some formal clothes then," I said, the corners of my mouth twitching upwards at the thought of Jace in a tailored suit. "You know, to complete the distraction."

He chuckled, a sound that resonated within the quiet library like music. "Oh, I can't wait to see you in a gown. Just don't trip over the hem when you're trying to chase down our enemies."

"Ha! You just wait. I've got moves that would put a ballet dancer to shame," I retorted, enjoying the back-and-forth. "I won't be the one tripping up—at least not over my dress."

The days slipped by in a blur of preparation and playful banter, our dynamic evolving with every shared moment. We'd spend hours sifting through the gossip columns, diving into the web of social connections that tied our families together. I couldn't shake the feeling that every laugh we shared drew us closer to a precipice, a fragile balance between friendship and something more.

Yet, just as the excitement built, so did the underlying tension. One evening, as we sat poring over potential attendees of the gala, the atmosphere shifted. The warmth of our laughter faded into an uneasy silence as I stumbled upon an article that felt like a punch to the gut.

"Jace, look at this." I turned the screen toward him, my heart racing as I pointed at the bold headline. "They're saying there might be a serious threat at the gala. Something about a security breach."

He leaned closer, his brows furrowing as he read the article. "This is bad," he murmured, the lightness in his tone evaporating. "If they're planning something during the event... we need to figure out what it is before it's too late."

My stomach dropped, a wave of dread washing over me. "What if it's aimed at our families? What if—"

"We'll deal with it," he interrupted, his voice steady but fierce, the protective undertone unmistakable. "Together. That's the whole point, right? You and me against the world?"

I nodded, but the gnawing fear in my gut refused to dissipate. It was one thing to plan, to pretend that we were in control; it was another entirely to face the reality of the danger lurking just beyond our carefully constructed bubble.

"Okay, let's regroup and come up with a strategy," I said, forcing myself to focus on the task at hand. "We can't let panic dictate our next move."

Jace stood, his posture shifting into that of a leader, and it filled me with a strange mix of admiration and something else I dared not name. "I'll make a few calls, see what I can dig up about the security arrangements. Meanwhile, you should reach out to your dad's contacts. If we can get ahead of this, we might be able to prevent it from escalating."

"Right. We'll both do what we can." I took a deep breath, the gravity of the situation settling around us like a heavy fog. "Let's get to work."

As the night unfolded, I couldn't shake the sense that our alliance was about to be put to the ultimate test. Trust hung in the air like a fragile thread, and every moment felt charged with an electricity I couldn't ignore. In the midst of all the chaos, I found myself wondering how much longer we could maintain our playful façade while navigating the storm that threatened to engulf us. The line between friendship and something deeper blurred further, creating a tension that left my heart racing and my thoughts tangled in a web of uncertainty.

With the gala looming just days away, the atmosphere crackled with a mixture of excitement and dread. Jace and I had poured over every detail, sifting through our meticulously gathered information like archaeologists uncovering a lost city. The library felt less like a sanctuary and more like a war room, each whisper of our plans resonating off the aged oak shelves.

"Okay, so I've got my suit ready, and you'd better believe I'll be bringing my A-game," Jace said, leaning back in his chair with an air of exaggerated confidence. "What about you? Are you prepared to stun the crowd into silence?"

"Is that your way of saying I should wear something that distracts from your very existence?" I shot back, the corner of my mouth twitching up in a playful smile. "Because if so, I might just take you up on it."

His laughter rang through the room, rich and warm, pulling me further into the moment. "Not a chance. I need everyone's attention focused on our mission, not me striking a pose in a fancy suit."

We exchanged plans, building a strategy that felt like constructing a bridge over a chasm of uncertainty. As the sun dipped lower in the sky, casting golden rays through the window, the world outside seemed to fade away. The threat that loomed over our families had shifted from a distant worry to an imminent storm, and with every laugh we shared, I could feel the tension coiling tighter around us.

"Alright, so we'll meet at the gala and keep our ears open," I said, straightening up and trying to channel my focus. "You watch for anything suspicious while I—"

"While you charm the crowd, right?" He interrupted, winking at me. "Let's be honest, you're the one who could turn heads in a paper bag."

"Oh, stop it," I replied, rolling my eyes, but warmth flooded my cheeks at his compliment. "I'm serious. I'll be the one mingling with my dad's friends. We need to figure out who has their fingers in this mess."

"And I'll mingle with the people who think they're above us," Jace said, his tone growing serious. "You know I can get information from those kinds of folks. They love to talk about their money and connections—if you know how to ask the right questions."

"Just remember to play nice," I said, half-joking. "We can't have you charming our potential enemies into plotting their next move against us."

His expression turned serious as he met my gaze, the lightness fading. "If things go south, promise me you'll stay close. I don't want to lose you in that crowd."

The vulnerability in his voice struck a chord within me, igniting a fierce protectiveness. "You don't have to worry about me. I'm tougher than I look," I replied, a playful edge to my voice. "But I'll keep an eye on you too. We're in this together."

As the evening shadows crept in, our laughter faded, replaced by the weight of our looming reality. The idea of facing the unknown at the gala stirred a whirlwind of nerves in my stomach. Would we be able to see through the layers of deception surrounding our families?

The day of the gala arrived, vibrant and filled with possibility, yet I felt a pit of anxiety resting deep in my gut. I dressed slowly, pulling on the gown that hugged my curves just right, a deep sapphire blue that reminded me of twilight skies. It was the kind of dress that transformed me into someone else, someone who could stand against the shadows creeping at the edges of my life. I brushed my hair back, letting it fall in soft waves around my shoulders, and the reflection in the mirror startled me with a sense of confidence I hadn't felt in a long time.

"Wow," my younger sister exclaimed from the doorway, her eyes wide with admiration. "You look like you stepped out of a fairy tale."

"Thanks, but I'd rather not be the damsel in distress tonight," I shot back, trying to inject humor into my nerves. "More like the hero ready to save the day."

As I made my way to the gala venue, my heart raced with each step, anticipation mingling with anxiety. The grand ballroom, bathed in golden light and adorned with opulent decorations, came alive as guests mingled, their laughter and chatter mingling with the soft strains of a string quartet. It was both enchanting and suffocating, a labyrinth of potential allies and hidden threats.

I spotted Jace across the room, his tall frame commanding attention in a fitted black suit. He was engaged in conversation, his charisma undeniable, as he effortlessly navigated the crowd. I felt a flutter of pride knowing we were in this together, even if it felt like walking a tightrope without a safety net.

"Time to charm the masses," I murmured to myself, slipping into the fray. I approached the bar, pretending to study the cocktail menu, my mind racing with thoughts of what to do next.

"Excuse me, but are you planning to stand here all night?" a voice interrupted, smooth and teasing. I turned to find a tall, impeccably dressed man with dark hair and a knowing smile. "Because I have to say, you're far too stunning to be tucked away in a corner."

"Flattery will get you everywhere," I replied, playing along, grateful for the distraction. "But I'm actually here on business."

"Ah, a woman of dual purposes. How refreshing." He extended his hand, a sly grin on his face. "I'm David. And you are?"

"Melanie," I said, shaking his hand, my instincts alert. "And yes, I am here to make some connections. Do you happen to know what's brewing beneath all this glamour?"

David's eyes flickered with interest. "The usual rumors, I suppose. But I wouldn't worry too much. The biggest threats come from those hidden in plain sight." His gaze drifted over my shoulder, and I turned just in time to catch Jace approaching, a wary expression on his face.

"Melanie," Jace called, cutting through the throng of guests, a hint of urgency in his voice. "Can we talk? Now."

The smile faded from David's face, replaced by a curious frown as he looked between us. "Is everything alright?"

I shot Jace a questioning glance, sensing the tension that radiated from him. "What's going on?" I asked, trying to keep my voice steady.

He leaned in closer, lowering his voice. "I overheard something. There's talk of a security breach, and it's happening tonight. We need to find out where and when. We can't let our families be caught in the crossfire."

My stomach dropped, the reality of our mission crashing over me like a wave. "Are you serious? Can we trust anyone here?"

"I don't know," he replied, his expression grim. "But we need to act fast."

Just then, the lights flickered, casting the room into an eerie half-light, and a low murmur swept through the crowd. "What's happening?" I whispered, the weight of dread settling over us.

Before Jace could respond, a commotion erupted at the entrance, and my heart raced as I turned to see figures in dark suits, faces obscured by shadows, pushing through the throng. They moved with an unsettling purpose, and an icy chill raced down my spine.

"Jace," I breathed, gripping his arm, the laughter and chatter fading into a haunting silence. "This isn't just a party anymore."

"Stay close," he said, his voice low and urgent, and in that moment, as the shadows closed in around us, I realized that we were standing on the brink of something far more dangerous than we'd anticipated.

And just like that, the night turned from a glimmering promise into a nightmarish reality, leaving us teetering on the edge of chaos.

Chapter 5: Unraveling Threads

The evening sun cast a golden hue over the city, filtering through the floor-to-ceiling windows of Julian's sleek apartment. The light danced across the polished surfaces, illuminating the scattered documents that covered the glass table, each page a potential key to unraveling the tangled web that had ensnared us both. My heart raced, a heady mix of anxiety and determination propelling me forward as I flipped through the papers, my fingers brushing over the inked words like a musician tuning an instrument, searching for harmony amid the discord.

"Do you think he knew?" I asked, my voice barely rising above a whisper as I glanced at Julian. He leaned back in his chair, the shadows playing across his chiseled features, his brow furrowed in thought. There was an intensity in his gaze, a flicker of something deeper than concern that made my heart leap and my stomach churn all at once.

"Hard to say," he replied, his tone smooth, but there was an edge to it that suggested we were both skirting around the real issue. "Whoever this is, they're not just playing games. They're ruthless." His eyes darted to the documents, then back to me, as if he were assessing the risk of our next move. The air in the room thickened, charged with unspoken fears and burgeoning possibilities.

I let out a breath I hadn't realized I was holding. "We need to dig deeper. If there's even a chance that someone is pulling strings behind the scenes, we can't afford to back down now." The urgency in my voice was met with a silence that felt heavy, almost suffocating. I could sense the invisible thread of fate weaving us together, drawing us closer as the stakes grew higher.

"Right," he said, leaning forward, elbows resting on the table, his fingers steepled in front of him. "But it's not just about finding answers. It's about what happens when we do." The weight of his words hung between us, a challenge and a warning all at once.

I met his gaze, willing my pulse to slow. "We can handle it. Together." The resolve in my voice surprised even me. In the midst of the chaos swirling around us, this strange bond we shared had become a lifeline, tethering me to something beyond the murky waters of our investigation.

He held my gaze for a moment longer, and the tension shifted. The atmosphere crackled, and I felt a magnetic pull between us, something far more potent than fear or ambition. It was raw, electric, and terrifying all at once. Just as I began to lean into that moment, caught in the gravitational pull of his presence, a sudden sound shattered the fragile tranquility.

A faint rustling echoed from the hallway outside, like whispers of secrets long buried, bringing me back to reality with a jolt. I straightened, heart racing again, my instincts on high alert. "Did you hear that?" I asked, my voice a harsh whisper now.

Julian nodded, his expression shifting to one of focused determination. "Stay here," he said, his tone leaving no room for argument. But I was having none of that. The thrill of danger coursed through my veins, pushing me to stay close, to face whatever was lurking just beyond the door.

As he moved to investigate, I felt a surge of adrenaline. The thrill of the unknown beckoned me, a seductive invitation to embrace the chaos. The space between us felt charged, and for a fleeting second, I almost wished for an interruption—a distraction from the inevitable pull we felt towards each other. I could sense that the deeper we dove into this mess, the more tangled our lives would become, yet a part of me craved that connection, the complexity of it all.

The door creaked open, and he peered into the dim hallway, his posture taut and ready. The tension in the air seemed to thicken, each moment stretching out as I held my breath, waiting for something—anything—to happen. The rustling continued, punctuated by the faint sound of footsteps retreating down the hall.

"Nothing," he said finally, stepping back inside and closing the door behind him. The disappointment in his voice was palpable, and it was a reminder of the uncertainty we faced. I felt a rush of adrenaline, the chase fueling a desire I hadn't quite acknowledged.

"Maybe it was just the wind," I suggested, trying to lighten the mood, but my attempt felt flimsy against the weight of the situation. We both knew that nothing was simply 'just the wind' anymore.

Julian returned to the table, his brow still furrowed in thought. "Or it could be someone watching us." He ran a hand through his hair, a gesture of frustration that only served to deepen my attraction to him.

In a moment of vulnerability, I caught his eye and, without thinking, reached out to grasp his hand. His warmth radiated through me, igniting something that had been smoldering beneath the surface. "Whatever happens, we face it together," I declared, and as my heart raced, I could almost hear the strings of fate tugging tighter around us.

His lips curled into a half-smile, a flicker of something brighter breaking through the tension. "And if it all goes sideways?" he teased, but there was a sincerity in his tone that made me lean closer.

"Then we'll make it a hell of a story," I replied, a smile breaking free despite the gravity of our situation.

In that moment, the world outside faded, the darkness beyond our walls feeling distant and insignificant compared to the burgeoning connection that enveloped us. Our lips brushed softly, a tentative exploration that sent a wave of heat through my body. But just as quickly, the memories of the danger looming over us crashed back, and I pulled away, breathless, heart racing.

"Maybe later," I murmured, my cheeks flushing, and I could see the flicker of understanding in his eyes—an unspoken agreement to hold off on the chaos of our emotions until we navigated the storm that lay ahead. But as we returned to our documents, the room felt different, the air thick with possibilities, a haunting reminder of how easily the line between danger and desire could blur.

The glow from the city outside bled into the room, each flickering light telling tales of lives lived in unyielding pursuit of happiness, while we found ourselves mired in the shadows of secrets and lies. I tried to shake off the remnants of that brief kiss, a spark that had ignited a longing I wasn't ready to confront. Instead, I refocused on the stack of papers in front of me, hoping to drown out the intoxicating possibilities that lingered between us.

Julian had resumed his own search, his brows furrowed as he leafed through the documents with the meticulousness of a surgeon. Every now and then, he glanced up at me, a mix of curiosity and something warmer flitting across his features, as if he were trying to decode the enigma that was unfolding between us. "You know," he said, breaking the silence that had draped over us like a heavy blanket, "if this were a movie, we'd be the intrepid duo unraveling a conspiracy while dodging bullets."

I chuckled softly, shaking my head at the image. "Right. And I'd probably trip over my own feet right before the climactic showdown." I leaned back in my chair, folding my arms. "More likely, I'd be the one who accidentally sends an email to the entire office, exposing our entire operation."

His laughter was a welcome sound, easing the tension that threatened to suffocate us. "Well, if that happens, I'll be there to rescue you, even if it means throwing myself in front of a metaphorical bus," he replied, his eyes sparkling with mischief.

"Rescue me? In that case, I'd prefer a motorcycle chase over a bus. Much more stylish." I shot him a grin, feeling a warmth bloom in my chest, a flicker of normalcy in a situation that was anything but.

"Motorcycle it is," he said, his voice rich with mock seriousness. "But only if you promise not to scream too loud when I hit the brakes."

"Trust me, my scream would be entirely justified," I retorted, rolling my eyes. We fell into an easy banter, the kind that turned the suffocating atmosphere into a light, buoyant breeze. But the laughter was a thin veil over the seriousness of our task, the danger still lurking just outside our door, waiting for us to let our guard down.

After a few moments, the humor began to wane as reality seeped back in. "So, back to this powerful figure you mentioned," I said, my tone shifting. "What are we really up against?"

Julian's expression hardened, the humor draining away as he leaned back in his chair, fingers tapping a slow, contemplative rhythm on the table. "Someone influential, that much I can tell you. The kind of person who doesn't just have power but wields it like a sword." He paused, searching my face for understanding. "And they're not going to let us waltz in and dismantle their plans."

I nodded, the weight of his words sinking in. "So we need to be strategic. Maybe lure them out somehow?"

"Exactly. We need to play the game but on our terms." His eyes met mine, and for a moment, it felt as if we were standing at the edge of a precipice, teetering on the brink of something monumental.

We returned to our documents, sifting through names and connections, our minds working in tandem, weaving threads of information into a clearer picture. The names on the pages began to blur together, and soon, I found myself lost in thought, pondering the twisted paths that had led us to this point.

Just then, Julian let out a soft exclamation, breaking the spell. "Look at this." He held up a sheet, his expression intense. The name at the top sent a shiver down my spine—Margaret Wells. The powerful businesswoman had her hands in a little bit of everything, her influence spreading like a web through the city, sticky and treacherous.

"I've heard of her," I murmured, leaning closer. "She has a reputation for getting what she wants, no matter the cost."

"Exactly. And from what I've been able to piece together, she's been connected to some questionable dealings lately. If she's involved in whatever is happening here, then we're in deep." His voice dropped to a conspiratorial whisper. "And that's not the worst of it."

I raised an eyebrow, a spark of curiosity igniting in me. "What do you mean?"

"I found a trail that connects her to some high-profile disappearances," he said, eyes narrowing as he continued. "People who were once in her circle, now completely off the grid."

A chill crawled up my spine. "You're serious? If she's involved in something like that, we're playing with fire."

"Fire? More like a raging inferno," he replied, his expression a mixture of concern and determination. "We need to figure out how to approach her without putting ourselves in direct danger. If she gets a whiff of what we're doing..." His words trailed off, leaving an ominous weight hanging in the air.

"I say we act like we belong in her world," I suggested, my mind racing with possibilities. "Maybe we can get close enough to learn more, find out what she's really up to."

Julian considered this, and I could see the gears turning in his mind. "That could work, but it requires finesse. We need to be cautious—she'll see right through anything less than genuine."

"Cautious? You know I've got that in spades," I teased, trying to lighten the mood. "Just wait until you see my poker face; I can bluff my way through anything."

"Your poker face?" he echoed, a grin breaking through the tension. "I think I'd like to see that in action. Maybe we should get you a pair of shades and a trench coat for effect."

"Now you're talking," I laughed, imagining myself as a glamorous spy, a persona that would certainly require an extensive wardrobe overhaul. But underneath the humor, my heart raced at the thought of stepping into that world—dangerous, unpredictable, but thrillingly alive.

As we plotted our approach, the evening stretched on, shadows lengthening around us as the city continued its relentless pulse outside. I felt the excitement building, igniting a sense of purpose within me, and in that moment, I realized how intertwined our fates had become. The lines of our lives were no longer straight; they looped and tangled, creating an intricate pattern that held both danger and undeniable allure.

Then, just as I was beginning to envision our next steps, the power in the apartment flickered ominously, plunging us into darkness. I froze, the sudden absence of light amplifying every sound—the distant hum of the city, the faint rustling of papers, the quickening beat of my heart.

"Stay close," Julian whispered, his voice low and steady. I could feel his presence beside me, a comforting reminder that I wasn't alone in this tangled web. We were in this together, whether we were unraveling threads or weaving new ones, and somehow, that made all the difference.

The room lay shrouded in an unsettling darkness, the city outside continuing its vibrant life, oblivious to the drama unfolding within the sleek walls of Julian's apartment. My pulse raced as I strained my eyes against the blackness, feeling the oppressive weight of the unknown pressing in. The flickering power had thrown us into a realm of uncertainty, and I could sense the tension thickening around us like a storm about to break.

"Great, just what we needed," I quipped, trying to inject some levity into the situation. "Darkness and danger—sounds like the title of a terrible thriller."

Julian chuckled softly, the sound a reassuring balm in the gloom. "I'd rather be in a rom-com with you, dodging awkward situations instead of potential threats." He moved closer, his presence grounding me amidst the swirling anxiety.

"Rom-coms don't usually have this level of intrigue," I replied, shifting in my seat. "What's the plot twist here? Do we get mistaken for spies and end up at a high-stakes gala?"

"Only if you're prepared to wear something stunning," he shot back, a playful grin breaking through the darkness. "I can see you in a dazzling red gown, sweeping through the crowd like you own the place."

"Oh please," I laughed, though the thought of strutting into a glamorous event with him at my side sent a thrill through me. "I'd probably trip over my own heels and make a scene."

"Even better," he replied, his voice laced with amusement. "A dramatic entrance always catches attention."

As the banter continued, I felt the tension begin to dissipate, momentarily forgotten in the haze of humor and closeness. But reality had a way of crashing back in, and the laughter faded as I noticed the weight of silence settling around us again. "We should check the flashlights," I suggested, breaking the spell. "We can't stay in the dark forever, no matter how cozy it feels."

"Right. Let me grab one." Julian turned, and I could hear the sound of him rummaging through a nearby drawer, the scrape of metal against wood echoing in the quiet. The stillness outside seemed to intensify, as if the world was holding its breath, waiting for something to happen.

Suddenly, the doorbell rang, a sharp, jarring sound that shattered the tranquility we had momentarily embraced. I jumped, my heart leaping into my throat. "Who could that be?" I whispered, my mind racing through the possibilities.

"Stay here," Julian said, his voice now all business. He moved toward the door, every muscle in his body tense, poised for action. I watched, torn between the instinct to follow and the urge to remain hidden, knowing that whoever was on the other side could either be a friend or a threat.

"Wait," I called softly, just as he reached for the doorknob. "Maybe we should—"

But before I could finish, he swung the door open, and a figure stood framed in the doorway, backlit by the dim hallway light. The silhouette was familiar yet unsettling, the contours of their face barely discernible.

"Jack," I breathed, my heart racing at the sight of him.

"Sorry to interrupt your little rendezvous," he said, stepping into the room with a casualness that belied the tension crackling in the air. His gaze flitted between Julian and me, a knowing smirk curling his lips. "Looks like I'm the third wheel here."

"Not quite how it is," I replied, irritation and relief mingling in my voice. "We were just... researching."

"Researching? Or are you two playing detective?" Jack raised an eyebrow, arms crossed, clearly not buying my attempt at deflection.

"Detective work doesn't usually involve candlelight dinners," Julian said dryly, stepping back to allow Jack to enter fully. "What are you doing here?"

"I came to check in on you both. Heard about the power outage. Thought I'd bring a little light," he said, nodding toward the small lantern he carried. "But it seems you've got enough mystery to keep you entertained."

I shot a glance at Julian, who remained stoic, arms crossed defensively. There was a sharpness in his expression, a flicker of tension that told me he was assessing Jack's presence, and the implications it might have.

"Did you find anything?" Jack pressed, his attention snapping back to the mess of papers strewn across the table.

"We found a name," Julian replied, his tone measured. "Margaret Wells."

Jack's expression shifted, surprise coloring his features. "That's a big name. You're diving deep, aren't you?"

"Maybe deeper than we should," I admitted, feeling a chill at the thought. "But if she's involved, we need to know what we're dealing with."

Jack's eyes narrowed, and he leaned closer, lowering his voice. "Just be careful. You don't want to attract her attention. People like her don't play nice."

Before I could respond, the lights flickered back on, bathing the room in a sudden glow. The momentary brightness seemed almost surreal, like a spotlight shining on a stage where we were all performers, each playing a role in a dangerous game.

The atmosphere shifted again, the playful banter of moments before receding as the reality of our situation loomed larger. "What's your plan?" Jack asked, crossing his arms, a challenge in his gaze.

"We go after her," Julian said, his voice firm. "But we need to be smart about it. We'll need information, connections. We can't just walk into her world without preparation."

"Connections? You mean like the ones you were trying to avoid making earlier?" Jack shot back, a hint of sarcasm lacing his words.

"Let's just say our methods might need to be a little more… unconventional," Julian replied, a smirk ghosting across his lips.

"You mean your methods," I interjected, narrowing my eyes playfully. "I'll just be here looking fabulous and saving your backs."

Jack laughed, but there was an edge to it. "Just remember, glamour won't save you if things go south."

"Nothing ever goes south in a rom-com," I countered, though the uncertainty gnawed at me. "But let's be real, we need a plan that doesn't involve tripping over heels or stumbling into trouble."

"I'll see what I can dig up," Jack said, his expression sobering. "But you need to be careful. Wells has eyes everywhere."

The room fell silent as we exchanged wary glances, the reality of our undertaking settling in like a heavy mist. Just as I was about to suggest a specific course of action, the apartment door swung open again, this time with an ominous creak that sent a chill skittering down my spine.

A shadow loomed in the entrance, a figure I hadn't expected, one that sent my heart plummeting into my stomach. The last thing I heard before everything spiraled into chaos was a voice that froze the blood in my veins, thick with authority and menace. "Looking for me?"

The door slammed shut behind them, and in that instant, I realized we were no longer just playing a game; we were now full participants in a perilous dance, and the stakes had just been raised to an unforgiving height.

Chapter 6: A Web of Lies

The cool air in the dimly lit room wrapped around me like a shroud, heavy with the scent of sandalwood and lingering whispers of betrayal. Shadows danced across the walls as the flickering candlelight struggled to hold its ground against the encroaching darkness. I leaned against the wooden table, my fingers tracing the intricate carvings as I wrestled with the news that had just unraveled my world. Nathan, the man who had once been my anchor, now felt like a ghost slipping through my fingers, taunting me with his secrets. The betrayal lay thick in the air, palpable and suffocating.

He stood across from me, arms crossed defensively over his chest, his expression a mixture of defiance and something darker, something I couldn't quite decipher. The lines of his jaw clenched tight as if he were bracing himself against the storm brewing between us. "You have to understand, Alina," he said, his voice low, laced with an urgency that sent shivers down my spine. "I had my reasons for keeping this from you."

"Reasons?" I echoed, incredulity flaring within me. "Is that what you call lying to me? Feeding me false information while I risk everything to trust you?" My heart raced, the adrenaline surging through my veins as anger coursed alongside the betrayal. I wanted to scream, to shake him until the truth spilled from his lips like a waterfall, but instead, I found myself frozen, caught in the web of our shared history, our laughter, our whispered dreams that now felt like cruel mockeries.

He stepped closer, the distance between us evaporating as his gaze bore into mine, searching for something—perhaps forgiveness, perhaps understanding. "I didn't want to put you in danger. You have no idea what's at stake," he implored, the rawness of his emotions flickering in his eyes like a dying ember.

"Then enlighten me, Nathan. Because right now, all I see is a liar wrapped in shadows." The accusation slipped from my lips like a serpent, venomous and sharp. The accusation hung in the air, a ghost that clung to us, choking any warmth that remained. I could see the hurt etched across his face, the way his shoulders drooped as if the weight of the truth had physically crushed him.

Silence engulfed us, thick and heavy, until it felt like the world outside had ceased to exist. I could almost hear my heart hammering against my ribcage, drowning out the whispers of the candle flames. "What if I told you I was trying to protect you from something far worse than I ever could?" His voice trembled, revealing a vulnerability that tugged at the edges of my anger.

"Protect me? Or control me?" The words tumbled out before I could stop them, each syllable dripping with bitterness. Memories of our late-night talks, the way he'd always seemed to know what was best for me, now felt like chains binding me to a past I could no longer trust. My heart was a battlefield, warring against the fragments of love and loyalty that had once made me believe in him. "You've kept me in the dark, Nathan. How can I believe anything you say now?"

His gaze flickered, and for a fleeting moment, I saw the mask crack, the raw fear and desperation in his eyes betraying the façade he worked so hard to maintain. "Because I need you to trust me now more than ever," he urged, stepping forward until there was barely an inch between us. The air crackled with tension, an electric charge that both terrified and excited me. "There's someone among us feeding lies, manipulating everything from the shadows. You've been used, Alina, and if we don't find out who it is, we're both in danger."

My pulse quickened, battling between the urge to flee and the desire to pull him closer, to wrap myself in his warmth and chase away the chill of uncertainty. "Who?" I whispered, the question hanging in the air like a loaded gun. "Who's doing this?"

"I don't know yet," he admitted, the frustration bubbling to the surface. "But we can't trust anyone—especially not those who have been closest to us." His breath was warm against my skin, and in that moment, the distance between our hearts felt as insurmountable as the lies that separated us. Yet the desire to believe him surged, a flicker of hope amid the chaos.

"Then what do we do?" I asked, my voice barely above a whisper. In that instant, I felt the weight of the world crashing down around us, yet beneath the surface, a flicker of resolve ignited within me.

"We fight," he said, determination hardening his features. "Together."

A rush of adrenaline coursed through me, igniting a fire that had been stifled by doubt. In the swirling maelstrom of confusion, a profound connection tugged at me, pulling me closer to him despite the distance our confrontation had created.

I looked into his eyes, searching for answers, for clarity in the midst of turmoil. Instead, I found passion—fierce, unyielding, and impossible to ignore. In that moment of vulnerability, of raw truth, the air around us shifted, tension morphing into something else entirely. As if in slow motion, Nathan leaned closer, his hands reaching out to cradle my face, and the world fell away.

Our lips met, hesitantly at first, like a delicate dance of trust reborn from the ashes of doubt. The kiss deepened, a desperate mingling of fears and hopes, a promise made in silence as the storm outside raged on, mirroring the tempest within us. I felt the walls I had built around my heart begin to crumble, the sweetness of his kiss igniting something dormant inside me. But just as quickly, the shadows loomed large once more, a reminder that our battle was far from over, and the truth still lay hidden in a web of lies.

The moment lingered, sweet yet fraught with uncertainty, our lips brushing against the remnants of trust that hung precariously between us. Nathan's fingers tangled in my hair, and I felt a thrill race through me, but it was tempered by the weight of our unspoken fears. The kiss, while igniting a spark of hope, could not mask the shadows lurking just beyond the flickering candlelight. When we finally pulled away, the tension returned, heavy and suffocating, as if the air had thickened with unsaid words and unaddressed questions.

"Let's get to the bottom of this," I said, my voice steadier now, bolstered by the resolve coursing through me. "We need to figure out who's manipulating our lives." The fire in my gut had rekindled; I could almost hear the cogs of determination grinding into motion.

Nathan nodded, the flicker of determination in his eyes returning as he stepped back, the cool air rushing in to fill the space he had left behind. "There are too many pieces moving around us. We have to find out who can be trusted." He ran a hand through his tousled hair, a habit I'd grown to find endearing, yet in that moment, it felt more like a sign of his own burgeoning frustration.

"Great, a mystery." I rolled my eyes, attempting to inject some levity into our dire situation. "Just when I thought my life couldn't get more exciting." The irony dripped from my voice like honey, sweet but heavy with the truth. The whole situation felt like a poorly plotted novel, and I could almost see the cliché character swooping in for the dramatic rescue. Except this time, I was the protagonist caught in a web of lies, with Nathan as my reluctant sidekick.

"We need to gather information," he said, ignoring my sarcasm, his brow furrowing in that way it always did when he was deep in thought. "Let's start with those closest to us. If someone is feeding us lies, it could be anyone."

The enormity of his words settled like a stone in my stomach. The thought of questioning our friends, our allies, felt daunting. "What about Liz?" I suggested, recalling my best friend who had always been a steadfast ally, but lately, her behavior had been uncharacteristically evasive. "She was acting strange at the last gathering. Almost... defensive."

Nathan's gaze sharpened, a flicker of recognition sparking behind his eyes. "You think she could be involved?"

"I don't want to believe it, but who knows? We need to consider every possibility, even the ones that hurt." I sighed, the weight of suspicion gnawing at my heart. Trust was a fragile thing, and it felt as if we were caught in a game where the rules shifted with every breath.

"Let's talk to her," he replied, his tone a mixture of resolve and uncertainty. "But we need to be careful. If she's involved, we can't tip her off."

A plan began to form, woven from threads of hope and apprehension. We decided to meet Liz at our favorite café, a cozy little nook nestled between old bookshops, where the aroma of coffee and freshly baked pastries danced in the air like a welcoming embrace. As we made our way through the city streets, the sun began to dip below the horizon, casting long shadows that mirrored the unease settling within me. The vibrant colors of autumn leaves fell around us, beautiful yet brittle, like the delicate nature of our alliance.

Once we arrived, the warmth of the café enveloped us, but the bright atmosphere did little to quell the tension coiling in my stomach. We found Liz seated at our usual table, her fingers wrapped around a steaming mug, the steam rising like ghostly tendrils. Her smile was bright, yet there was something off about her eyes—a glint of wariness that made my pulse quicken.

"Hey, you two! So glad you could make it!" she exclaimed, her cheerfulness almost too bright, too forced. I exchanged a glance with Nathan, who was already assessing the situation with that keen look I had come to rely on.

"Hi, Liz!" I responded, forcing a smile, though my heart raced as I took a seat across from her. "How've you been?"

"Oh, you know, same old," she said, but her eyes darted away, avoiding mine as she stirred her drink. "Busy with work and all that."

"Right," Nathan interjected smoothly, "busy is the word of the day for everyone, it seems." His tone was casual, but there was an edge that hinted at our shared purpose. "Any exciting projects on the horizon?"

Liz shrugged, her gaze flickering towards the window as if searching for an escape. "Just the usual stuff. You know how it is."

A silence settled, thick with unspoken words. I could feel Nathan's tension vibrating beside me, a taut string ready to snap. It was time to dig deeper. "Actually, we were hoping to talk about something important," I said, trying to keep my tone light while the gravity of our conversation loomed large.

Her gaze snapped back to mine, a flicker of alarm flitting across her face. "Important? Like what?"

I leaned in, my heart racing. "We've been hearing some unsettling things lately. About our... situation. And we thought you might have some insights."

Liz's expression changed, a flash of something—fear, perhaps—crossing her features. "What kind of insights?"

Nathan stepped in, his voice calm but firm. "We need honesty, Liz. If someone is manipulating us, we can't afford to have anyone holding back."

A nervous laugh escaped her lips, but it felt brittle, like glass ready to shatter. "You know I'd never keep anything from you guys. We're friends. Always have been."

"Then why do you seem so uneasy?" I pressed, my voice softer now, coaxing. "We're on the same side here."

Her facade cracked slightly, and for a moment, I glimpsed the worry that lay beneath her cheerful exterior. "It's just... everything is so complicated. You don't understand."

"Try us," Nathan urged, leaning closer, his intensity palpable. "We can't help if you don't share."

The silence that followed was deafening, punctuated only by the clinking of cups and the murmur of other patrons. Liz's gaze flicked to the door, her body language tense, as if she were weighing the risks of what she might reveal.

"Okay, fine," she said finally, her voice barely above a whisper. "But you have to promise me you'll be careful."

As she leaned in, I felt the tension in the air shift once more, an electric pulse of uncertainty mingling with anticipation. The truth was teetering on the edge, ready to tumble into the open, and I braced myself for whatever came next. The web of lies we had been caught in was beginning to unravel, and with it came a sense of both dread and exhilaration. Whatever Liz was about to say could change everything.

The tension in the café hung thick as Liz leaned in closer, her voice dropping to a conspiratorial whisper, the kind that always seemed to ignite a spark of mischief in my heart. "You both have to understand something important," she began, her eyes darting toward the door again, ensuring we were not being overheard. "I've heard things... things that make me question who we can really trust."

Nathan and I exchanged a glance, our pulse quickening with anticipation and dread. "Like what?" Nathan pressed, leaning so far forward that he nearly toppled over his chair.

Liz's hands trembled slightly as she wrapped them around her mug, almost as if it were a lifeline. "I've been hearing whispers about a group—someone is planning something big, and it involves all of us. I don't know the details, but they're watching. They know who we are, and they're not just after secrets. They want control."

Control. The word echoed in my mind, sending icy tendrils of fear creeping down my spine. I had sensed the unrest, the uncertainty brewing in the air, but hearing it spoken aloud twisted my insides in a way I couldn't ignore. "Who is this group?" I demanded, unable to mask the urgency in my voice. "What do you mean they're watching?"

She took a shaky breath, clearly grappling with the weight of the knowledge she held. "I can't say for sure. All I know is that people have gone missing—friends of mine, people who were once part of our circle. They just... vanished." Her eyes locked onto mine, searching for understanding, and I felt my stomach twist.

"Why didn't you tell us this sooner?" I shot back, frustration bubbling to the surface, mixing with the fear clawing at my insides. "We could have done something!"

"I didn't want to cause panic! And honestly, I thought it was just rumors." Liz's voice quivered, the tension evident in her frame. "But then I started seeing patterns. It's like a puzzle, and every piece points to something darker. I thought... I thought if I kept my head down, maybe it wouldn't touch us."

Nathan interjected, his tone sharp yet steady. "We can't afford to keep our heads down anymore. Not if people are disappearing." He leaned closer, the determination in his eyes igniting a flicker of hope within me. "We need to find out who's behind this and why they're targeting us."

Liz looked between us, her expression shifting from fear to determination. "Okay, then what's our plan? We need to be smart about this. If they're watching, we can't just go charging in blindly."

"Agreed," I said, glancing around the café, suddenly feeling exposed. The patrons seemed blissfully unaware, their conversations flowing freely, but I couldn't shake the sensation that shadows lurked just beyond the cheerful chaos. "We need to be strategic. Maybe we can gather intel from those who've been around the circle longer. Anyone who might have heard something unusual."

"People are cautious," Liz warned, her brow furrowed. "If they think we're probing too deeply, they might cut us off or worse. We need to be careful."

"What about some of our old contacts?" Nathan suggested, a glimmer of hope in his voice. "The ones who left the group a while back. They might have insights into what's been going on. Maybe they've seen or heard something."

A moment of silence fell as we considered this. It was risky to reach out to those who had distanced themselves, but they might also be the key to unraveling this web of lies.

"Alright, let's start with Mark. He left last summer and hasn't really been around since," I proposed, recalling his charming smile and penchant for knowing everyone's business. "He might have heard something. And if anyone can navigate this mess, it's him."

"Let's do it," Nathan said, determination flooding his voice. "But we need to keep our plans tight-lipped. No one else can know we're looking into this."

As we settled into our new focus, the atmosphere around us began to shift. The café buzzed with the warm hum of conversation, but I couldn't shake the unease creeping back in. The shadows in the corners of the room felt longer, more sinister, and I glanced over my shoulder, half-expecting someone to be eavesdropping.

"Alina?" Liz's voice broke through my thoughts. "Are you okay?"

I forced a smile, pushing the anxiety aside. "Yeah, just... thinking about how far we've fallen into this mess."

"Falling or diving?" Nathan quipped, his eyes sparkling with that familiar mischief that often masked deeper thoughts. "We could be the stars of a terrible mystery novel."

Liz laughed lightly, though I could tell her heart wasn't in it. "More like a thriller. One where we don't survive the last chapter."

I chuckled, though the reality stung. This wasn't just a plot twist in a book; it was our lives on the line. Just as I was about to speak, the café door swung open with a jingle, and a rush of cold air swept through, bringing with it a familiar figure.

"Mark?" I exclaimed, recognizing him instantly, my heart leaping with a mix of relief and disbelief. He strolled in as if he owned the place, his confident demeanor making him stand out even in a crowded café.

"Surprise!" he grinned, and I couldn't help but smile back, the warmth of his presence a balm against the rising tension. "I thought I'd pop in for a coffee and some gossip. I hear you've been stirring the pot."

Before I could respond, his gaze shifted past me, narrowing as he caught sight of Liz. "You look like you've seen a ghost."

"Or a conspiracy," I murmured under my breath, the irony of our situation settling heavily on my shoulders.

"Maybe both," Nathan said softly, the sudden gravity in his voice pulling my attention back to Mark. "We need to talk."

Mark raised an eyebrow, his expression shifting from playful to serious in an instant. "About what? You guys look like you've just stumbled into a horror movie plot."

"We might be," I said, my heart pounding as I braced myself for what was to come. The energy in the café shifted again, the lightness replaced with an undercurrent of urgency.

As we drew closer, I felt the air thicken with unspoken words. "There's something happening, Mark. Something dangerous," I began, but before I could delve deeper, the door swung open once more, the bell chiming like a warning.

The atmosphere froze, and I turned, my heart racing as a tall figure stepped in, cloaked in shadows. Recognition hit me like a thunderclap, and my breath caught in my throat. The familiar features were unmistakable, though the cold smirk on his face sent chills racing down my spine.

"I see you've been busy," he said, his voice smooth and mocking, piercing through the hum of chatter as he scanned our table with a predatory gleam in his eyes.

And in that moment, the world around us slipped away, leaving only the impending chaos and the unmistakable sense that the web of lies was tightening around us, suffocating in its embrace.

Chapter 7: The Calm Before the Storm

The evening was an exquisite tapestry woven with the golden threads of dusk, the air thick with the scent of blooming jasmine that clung to the warm, languid breeze. Each breath felt like inhaling the essence of summer itself, heavy with the promise of secrets yet to be uncovered. Sitting on the edge of the old wooden pier, I dipped my toes into the cool, shimmering water below, a stark contrast to the soft heat radiating from the sun as it nestled below the horizon. The water lapped at the wood, creating a rhythmic song that echoed the cadence of my heartbeat, as if the world held its breath, waiting for something monumental to happen.

Next to me, he was a silhouette against the dimming light, his features partially obscured, but I felt the intensity of his gaze more than I could see it. Nathaniel Parker—my sworn enemy, at least that's what we both believed, clinging to that notion like a child to a security blanket. In the tender light of the setting sun, though, the sharp lines of animosity between us began to blur, revealing the complexities beneath our rivalry. I stole a glance sideways, catching the play of shadows across his jawline, the way his dark hair danced lightly in the breeze, and for a moment, I forgot our history, the petty squabbles that had become the backdrop of our lives.

"Did you ever think we'd end up here?" I asked, breaking the silence that had thickened like fog between us.

He chuckled softly, the sound low and rich. "Honestly? I always thought you'd throw me off this pier the moment we were alone." His eyes sparkled with mischief, and I could almost believe there was warmth in his voice instead of the biting sarcasm I had grown accustomed to.

"Maybe that's still an option," I replied, the corners of my lips tugging upward. "You did try to sabotage my presentation last week."

"Just a minor technical glitch," he countered, the banter lightening the atmosphere, weaving an unexpected thread of camaraderie. "You would have pulled through, as usual."

A comfortable silence enveloped us, filled with the distant calls of night creatures and the gentle rustle of leaves overhead. It was in this tranquility that I found the courage to peel back the layers of pretense, exposing the raw truths of our lives. "What was it like for you growing up?" I asked, my curiosity tinged with the genuine desire to understand the man beside me, not just the adversary who had spent years trying to undermine my every effort.

He paused, staring out at the darkening water, his brow furrowed in thought. "There was always an expectation to excel. My father..." His voice trailed off, the unspoken weight hanging between us like a dense fog. "He never allowed failure. It was as if the only acceptable outcome was victory."

"Sounds exhausting," I said, feeling the weight of his words settle into my bones. "I thought it was just me. My mother had plans for my future before I even took my first steps. A doctor, a lawyer, something respectable. There was no room for mistakes."

His gaze turned to me, eyes glimmering with a mixture of understanding and something deeper—an acknowledgment of shared burdens. "And here we are, both trying to break free from the shackles of those expectations," he mused, a thoughtful expression softening his sharp features.

The air grew thicker with unspoken desires, and as the last vestiges of sunlight slipped away, the stars emerged, twinkling like tiny diamonds scattered across a velvet canvas. It was beautiful and mesmerizing, but the atmosphere crackled with a tension that thrummed beneath our words.

"Tell me something you want," I challenged, leaning closer, feeling the magnetic pull between us intensify. The shadows of our past faded in the glow of the constellations above us.

He hesitated, searching my face as if trying to decode the secrets hidden in my eyes. "I want to be more than just the son of a businessman," he finally admitted, his voice barely above a whisper, yet it resonated deeply within me. "I want to create something that's mine, not just an extension of my family's legacy."

His vulnerability surprised me, unraveling the animosity that had so defined our interactions. "I think we all want that," I said softly. "To carve our own path." The words hung in the air, heavy with promise and the potential for change.

But just as the moment reached its zenith, an unexpected chill swept through the air, snatching the warmth from my skin. A figure emerged from the shadows of the trees lining the pier, moving with a stealth that sent a shiver down my spine. I straightened, instinctively drawing away from Nathaniel, the weight of reality crashing back into our ephemeral connection.

"Who—?" I began, but the figure was already stepping closer, a silhouette against the starry backdrop.

"Stay where you are!" a voice called out, sharp and demanding. It pierced the tranquil night, sending a jolt of adrenaline racing through me. The calmness of the moment shattered like glass, and all the warmth that had been blossoming between Nathaniel and me dissipated in an instant, replaced by a dread that coiled tightly in my stomach.

Nathaniel shifted beside me, his earlier bravado replaced with an alert tension. "What do you want?" he demanded, his voice steady but laced with an undercurrent of warning.

"I'm here for answers," the figure replied, emerging into the light, revealing a face I recognized, yet had never hoped to see again. The very person whose presence could unravel everything we had begun to stitch together on this tranquil evening, pulling us back into the fray just as we dared to dream of escape.

The figure stepped into the light, revealing a face that made my heart drop into my stomach—a face I had thought was safely tucked away in the annals of my past. It was Marcus, my older brother, his presence as disconcerting as a sudden downpour on a sunny day. His confident stride, marred by the tension of this unexpected reunion, carried an unsettling energy that seeped into the very air we breathed.

"Marcus," I managed, my voice barely a whisper. I tried to mask my unease, but the words clung to my throat like barbed wire. He had always been the ambitious one, fueled by dreams that soared high and expectations that crushed beneath their weight. "What are you doing here?"

His lips curled into a smirk that could only be described as devilish. "Surprised to see me?" The teasing lilt in his voice felt at odds with the shadows that encroached upon us. "I thought you'd be off playing princess with your new friend here." He gestured lazily towards Nathaniel, whose posture had shifted into one of guarded readiness, the playful banter we had shared now a distant memory.

"New friend?" Nathaniel echoed, his eyes narrowing as he assessed Marcus. "What do you know about her, and what do you want?"

Marcus stepped closer, the glow from the stars illuminating his features with a harsh clarity. "Only what I need to know," he replied smoothly. "And I'm here because, let's face it, sis, you've stumbled into something a bit deeper than your typical high school rivalry." He chuckled, the sound slicing through the night, infusing it with a chill that made my skin prickle.

"What are you talking about?" I shot back, instinctively pulling my knees up to my chest, trying to shield myself from the creeping dread that had settled around us like an unwelcome fog. The pier felt suddenly smaller, the air thicker, and the moonlight cast long, foreboding shadows that danced across the water.

"Let's just say there are things at play here that you haven't quite grasped," Marcus said, his voice dropping to a conspiratorial whisper that sent shivers down my spine. "You've been poking your nose where it doesn't belong. And that," he pointed a finger at me, "could get you hurt."

Nathaniel moved in front of me, protective yet visibly bristling. "If you think you can intimidate her, you've got another thing coming. You need to back off."

Marcus's gaze flickered between us, amusement dancing in his eyes, as if he were witnessing a performance rather than a confrontation. "Cute. Really." He leaned casually against a nearby post, crossing his arms as if he had all the time in the world. "But trust me, Nathaniel, I'm not the one you should be worried about."

"Stop playing games," I said, my voice steadier than I felt. "What do you want from me? I've already distanced myself from the family drama."

"Family drama," he repeated, his tone dripping with sarcasm. "Ah, yes. That's what you think it is. But it's much bigger than that." His expression hardened. "You think this is about you and Nathaniel? You're both pieces in a much larger puzzle."

The implications of his words hung in the air, heavy and oppressive. The water lapping against the pier became a distant murmur, swallowed by the sudden intensity of the moment. My heart raced as I tried to piece together what Marcus was hinting at. "What are you talking about? Just spit it out, Marcus."

He stepped closer, dropping his voice further. "There are forces at work that want to keep us—this—under control. There's a reason you were thrust into this rivalry with Nathaniel, and it's not just a petty squabble. There's power in the connection between our families, and it's time you understood what that means."

Nathaniel shifted, clearly agitated, and I felt the tension radiating off him like heat from a flame. "What connection? I don't want anything to do with your family's schemes."

Marcus chuckled darkly. "You say that now, but you're already caught in the crossfire. It's too late to pull out." He turned his attention back to me, his gaze sharp as he gauged my reaction. "You think you're so different, don't you? But you're as much a player in this game as I am."

I took a step back, the weight of his words slamming into me like a freight train. "You don't get to dictate my choices, Marcus. I'll decide what I want to be a part of." My voice trembled with a mix of defiance and uncertainty.

"Oh, but you don't realize the choices you've already made," he shot back, a glint of something sinister in his eyes. "Whether you want it or not, you've opened a door that can't be closed."

Before I could respond, Nathaniel's hand shot out to grab my arm, his grip firm yet comforting. "We need to go," he said, his voice low and urgent. "Whatever you think you're here for, it's not safe. Not with him around."

Marcus straightened, an amused smile playing at the corners of his lips. "Running away, are we? Always the coward's choice."

"Coward? That's rich coming from you," I snapped, fueled by an adrenaline rush. "You're the one lurking in the shadows, hoping to scare us with your threats."

His smile vanished, replaced by a more serious expression. "I'm trying to save you, but you're too stubborn to see it. Just know that your actions have consequences." With that, he stepped back, fading into the darkness from which he had emerged, leaving behind an unsettling tension that hung heavily between Nathaniel and me.

As we stood there, the night felt different—charged, electric, as if the universe was holding its breath, waiting for our next move.

"What just happened?" I breathed, glancing up at Nathaniel, who wore an expression that mixed concern and determination.

"I don't know," he replied, his brow furrowing. "But we can't ignore it. He's right about one thing; this isn't just about us anymore."

The weight of his words settled in the pit of my stomach, mingling with the remnants of my earlier bravado. As the stars twinkled overhead, I realized that the calm we had enjoyed was nothing but an illusion, and the storm was gathering on the horizon, ready to sweep us into its depths.

The silence left in the wake of Marcus's departure was a tangible thing, thick and suffocating, wrapping around us like a fog. The stillness of the night, once a gentle embrace, now felt charged, as if the universe itself were vibrating with tension. I looked up at Nathaniel, who stood rigid beside me, his face a mask of concern that seemed almost out of place against the backdrop of our earlier banter.

"What do we do now?" I asked, my voice barely above a whisper, the weight of uncertainty settling heavily on my shoulders.

Nathaniel's gaze swept the surrounding darkness, his body taut like a coiled spring. "We need to regroup. Whatever game Marcus is playing, we can't let him control the narrative." He shifted closer, and I felt the warmth radiating from him, a stark contrast to the icy grip of fear curling in my stomach.

"Control the narrative? Is that what this is all about?" I said, incredulous. "I thought this was about us, about figuring out who we are away from the expectations."

"Maybe it was. But Marcus has a knack for complicating everything." He ran a hand through his hair, frustration flickering in his eyes. "He knows how to push buttons, and he'll use whatever he can against us."

The reality of our situation sank in deeper, each revelation like a stone dropped into a still pond, creating ripples of unease. "So, what's next? We can't just sit back and let him dictate the terms." The fiery spirit I often relied on flared to life within me, igniting a determination I hadn't fully realized was there.

Nathaniel regarded me, his expression softening slightly. "You're right. We need to find out what he's up to. We can't let him keep us in the dark."

I nodded, emboldened by his words, yet doubt still whispered at the edges of my resolve. "But how? He's always one step ahead, and we're just... us."

"Us is enough," he said, a hint of a smile breaking through the tension. "Besides, we have each other. And if I know Marcus, he's not as infallible as he likes to believe. We just have to outsmart him."

The idea sparked something in me—a flicker of rebellion against the oppressive expectations that had loomed over my life for too long. "Fine. But I want to know everything. I refuse to be a pawn in someone else's game."

"Deal," Nathaniel replied, and we exchanged a look that was charged with mutual understanding, the kind of connection forged in the fires of conflict.

We gathered our things, the night's earlier romance dissipating into a shared mission. As we made our way back along the path leading away from the pier, I felt the air grow denser, as if the world were holding its breath. The trees whispered secrets overhead, and the moon, shrouded in clouds, cast an eerie glow that heightened my senses.

"Do you think he's watching us?" I asked, glancing over my shoulder, half-expecting to see Marcus lurking in the shadows.

"Probably," Nathaniel replied, his voice low. "But let him watch. It'll just make our victory that much sweeter."

A nervous thrill ran through me. "You're really confident about this, aren't you?" I teased, trying to lighten the heavy atmosphere.

"I'm a lot of things, but I prefer 'realistic.' Besides," he added with a smirk, "having you on my side makes me feel like we've got a fighting chance."

I rolled my eyes, playfully nudging him as we walked. "You flatter me. But you're right; I'm not going to let my brother's shadow loom over me anymore. If this is a fight, then let's bring it."

We made our way to a small café that was still buzzing with life, the aroma of coffee and baked goods wafting through the air. Inside, the atmosphere was warm and inviting, a stark contrast to the chill that lingered outside. We settled into a corner booth, the soft glow of string lights providing a cozy cocoon against the chaos swirling in our minds.

"I think we should start by gathering intel," Nathaniel suggested as he sipped his coffee, the steam curling upwards like the questions swirling in my head. "We need to find out what Marcus is really up to. If he's making moves behind the scenes, we need to be prepared."

"Sounds like a plan. But how do we do that without drawing attention?" I asked, already brainstorming the potential risks.

Nathaniel leaned in closer, the confidence in his posture reassuring. "We play it cool. We act like nothing's wrong, while we dig for information. You still have connections at school—friends who might overhear something."

"True, but I don't want to put them at risk," I replied, biting my lip. "What if Marcus finds out?"

"Then we make sure they don't know too much. Just enough to keep their ears open." He paused, considering. "And I can reach out to a few contacts of my own. We need to widen our network."

A sense of excitement bubbled beneath the surface, mingling with the tension still wrapped around us like a blanket. "I like this.

But if we're going to do this, we need to be smart. No reckless moves."

"Agreed," he said, a serious look crossing his face. "One misstep could lead to disaster."

As we plotted and planned, the café buzzed around us, the laughter of friends and the clinking of dishes forming a comforting backdrop to our conversations. We worked together, each idea building off the other, and with every shared thought, I felt the weight of my familial expectations lessen just a little more.

But just as I began to feel a flicker of hope, the door swung open, and the cold air rushed in, accompanied by the unmistakable figure of Marcus. He strode in confidently, his eyes scanning the room until they landed on us, a sly smile curling at his lips.

"Fancy meeting you here," he called out, his voice smooth and dripping with sarcasm. "Planning your next move, are we?"

The world around me slowed, my heart pounding in my chest as realization struck. We were no longer the hunters; we were the hunted.

Chapter 8: Shadows of the Past

The inn stood steadfast against the bracing wind that whistled through the trees, its wooden façade glowing warmly in the encroaching twilight. Flickering lights danced behind the lace curtains, illuminating the laughter and chatter within. The scent of rosemary and garlic wafted from the kitchen, weaving itself through the air, a comforting reminder of home even as an undercurrent of tension crept through the gathering shadows. I had always found solace here, amidst the creaking floorboards and the eclectic mix of guests, each with their own stories and secrets. Tonight, however, an air of foreboding settled over the place like an unwelcome guest.

It began with a knock at the door, sharp and insistent. I glanced at Ella, my closest friend and partner in this chaotic world we called the Ravenwood Inn. She was drying her hands on a flour-dusted apron, her brow furrowed with curiosity and concern. We exchanged a glance; the kind that said everything without uttering a word. As I approached the door, my heart raced, each beat echoing in the stillness that followed.

Swinging it open, I was met with a nondescript cardboard box sitting awkwardly on the doorstep. There was no return address, just a heavy sense of dread hanging in the air. I hesitated, a shiver of instinct telling me to turn back, but the curiosity burned brighter than my caution. I crouched down, examining it, the dull brown of the cardboard absorbing the light, as if it were cloaked in shadows. With a swift motion, I lifted it, feeling the weight of uncertainty in my hands.

"Are you going to open it or just stare at it?" Ella quipped from behind me, her voice laced with the teasing edge that always calmed my nerves. She sidled up next to me, peering over my shoulder. "Maybe it's a treasure map."

"Or a bomb," I replied dryly, shaking my head. "Either way, we're about to find out."

I pulled a utility knife from my pocket and sliced through the tape, my hands trembling slightly. The cardboard flaps fell open, revealing a tangle of shredded paper and a small envelope, its edges frayed and yellowed. I removed it gingerly, the paper crisp and fragile beneath my fingers. There was something ominous about the way it felt, as if it were charged with a warning that danced just out of reach.

"Read it," Ella urged, leaning closer, her excitement tinged with anxiety.

I unfolded the note, the faint scent of aged paper wafting up. My eyes skimmed over the scrawled handwriting, the words coming into focus like a slowly emerging photograph. A chill raced down my spine as I read aloud, each syllable heavier than the last.

"We know your secrets. We will come for what is ours."

The silence that followed was palpable, thick with an unspoken fear that seemed to wrap around us. I could feel Ella's breath hitch in her throat as the implications of the message sank in. The warning wasn't just vague; it was personal. It sent tendrils of panic curling around my heart, a visceral reminder of the chaos that had erupted in our lives not long ago.

"This is not good," I murmured, my voice barely above a whisper. "Not good at all."

"Do you think it's about... him?" Ella asked, the question hanging in the air between us like a ghost.

My thoughts raced back to him—Evan. The man who had stormed into our lives, a whirlwind of charm and danger wrapped into one tantalizing package. There was a connection between us, undeniable and electric, even in the midst of the chaos. But he was also the enemy, a fierce rival vying for the same resources we were. How could I reconcile those feelings with the threat looming over us?

"We have to warn the others," I finally said, determination slicing through the fear. "They need to know."

Ella nodded, her expression shifting from shock to resolve. "Let's gather everyone in the common room. We can figure this out together."

The walk to the common room felt like traversing a battlefield. Each step echoed in my ears, a stark reminder of the burden we bore. The flickering lights cast dancing shadows across the walls, and I could almost hear the whispers of history trapped within the woodwork. It was a place filled with laughter and shared memories, but tonight it felt different—a gathering storm brewing just beyond the horizon.

As we entered, I found the others clustered around the fireplace, their faces illuminated by the warm glow. Laughter and chatter faded into a hushed murmur as they noticed our arrival. The air thickened with curiosity and concern as I stepped forward, holding the note like a talisman against the dark.

"I have something important to share," I began, the weight of my words hanging in the air. "We received a warning, a clear threat against us."

Gasps filled the room, and the warmth of the fire was suddenly overshadowed by a chill that crept into our bones. I glanced around, meeting the eyes of friends turned family, each face reflecting the chaos that had woven itself into the tapestry of our lives.

"Do you think it's about Evan?" Liam, the ever-practical owner of the inn, asked, his brow furrowed as he leaned forward, concern etched in every line of his face.

"I don't know," I replied, the uncertainty clawing at my insides. "But we can't take this lightly. We need to confront whatever this is head-on."

In that moment, surrounded by the people I cared for most, I felt the fragile threads of unity binding us together. The shadows outside might be closing in, but we were not about to let fear dictate our actions. We would stand firm against the darkness, come what may.

As the fire crackled, casting flickering lights across our faces, I felt a surge of defiance welling up within me. I would not be the victim of this threat. Whatever it took, I was determined to protect my family—our family. And if it meant confronting the very feelings that complicated everything, then so be it. After all, life had never been simple, and I wasn't about to let fear unravel the bonds we had forged.

The air in the common room was thick with a mix of apprehension and determination as my friends leaned in, each of their expressions a reflection of the unspoken fears that had begun to seep into the corners of our sanctuary. Ella stepped forward, her voice steady but tinged with urgency. "We need to come up with a plan, something solid. We can't let this message intimidate us into hiding."

I nodded, grateful for her unwavering resolve. "Exactly. We need to figure out who might be behind this and what they want from us."

As the others chimed in, tossing around ideas and half-formed theories, I allowed my gaze to drift to the fire flickering in the hearth, each flame a reminder of the warmth and safety we had built together. It was strange to think that something so small—a note, a threat—could unravel it all. But as the embers glowed brighter, I felt a surge of strength. We were in this together, and whatever awaited us, we would face it head-on.

Liam leaned against the mantel, arms crossed, his sharp eyes darting around the room. "Let's not forget that there's a lot at stake here. If this is about Evan, then we need to tread carefully. He might be a rival, but he's also tied to some pretty powerful people."

"Powerful people who might be trying to scare us off," I said, frustration bubbling just beneath the surface. "But if we show fear, we lose everything we've built. We have to take a stand."

"Then let's do it," Ella said, a fire igniting in her voice. "Let's find out what he knows and how this ties back to us."

The collective murmurs of agreement filled the room, a chorus of determination that fueled my resolve. I could feel the weight of their trust resting on my shoulders, and though the prospect of facing Evan again sent a shiver down my spine, I also felt a strange thrill at the thought. There was something intoxicating about the man—a pull that made it hard to breathe at times, even amidst the chaos.

"I'll reach out to him," I said, surprising even myself with the audacity of my suggestion. "But I need to be careful. We have to keep this quiet. If there's anything he's planning, we can't let him know we're onto him."

The others nodded, some sharing glances that conveyed the weight of my decision. It was a risk, undoubtedly, but something told me that confronting him was the only way to unveil the truth behind the threat.

That night, after the laughter and light faded, I lay in my room, the shadows of the inn stretching across the walls like dark fingers. I couldn't shake the feeling that the walls had ears, that every creak of the floorboards was a reminder that our sanctuary could easily become a prison if we weren't careful. I found myself staring at the ceiling, the words from the note echoing in my mind, the threat a haunting melody.

As dawn crept in, casting soft hues of pink and gold across the sky, I knew what I had to do. I pulled on a sweater and ventured out into the brisk morning air, the cold biting at my cheeks as I made my way down the gravel path leading to the stables. The horses were restless, their breaths forming puffs of fog in the early light, and the scent of hay and leather filled the air, grounding me. I needed the clarity of thought that riding often brought.

After saddling up Bella, my spirited mare, I kicked her into a canter, the world around me blurring into a symphony of colors and sounds. The wind whipped through my hair, and for a fleeting moment, I forgot about the shadows threatening our peace. I rode hard, letting the adrenaline fuel my resolve, pushing past the trepidation that had been gnawing at my insides.

When I finally slowed to a stop by the edge of the woods, my heart racing from the thrill, I felt a sense of purpose settle over me. The trees loomed tall and ancient, their branches whispering secrets that seemed to weave through the air. It was here, amidst the natural world, that I often found my solace. But today, it felt more like a battleground.

The connection I felt with Evan bubbled to the surface again, and I had to push it away. He was a complication I couldn't afford, a dangerous allure that might pull me into a spiral of chaos. But as I gathered my thoughts, a voice echoed through the clearing, startling me.

"Riding alone? You do realize that can be dangerous, don't you?"

I turned sharply, a familiar figure stepping out from behind a tree. Evan's presence was magnetic, his smile both disarming and infuriating. His dark hair ruffled by the breeze, he looked effortlessly charming, as if the very sunlight conspired to highlight his features.

"What are you doing here?" I demanded, fighting the urge to smooth my hair and appear unaffected. "This is private property."

"Ah, but you see, I have a vested interest in the happenings around here," he replied, crossing his arms casually, a confident glint in his eye. "Especially when it comes to messages being delivered to my friends."

I swallowed hard, the tension between us electrifying. "You know about the note?"

"Not all the details, but I have my sources. I was hoping we could discuss it—just the two of us."

His tone was smooth, but there was an edge to it, a layer of urgency lurking beneath the surface. I weighed my options, every instinct screaming at me to turn and ride away, to seek safety within the walls of the inn. Yet, part of me was drawn to him, as if an invisible thread connected us, pulling me into his orbit despite the danger.

"Fine," I finally said, my voice steadier than I felt. "But we do this on my terms. If you think you can intimidate me with your charm, you're sorely mistaken."

He chuckled softly, the sound reverberating through the air. "Intimidate? Not at all. I'm merely here to offer you a chance to learn the truth. The stakes are higher than you realize."

With a deep breath, I steeled myself for the conversation that lay ahead. The winds whispered around us, carrying secrets of their own, and as I looked into his eyes, I knew this would either be a turning point or a descent into chaos. Whatever happened next would demand every ounce of courage I possessed, and I was ready to dive into the unknown, one heartbeat at a time.

The tension in the air was almost palpable as Evan and I stood amidst the towering trees, the rustle of leaves creating a backdrop to our burgeoning confrontation. I felt my heart hammering against my ribcage, both from the chill of the morning air and the weight of the moment. His presence was magnetic, yet threatening, like the calm before a storm.

"You're not here to intimidate me, but you certainly know how to make a dramatic entrance," I said, folding my arms defiantly across my chest, attempting to project a confidence I didn't entirely feel.

"Dramatic is my middle name," he quipped, a playful grin dancing on his lips. "But really, I'm here to help you understand what's really at play."

"And you think I'll just take your word for it?" I shot back, narrowing my eyes. "You're the last person I'd trust right now, especially with a note that implies you might have some involvement in whatever's happening."

"Touché," he admitted, his tone turning serious. "But consider this: the threat is more than just a warning; it's a message from a group that has been watching you. They want to exploit the chaos."

"Exploit? What do you mean?" My curiosity piqued despite the caution swirling in my mind.

Evan stepped closer, his voice lowering to a conspiratorial whisper. "I suspect they're trying to drive a wedge between us, to make us doubt one another. If they can manipulate your fear, they can control the narrative. We can't let them win."

His words hung in the air, dense with the weight of truth. I wanted to dismiss his theory outright, but a flicker of doubt crept in, gnawing at my confidence. "What do you know about this group?" I asked, my resolve momentarily wavering.

"Enough to understand their motives," he replied, frustration edging into his voice. "They thrive on discord and distrust. It's how they operate. The more we bicker and distrust each other, the stronger they become."

"What's in it for you?" I pressed, skepticism lacing my words. "Why would you want to help us?"

"Because I know what it feels like to be hunted," he confessed, his eyes darkening with something that felt far too personal. "And because I don't want to lose anyone else to fear."

For a moment, I saw a flicker of vulnerability beneath his bravado, a glimpse into a past that perhaps mirrored my own experiences with loss and chaos. It was enough to make my heart ache, but not enough to let my guard down.

"Okay, I'll bite," I said, trying to maintain an air of bravado even as the unease churned in my gut. "What's the plan?"

He took a step back, considering. "We need to gather more information. Find out who's behind the message. There are contacts I can reach out to—people who might have insight into what's happening."

"And then what? Wait around until they strike?" I countered, my voice sharp. "We need to take action."

Evan rubbed the back of his neck, clearly frustrated. "I agree, but we need a strategy. We can't charge in blindly, or we'll end up as pawns in their game."

"You're telling me to play it safe?" I raised an eyebrow, amused despite the seriousness of the situation. "I've never been good at that."

"Then maybe it's time to learn," he shot back, a spark of mischief returning to his eyes. "Besides, who would I have to spar with if you get yourself captured?"

"Charming," I retorted, shaking my head, but a reluctant smile crept onto my lips. "Alright, let's say I'm in. What's the first step?"

"First, I need to know who you've talked to about the note. Anyone who might be at risk," he said, the shift in tone making the gravity of our situation clear.

I hesitated, the weight of the truth pressing down. I had confided in Ella, of course, and Liam—my confidants, my family in this mess. But I had also exchanged words with others, people who had wandered in and out of our lives, leaving breadcrumbs of their pasts behind.

"Ella and Liam, but I've also spoken to a few guests who have been around lately," I admitted, the names slipping from my lips like a confession. "They could be in danger too."

"Good," Evan replied, his expression growing serious once more. "Let's start with them. We need to keep our circle tight and watch each other's backs. If they're watching you, they're likely keeping tabs on the inn too."

The notion made my skin crawl, but I nodded, determined to confront the darkness that loomed over us. "I'll gather everyone in the common room. We can discuss the next steps and how we can safeguard ourselves."

As we turned to leave, a sudden rustle in the underbrush caught my attention. I paused, instinctively reaching for Evan's arm, my heart racing as I scanned the shadows. "Did you hear that?"

Before Evan could respond, a figure emerged from the trees, stepping into the dappled sunlight that filtered through the leaves. My stomach dropped when I recognized the familiar silhouette, one I had not expected to see.

"Thought you could use some backup," said a voice that was both unexpected and alarmingly familiar. It was Caleb, my estranged brother, his expression a blend of determination and unease. "I've been following your trail, and it seems we have more than just a simple threat on our hands."

Evan and I exchanged a look, both surprised and wary. "What do you know?" I asked, unable to hide the urgency in my tone.

Caleb stepped closer, his gaze flicking between us. "More than you'd like to hear. I've uncovered something about the group that's been watching you, and I don't think you're prepared for what I've found."

The way he said it sent a jolt of apprehension through me, the kind that pulled tight in my chest. "What do you mean?"

Before he could answer, a rustling from the path behind us drew my attention once more. The chill of dread washed over me as I turned, my heart sinking. Emerging from the shadows was a trio of figures, their expressions masked but their intentions clear.

"Looks like you've all been quite busy," one of them said, a smirk slicing through the tension. "We've come to have a little chat."

The air crackled with danger, every instinct in me screaming to run, to hide. But as I stood there, surrounded by both allies and foes, I realized I had no choice but to confront whatever lay ahead. I had opened the door to this chaos, and now it was time to step through, even if it meant facing the darkest corners of my past.

Chapter 9: Tension in the Air

The night sparkled like shards of shattered glass, a dizzying array of lights flickering across the grand ballroom, which stretched beneath a magnificent crystal chandelier that seemed to hum with whispers of secrets untold. My heart thudded in my chest, not merely from the thrill of the evening, but from the palpable tension that crackled in the air, an electric reminder of the looming danger we were about to face. I stood in front of the mirror, taking in the reflection of my own emerald gown, the fabric cascading around me like a waterfall of color, its rich hue complementing the golden flecks of my eyes. I felt both radiant and exposed, the deep V of the neckline daring the world to look deeper while I tried desperately to keep my composure.

As I turned away from the mirror, the slight rustle of the gown echoed my internal conflict. There was an unsettling duality to my existence tonight—I was stepping into a world of glitz and glamour, but underlined by a heavy sense of foreboding. The warning loomed large in my mind, the cryptic message echoing back to me as I met his gaze across the room. Ethan, dressed in a tailored black suit that hugged him in all the right places, approached with a confidence that made my heart flutter despite the gravity of our mission. His presence grounded me, a steady anchor amidst the whirlpool of uncertainty swirling around us.

"Ready to dive into the shark tank?" he asked, his lips curling into a teasing smirk that softened the tension in his deep-set eyes. The way he leaned against the doorframe, arms crossed casually yet protectively, made me wish the stakes were lower. I appreciated the way he carried himself, effortlessly blending into the opulence surrounding us, yet I knew that lurking just beneath his easy charm was an urgency that matched my own.

"Only if you promise to keep me safe," I replied, my voice lighter than I felt. We both knew the stakes. This gala wasn't just an evening of wine and laughter; it was a gateway into the underbelly of power and deceit. I could almost feel the whispers of danger curling around my ankles, like tendrils of smoke, as I stepped into the fray.

Ethan extended his arm, a gentleman's offer that made my heart race and my pulse quicken. I took it, and together we stepped into the ballroom, the world falling away as the intoxicating scents of expensive perfume and aged whiskey enveloped us. Laughter bubbled up like champagne, bright and fleeting, masking the unspoken threats simmering beneath the surface. Guests glided by, each more opulent than the last, shimmering like precious stones under the soft glow of chandeliers.

I couldn't help but feel small amongst them, but there was a thrill in the vulnerability. With every step, I felt more like a player in this grand game, determined to uncover the truths hidden behind charming smiles and polite conversations. I glanced at Ethan, whose presence radiated warmth and strength. He seemed to understand the unvoiced fears that tangled in my stomach, the adrenaline coursing through me like a live wire.

"Stick close," he murmured, leaning in just enough for me to catch the faint scent of his cologne—a mix of sandalwood and something intoxicatingly fresh. "I have a plan, but we need to blend in first. Just play the part."

I nodded, allowing the words to wash over me as I scanned the room, searching for familiar faces, the enemies we had yet to identify. Somewhere in this crowd, a shadowy figure lurked, their intentions as dark as the midnight blue sky outside.

The evening unfolded like a beautifully crafted tapestry, threads of laughter interwoven with moments of tension. I mingled with a group of elegantly dressed women, each one a picture of poise and sophistication, while my mind danced in a different rhythm, constantly analyzing every word and glance exchanged. One of them, a petite blonde with ice-blue eyes, leaned in closer, her voice a conspiratorial whisper, "Have you met Mr. Roth? He's positively enchanting—if you're into that sort of thing."

I smiled politely, though a flicker of unease rippled through me at the mention of the businessman who held sway over our lives. He was powerful, influential, and dangerously charming. I had no doubt that his gaze was already roaming the room, assessing potential threats, and sizing up those who dared to encroach upon his territory.

"Enchanting can often be a façade," I replied, my tone light but laced with caution. The blonde regarded me with curiosity, but the conversation shifted, and I felt a pang of regret for my own prudence. In a world where charm was currency, I had chosen the path of skepticism.

Ethan reappeared at my side, his expression a mixture of amusement and intrigue as he caught the tail end of the conversation. "Not a fan of Mr. Roth, I take it?"

I shrugged, my heart racing at his closeness. "He seems more like a puppeteer than a prince charming."

His laughter was low and warm, stirring something deep within me. "You may be right. But tonight, let's focus on the dance rather than the puppets."

The music swelled, pulling us into its rhythm. As we joined the swirling mass of bodies, I lost myself for a moment, the world around me fading as we twirled and swayed. The closeness of Ethan's body felt electric, the tension between us palpable, every brush of our hands igniting a spark that threatened to engulf me. But with every spin, every fleeting moment of laughter, I reminded myself of the danger that loomed just beyond the edges of our revelry.

We navigated the dance floor, each step drawing us deeper into the heart of the gala. And with every glance exchanged, I felt the weight of our shared mission pressing down on me, reminding me that beneath the glimmering façade of elegance, there lay shadows waiting to be unearthed. I needed to stay sharp, to keep my wits about me as we edged closer to the truth that threatened to unravel everything we held dear.

As the music swelled around us, transforming the ballroom into a pulsating heart of energy and intrigue, I felt the warmth of Ethan's presence grounding me amidst the chaos. The familiar rhythm of our bodies swaying together drew me into a state of blissful distraction. But as we spun beneath the glittering chandeliers, my gaze flickered across the room, scanning for any signs of the trouble we were here to uncover. Each face held a mask, some more convincing than others, but the weight of their secrets pressed down like a thick fog, obscuring the truth I desperately sought.

"Why do I get the feeling we're just two pieces on a chessboard?" I remarked, trying to keep the mood light while grappling with the unease gnawing at my insides.

Ethan grinned, a spark of mischief lighting up his eyes. "Because you're a queen, and I'm a very handsome knight, ready to save you from the pawns."

I couldn't help but laugh, the sound bubbling up between us like a burst of sunlight breaking through clouds. "Charming and modest. You do know how to flatter a girl."

"Only the ones who can handle a little danger," he replied, leaning in closer as the music faded momentarily. His breath was warm against my ear, sending a shiver of excitement coursing through me. "Speaking of danger, did you see Mr. Roth?"

At the mention of his name, my heart skipped a beat. I scanned the crowd, finally spotting the man who had woven himself into the fabric of our lives like a dark thread. He stood near the far wall, a commanding figure in his tailored suit, surrounded by a small entourage that seemed both enraptured and wary of his every word. Roth was the type of man who could silence a room with a single glance, and tonight, he radiated an aura of invincibility, a king surveying his domain.

"I'd recognize that smirk anywhere," I muttered, my lips tightening in distaste. "He's definitely the puppeteer."

"Let's not let him see us sweat," Ethan said, his tone shifting from playful to serious. "We'll stay close, keep our eyes open. The last thing we want is to draw attention."

As the music picked up again, I forced a smile, masking the tension in my gut. The gala was in full swing, the atmosphere thick with laughter and the clinking of crystal glasses. Yet I couldn't shake the feeling that we were teetering on the edge of something monumental. With every rotation, I felt the weight of expectations pressing down—expectations from our families, from the past, and from the shadows that followed us.

"Have you ever wondered," I began, my voice laced with curiosity, "what it would be like to just slip away from all of this? To leave behind the masks and the games?"

Ethan's eyes sparkled with intrigue as he led me into a more secluded corner of the ballroom, away from the prying eyes of the elite. "You mean, like running off to a tropical island and living off coconuts?"

"Something like that," I laughed, though the idea was far from ridiculous. In that moment, a sudden thrill of rebellion surged through me, tempting me to abandon the constraints of this carefully curated world. "Just a little place where no one knows our names and the only thing on our agenda is deciding between the beach and a hammock."

He tilted his head, studying me with an intensity that sent my heart racing. "Sounds idyllic. But would you really want to escape? What about the danger lurking in the shadows?"

I hesitated, the thrill of escape mingling with the sobering reality of our mission. "I guess that's the challenge, isn't it? To confront the shadows rather than run from them."

Before he could respond, a sudden commotion drew our attention across the room. A man had spilled red wine all over a woman in a dazzling sapphire gown, the liquid pooling around her feet like a crimson omen. Laughter erupted, but I noticed the flicker of annoyance cross her face, quickly masked by a smile. It was a stark reminder that, beneath the veneer of elegance, chaos lurked just beneath the surface.

"Looks like the night is getting messy," Ethan observed dryly. "But that's what makes it exciting, right?"

"Right," I replied, though a tinge of discomfort lingered. "This isn't just a party; it's a battleground. And we're the ones trying to uncover the hidden weapons."

We fell into an easy rhythm, the conversation flowing as effortlessly as the music. I allowed myself to be drawn into the moment, laughing at his witty jabs, each one accompanied by a glimmer of something deeper. But beneath the surface, my mind remained sharp, piecing together the puzzle of tonight's gathering.

"Let's go grab a drink," I suggested, glancing toward the bar at the edge of the room, which gleamed under the soft lights, laden with a variety of spirits that beckoned like sirens. "I need something strong to fortify my courage."

"Courage is overrated; a good cocktail will do the trick," he replied, winking as we wove our way through the crowd.

At the bar, the bartender flashed a smile, as if he were in on the secret of our adventure. I ordered a gin and tonic, the tartness promising to cut through the anxiety coiling in my stomach. Ethan ordered something dark and brooding, the name of which I couldn't quite catch over the din of chatter and laughter.

"Here's to courage, cocktails, and chaos," he toasted, raising his glass with a flourish.

I clinked my glass against his, a burst of warmth flooding through me as I met his gaze. "And to unraveling the secrets hidden in plain sight."

Just then, a sudden shout cut through the merriment, sharp and jarring. I turned, my heart racing as I caught sight of Roth, his face twisting into an expression of anger. The crowd around him recoiled, whispers rippling like a wave, and I felt a chill race down my spine.

"Who's he yelling at?" I asked, my voice barely above a whisper.

Ethan's expression hardened. "I don't know, but we should—"

Before he could finish, the crowd parted like the sea, revealing a figure standing defiantly before Roth, a striking woman with wild hair and fierce determination blazing in her eyes. She stood tall, unyielding, and every instinct screamed that she was someone important—a player in this deadly game who had finally chosen to step into the spotlight.

I held my breath as the tension in the room reached a fever pitch. The unexpected twist had thrown a wrench into our plans, and suddenly, our evening of charm and cocktails had transformed into something darker and infinitely more dangerous. With every heartbeat, the air thickened with anticipation, and I knew we were about to discover just how deep the shadows ran.

The atmosphere in the ballroom shifted dramatically, the tension like a taut string ready to snap. Roth's eyes flared with indignation as he stared down the defiant woman, her unwavering stance a stark contrast to the elegantly dressed elite around us. My heart raced, caught in a whirlwind of confusion and intrigue. Who was she? What had prompted Roth's fury?

Ethan's grip on my arm tightened as he leaned closer, his voice barely above a murmur, "We need to move. If this escalates, it could get ugly."

I nodded, my gaze still locked on the scene unfolding before us. The air crackled with unspoken words, the kind that linger just beneath the surface, threatening to burst forth and shatter the illusion of civility that enveloped us. The woman stepped forward, her chin lifted defiantly, and I could see a fierce determination radiating from her. It was intoxicating, like a siren's call, and I felt an inexplicable urge to know her story.

"Roth," she said, her voice steady and firm. "You can't keep using people as pawns in your game."

Gasps rippled through the crowd, the murmurs of shock blending with the clink of glasses and the steady thrum of music. My mind raced, trying to connect the dots. Roth had made a name for himself in ruthless business deals, but this was personal. The stakes were rising, and I could feel the impending confrontation in my bones.

Ethan pulled me to the side, a strategic maneuver that felt both protective and urgent. "Stay close, but keep your distance. If she's confronting Roth, it's not going to end well."

"Who is she?" I asked, my curiosity piqued despite the warning bells ringing in my head.

"Don't know," he admitted, eyes fixed on the pair. "But I've seen that fire before. She's not backing down."

Roth's face contorted with anger, his voice dripping with sarcasm. "Oh, please. Spare me the theatrics. You think you can sway public opinion with your little performance here? You're out of your depth."

"Maybe," she shot back, unfazed. "But at least I'm not afraid to speak the truth. Unlike you, who hides behind your money and influence."

It was a battle of wills, and I was mesmerized. The other guests around us were caught between their fascination and discomfort, much like I was. Some whispered behind gloved hands, others watched with open mouths, unsure how to react. I could feel Ethan's tension radiating beside me, but I was drawn in, a moth to the flame.

"What's your plan?" I whispered, turning to him. "Do we intervene?"

He shook his head, eyes still on the unfolding drama. "We need to know more. If she's got dirt on Roth, it could be our ticket to unraveling this whole mess."

My heart raced with the possibilities, but another part of me feared what might happen if this confrontation spiraled out of control. Just then, the woman took a bold step closer to Roth, her voice rising above the din of the crowd. "You think you're untouchable, don't you? But everyone has a breaking point, and yours is coming."

Roth's laughter was cold, devoid of humor. "You're making a mistake, sweetheart. You think this is a game, but you're playing with fire."

The crowd was hushed now, anticipation hanging in the air like smoke. I felt Ethan's breath quicken beside me, the tension between us palpable. We were standing on the precipice of something monumental, and I wasn't sure whether to hope for a resolution or brace for chaos.

"Do you really think you can just waltz in here and threaten me?" Roth continued, his eyes narrowing. "You've underestimated the consequences of your actions."

Before I could process the threat, Roth reached for his glass, his movements deliberate as he took a slow sip. The room felt suspended in time, everyone holding their breath as the confrontation reached a boiling point.

The woman didn't flinch, her expression fierce and unwavering. "You're right about one thing—this isn't a game. It's about the lives you've destroyed for your gain."

With that, she turned on her heel, her striking presence commanding the room. I caught a glimpse of her as she moved, a whirlwind of passion and defiance that left an electric charge in the air. My admiration mingled with an unsettling fear; she was playing a dangerous game, and the stakes were about to rise.

"Wait," I urged, suddenly aware of my own impulse. "We need to follow her."

Ethan's brow furrowed, a mixture of concern and determination etched across his features. "Are you serious? We don't even know what she's walking into."

"I can't just stand here," I insisted, my resolve hardening. "She's risking everything to expose him. We might be able to help."

He hesitated for a moment, the weight of the decision hanging between us. But then he nodded, a fierce determination igniting in his eyes. "Fine. But we stick together."

We maneuvered through the throng of guests, weaving our way toward the edge of the crowd, where the woman had disappeared. I felt the palpable tension lingering behind us, a reminder of the chaos Roth could unleash. As we reached the corner of the ballroom, I spotted her slipping through a set of double doors that led to a dimly lit hallway, and without a second thought, I followed.

The hallway was a stark contrast to the opulence of the gala—a narrow, dimly lit space that seemed to echo with the whispers of the past. The air felt heavier here, as if the walls themselves bore witness to secrets best left unspoken.

I turned to Ethan, urgency in my voice. "What if she's walking into a trap?"

"Then we'll have to outsmart it," he said, his tone firm. "Just stay alert."

We crept forward, our footsteps barely audible on the polished floor. As we approached the end of the hallway, I could hear the faint murmur of voices—Roth's unmistakable cadence threading through the air. My heart raced with the realization that we were inching closer to the confrontation I had hoped to witness.

Ethan motioned for silence, his eyes narrowing as he peered around the corner. I held my breath, the anticipation choking me. Just then, the door swung open, and Roth emerged, his expression a mixture of fury and disdain. He glanced down the hall, and for a fleeting moment, I thought he could sense our presence.

"Find her!" he barked, his voice cutting through the silence like a blade. "She can't escape. Not after what she's just done."

Panic surged through me. This was it; we had to act fast. But before we could retreat, a hand gripped my shoulder, spinning me around with a force that sent shockwaves through my body. I found myself face-to-face with a stranger—tall, imposing, and all too familiar with the darkness that permeated this world.

"What are you doing here?" he demanded, his eyes narrowing in recognition. "You shouldn't have come."

A thousand thoughts raced through my mind, but one word rose above the rest, resonating like an alarm bell. "Run!" I screamed, even as dread pooled in the pit of my stomach, knowing we were standing on the edge of a precipice—one that could swallow us whole if we didn't escape its grasp.

Chapter 10: Unmasking Deception

The gala hall shimmered like a jewel in the night, adorned with crystal chandeliers that cast a warm, golden glow over the sea of elegantly dressed guests. Laughter and clinking glasses created a symphony of celebration, but beneath the surface, an undercurrent of tension thrummed like a tightly strung bow, ready to snap. I felt the pulse of the room, a vibrant tapestry woven with secrets, half-truths, and carefully masked emotions. As I moved through the crowd, my heart raced—not just from the sheer opulence around me, but from the presence at my side.

Sebastian stood there, his tailored suit hugging his form in all the right places, the faintest hint of a smirk playing on his lips as he caught my eye. I hated that he was beautiful in a way that was both infuriating and magnetic. Every time I stole a glance at him, I was reminded of our history—a clash of wills and simmering animosity that felt as familiar as the silk of my gown brushing against my skin.

"Do you always wear that expression?" I quipped, my tone light, masking the turmoil beneath. "Like you just swallowed a lemon?"

He raised an eyebrow, an amused twinkle in his hazel eyes. "And yet, here you are, tethered to me like a moth to a flame." His voice was a low rumble, barely above the din, and I felt a flicker of warmth beneath my skin. There was a spark between us, igniting each time we exchanged words, charged and alive. It was maddening, really, how he had a way of unsettling me even in this sea of laughter and glamour.

"Hardly," I replied, feigning indifference as I scanned the room, taking in the swirling gowns and tuxedos, the glittering masks that concealed identities, much like the hidden agendas woven into the very fabric of our families. My gaze landed on a small group huddled in a corner, their whispers sharp and urgent. I strained to hear, my curiosity piqued. They spoke in hushed tones, the flickering candlelight casting shadows over their faces, revealing a tension that made my heart race.

"—cannot let them find out," one of them hissed, glancing around as if the walls themselves had ears. "It would ruin everything."

"Then we must act before the night ends," another voice responded, tight with fear and determination. My breath hitched; a conspiracy was brewing, one that wove our families into its sinister web. The urgency in their voices echoed in my mind, the realization dawning that tonight was not merely about celebration but something far more perilous.

"Are you going to keep ogling the gossipmongers, or are we going to mingle?" Sebastian's voice cut through my thoughts, a teasing lilt that pulled my focus back to him.

I rolled my eyes, though a smile tugged at my lips despite myself. "As if mingling with your crowd is any more appealing than listening to them plot our doom."

"You underestimate the power of charm," he replied, his smirk widening. "Come now, let's not be caught staring like common eavesdroppers." He took my arm, guiding me away from the encroaching shadows, yet I could still feel their whispers trailing behind us like a veil of intrigue.

As we meandered through the throng, the air thick with perfume and laughter, I found my heart racing not just from the thrill of potential danger but also from the intoxicating proximity of Sebastian. He was a puzzle, a contradiction wrapped in an enigma. His laughter was light, but his eyes held the weight of something deeper, something more profound. I couldn't decipher if it was passion or darkness lurking just beneath the surface.

"Tell me," I said suddenly, the words spilling out before I could think better of it. "What are you really doing here, Sebastian? Surely it's not just to torment me at a party."

He paused, and I could see the flicker of surprise in his gaze, quickly masked by that familiar nonchalance. "You wound me, Charlotte. I thought I was the highlight of your evening."

I couldn't help the laugh that escaped my lips, sharp and genuine. "You're not even in the top ten, and that includes the hors d'oeuvres."

"Perhaps I should step up my game," he mused, and the way he said it held an undercurrent of seriousness that set my heart racing anew. It felt like a challenge, one I was both eager and reluctant to accept.

Just then, the lights flickered, plunging the room into a momentary dimness before bursting back to life. Gasps echoed, and a slight hush fell over the crowd. It was as if the very air had shifted, charged with electricity. My instincts kicked in, and I glanced around, searching for the source of this sudden shift in atmosphere. It felt like a warning—a subtle nudge that something was about to unfold, and I was both terrified and exhilarated by the prospect.

"Do you feel that?" I asked Sebastian, my voice low, barely more than a breath.

"Like the world is about to change?" He was serious now, his gaze scanning the room with newfound intensity. "Yes."

Before I could respond, the murmurs I had overheard earlier swelled to a crescendo, voices rising above the music. People began to congregate, drawn toward the center of the room where a large projection screen had flickered to life, illuminating the crowd with an ominous glow. I squeezed Sebastian's arm, the sudden sense of foreboding wrapping around us like a shroud.

"Come on," I urged, dragging him toward the crowd. "Let's find out what's happening."

As we pushed through the throng, the whispers morphed into a cacophony of confusion. The screen displayed an image, a grainy photograph of two figures standing close together, their faces obscured. My stomach dropped. This was not merely a social gathering; it was a stage for unmasking hidden truths, a confrontation looming on the horizon like a storm. My heart raced as I turned to Sebastian, searching his expression for answers, but all I found was a resolve that mirrored my own fear.

"We need to know what's going on," I said, my voice firm as I held his gaze, grounding myself in the strength of his presence. "Whatever they're hiding, we have to unearth it before it's too late."

He nodded, determination igniting in his eyes. We stood on the precipice of a revelation, and despite the chaos swirling around us, I knew in that moment that I would protect him, no matter the cost.

The image flickered on the screen, the grainy photograph demanding our attention as the crowd hushed, anticipation thickening the air. A collective intake of breath passed through the guests, a wave of confusion that was palpable enough to make the crystal chandeliers tremble. I stood there, heart pounding, my gaze locked on the shadowy figures captured in that snapshot, an enigma poised to unravel before us.

"Is it just me, or does that look like someone we know?" Sebastian murmured, leaning closer, his breath warm against my ear, sending an unexpected shiver down my spine. His proximity felt both electrifying and unsettling, the tension between us charged with unspoken words.

I strained to focus, squinting at the screen. "That hair looks familiar," I replied, my voice barely above a whisper. "But the lighting is terrible. It could be anyone."

"You think it's someone from the board?" he mused, his brows furrowing, his voice laced with intrigue. "Or perhaps one of the families we've been told to steer clear of?"

"More like the families we're supposed to be allied with," I countered, my eyes narrowing as the plot thickened. The room was filled with murmurs, the whispers swirling around like the gentle rustle of silk against skin, laden with speculation. I felt as if we were trapped in a twisted fairy tale where nothing was as it seemed, the villains cloaked in designer suits and high-end jewelry.

As the image faded, the screen displayed the words "Secrets Revealed" in bold, dramatic lettering. My heart sank. This was no ordinary gala; this was a stage set for an unveiling that could shatter lives, and here we were, caught in the middle of a brewing storm.

"Do you think they'll show us who's behind it?" I asked, my voice tinged with dread. "Because I don't think I'm ready for this."

Sebastian's expression shifted from playful to serious, and for a moment, I saw the flicker of something deeper in his gaze—an acknowledgment of our shared vulnerability. "Ready or not, the truth has a way of coming out. Sometimes it's best to confront it head-on."

I caught the glint of determination in his eyes, and it sparked something within me. It was easy to forget how much I disliked him when he spoke like that, with such conviction. Yet, the thought of the truth unraveling left me feeling both exhilarated and terrified. Would I be able to handle whatever came next?

Suddenly, a figure stepped into the spotlight, a woman draped in a striking red gown that clung to her curves like a second skin. Her presence commanded attention, the fabric shimmering as she walked. Dark hair cascaded over her shoulders in elegant waves, and her face was painted with an expression that oscillated between confidence and menace.

"I see many familiar faces here tonight," she began, her voice smooth as silk, captivating the crowd like a spell. "But it's time to lift the veil on our hidden truths."

Sebastian and I exchanged glances, a silent understanding passing between us. This was it—the moment when the tangled threads of our lives would either come together or unravel completely.

"Who is she?" I whispered, my heart racing as I leaned closer to Sebastian, drawn by the gravity of the moment.

"That's Celeste Montgomery," he replied, his voice low. "Head of the Montgomery family. Her influence runs deep, and not just in the business world."

The crowd murmured, a mix of respect and apprehension rippling through them. I had heard whispers of the Montgomerys, of their connections and their power, but seeing Celeste in the flesh made it all too real. She radiated authority, and I couldn't shake the feeling that she was playing a game far beyond my comprehension.

"I think she might just enjoy this," I muttered, my eyes narrowing as I watched her command the stage.

She continued, "Tonight, we unveil the truth that has long lurked in the shadows—truths that bind us all together in a web of history, loyalty, and betrayal. We can no longer hide behind façades."

The words hit me like a cold wave, sending chills down my spine. Betrayal? History? My mind raced, recalling the conversations I had overheard earlier, the whispers of dark family secrets. What had I walked into?

Celeste gestured toward the screen, and the next image flickered to life—two figures standing in front of a lavish estate, the name of which sent a shockwave through the crowd. "This is the residence of the Hawthorne family, where a clandestine meeting took place just weeks ago."

Gasps echoed through the hall, eyes widening in disbelief. I felt my breath hitch, dread pooling in my stomach. The Hawthornes were intertwined with our family's legacy, a history marked by alliances forged in both love and rivalry.

"Tonight, we reveal who has been pulling the strings," Celeste declared, a glint of mischief dancing in her eyes. "Prepare yourselves, for the truth is about to shake our foundations."

"Do you think she's talking about us?" I whispered to Sebastian, my voice shaky. The very air seemed to vibrate with uncertainty, like the stillness before a storm.

"If she is, then we need to be ready," he replied, his expression steely. "We can't let them paint us into a corner."

A tension gripped my chest as I realized the stakes were higher than I'd imagined. If our families were truly bound in this conspiracy, our futures were at risk. But there was something else brewing within me—a fierce resolve.

"Let's figure this out together," I said, determination lacing my words. "I won't let them manipulate us. If they think they can unveil the truth and use it against us, they're mistaken."

Sebastian's gaze softened, and in that moment, I sensed a fragile alliance forming between us, one built not just on shared animosity but a mutual desire for truth and freedom.

"Agreed," he said, the corner of his mouth quirking up in that infuriatingly charming way. "But don't think I won't enjoy the chaos that ensues."

"Always the charmer," I retorted, the tension between us shifting into something lighter, teasing. "Just remember, if you end up in the doghouse, I won't be bailing you out."

"Fair enough," he shot back, his grin infectious. The fleeting levity of our banter made the impending chaos seem a little less daunting.

The spotlight dimmed again, the air crackling with suspense as Celeste prepared to reveal the next layer of this twisted tale. I grasped Sebastian's hand, feeling the warmth and strength of his presence grounding me amidst the uncertainty.

In this moment, as shadows danced across our faces and secrets threatened to consume us, I knew we would face whatever lay ahead together—an uncharted territory filled with danger, deception, and perhaps, just maybe, a flicker of hope.

The spotlight shifted once more, illuminating Celeste with an intensity that made her seem almost ethereal. Her voice rang out clear and commanding, slicing through the tension that hung heavy in the air. "Tonight is not just about unveiling truths; it's about accountability. We are all here because we have chosen to participate in a legacy that binds us, for better or worse. And some of us..." She paused, allowing her gaze to sweep over the audience, a predator assessing its prey. "Some of us are more entangled in this web than we would like to admit."

I felt my heart race, caught between the spectacle of her performance and the dread of what was to come. The flickering light bathed her in a warm glow, but her words sent chills down my spine. The crowd leaned in, captivated, while I found myself clutching Sebastian's hand a little tighter. The energy between us crackled, a mixture of anticipation and shared resolve.

"Who is she targeting?" I whispered urgently to Sebastian, my instincts on high alert.

"I don't know," he replied, his expression a mixture of curiosity and concern. "But it's clear she's about to expose something significant."

Celeste's voice rang out again, now laced with an undercurrent of menace. "Let us begin with the Hawthorne family's latest acquisition—the land that was once the pride of the Montgomerys. We all know the story, but what you may not know is the underhanded deal that secured it." She leaned forward, the dramatic pause stretching as the audience held its breath. "A deal brokered in darkness, one that involves collusion, deceit, and betrayal."

Gasps erupted from the crowd, and I felt the color drain from my face. The Montgomerys had always regarded the Hawthornes with suspicion, their bitter rivalry simmering beneath a veneer of civility. But to accuse them of underhanded dealings in such a public forum was tantamount to declaring war.

I glanced at Sebastian, who looked equally stricken. "We need to find out who she's referencing," I muttered, already scanning the crowd for anyone who might look guilty—or terrified. "This could get ugly."

"Agreed," he said, eyes narrowing as he surveyed the room. "If there's one thing I know about galas, it's that the real drama often happens behind closed doors."

As if on cue, Celeste gestured again, and the screen switched to a series of images—documents, signatures, and the faces of prominent figures. My stomach twisted as I recognized some of them. "And here," she continued, "we have the signatures of those who helped facilitate this betrayal. A web of deceit that ensnares not just the Hawthornes, but also several familiar faces from this very room."

The room erupted in a flurry of shocked murmurs. I exchanged a glance with Sebastian, a mutual understanding passing between us. The game was changing, and we were right in the thick of it.

"Look!" he pointed subtly to a figure in the crowd—Eleanor Hawthorne, her face ashen, desperately whispering to a companion. "She looks like she's about to bolt."

I turned my gaze back to the screen, my heart racing. "Do you think she's in on it? Or is she about to be outed?"

"Maybe both," Sebastian replied, his eyes glinting with a mix of mischief and seriousness. "We need to find out what she knows."

Before I could respond, Celeste's voice rang out once more, now filled with righteous fury. "We stand at a crossroads, ladies and gentlemen. Do we continue to allow these treacherous acts to dictate our lives, or do we stand united against this betrayal? We cannot afford to be complacent!"

I felt my pulse quicken as the room buzzed with renewed energy, the crowd now split between fear and defiance. The air crackled with tension, and I couldn't shake the feeling that this was a pivotal moment—one that could alter the course of our lives.

Sebastian leaned closer, his breath warm against my ear. "We should find a quiet corner and figure out our next move. This chaos is just beginning, and we can't let it swallow us whole."

I nodded, adrenaline coursing through me. "Lead the way, but let's avoid any dark alleys or secret chambers, shall we?"

He chuckled softly, his humor a welcome balm amid the swirling chaos. "I promise to keep our adventures above ground. For now."

As we made our way through the crowd, I caught snippets of frantic conversations and hushed accusations, each word amplifying my unease. The gala, once a celebration of wealth and glamour, had morphed into a battleground where alliances were tested and friendships dissected under the harsh glare of truth.

We slipped into a quieter corridor, the ornate decor contrasting sharply with the gravity of the moment. Here, away from the chaos, I could think more clearly, my mind racing with possibilities. "What do you think we should do next?" I asked, taking a breath to steady myself.

Sebastian ran a hand through his hair, a gesture of frustration mingled with determination. "We need to gather intel. Someone here must know the truth about the deal and the parties involved. If we can expose the real puppet masters behind this, we may have a chance to turn the tide."

I nodded, a sense of purpose igniting within me. "And what if it leads us back to our families?"

"Then we deal with it," he replied, his voice unwavering. "We can't let fear dictate our choices, Charlotte."

Just then, the sound of footsteps echoed down the corridor, drawing our attention. A figure emerged from the shadows—Eleanor Hawthorne, her expression frantic, her eyes darting as if she were being pursued. "You!" she gasped, spotting us. "You need to help me."

I exchanged a startled glance with Sebastian. "Help you? Why would we do that?"

"Because I'm not who you think I am," Eleanor insisted, her voice trembling with urgency. "They're planning something, something terrible. If we don't act fast, it could destroy everything."

"Who's 'they'?" I pressed, stepping closer.

"The families," she said, her voice barely above a whisper. "The ones who think they're untouchable. I overheard them plotting, and now they know I know."

My heart raced. "What did you hear?"

But before she could respond, a loud crash erupted from the main hall, followed by a scream that pierced the air like a knife. I felt a rush of fear course through me as the crowd reacted in shock, all eyes drawn to the chaos that was unfolding.

"Stay here!" Sebastian ordered, already moving toward the source of the commotion. But Eleanor clutched my arm, her grip like iron.

"No! We can't stay here!" she pleaded, panic radiating from her. "You don't understand—this is bigger than any of us!"

Before I could decide whether to follow Sebastian or heed Eleanor's warning, the corridor erupted into chaos. The sound of hurried footsteps thundered closer, and I felt the ground shift beneath me as everything I thought I knew began to unravel.

A shadow loomed at the entrance, silhouetted against the flickering lights, and my breath caught in my throat. The figure stepped forward, and my heart dropped. I recognized him instantly—one of the most powerful players in this intricate game, and he was not here for pleasantries.

"Let the games begin," he said, a sly smile creeping across his face.

In that moment, everything felt poised on the brink, ready to tip into an abyss of danger, and I could only hold my breath as the truth surged toward us, inevitable and dark.

Chapter 11: Fractured Alliances

The flickering candlelight danced across the polished surfaces of the grand ballroom, casting long shadows that stretched like anxious fingers across the marble floor. The air was thick with the mingling scents of lavender and something sweeter, a confection that masked the tension lingering like an uninvited guest. As I maneuvered through the crowd, my heart pounded in time with the pulsating rhythm of the string quartet, each note striking a discordant chord with the turmoil brewing inside me.

The gala was supposed to be a celebration—a night where dreams collided with reality under a canopy of opulence. Instead, it felt like an elaborate stage set for a tragedy, with me caught in a web of lies spun by those I had dared to trust. I forced a smile, the kind that felt more like a grimace, as I exchanged pleasantries with the guests. They were draped in jewels and silk, oblivious to the cracks forming beneath the surface of my carefully curated world.

Then there was him, my partner in this twisted dance of intrigue and desire, standing just beyond the cascading waterfall of silk curtains. His eyes, usually so bright with mischief, now carried the weight of secrets I had only begun to uncover. Just hours before, we had shared laughter over flutes of champagne, the bubbles racing to the surface like the thrill of newfound love. But the revelation of his family's underhanded dealings had shattered that illusion, leaving jagged pieces scattered in the corners of my mind.

The confrontation echoed in my thoughts—his defensiveness, my accusations. "You should have told me," I had insisted, my voice sharp enough to cut through the evening's festivities. The hurt in his eyes had mirrored my own, and in that moment, it felt like we were both standing on a precipice, the ground crumbling beneath us. I couldn't shake the feeling that every smile and every shared glance had been tinged with deceit. Was I merely a pawn in a game far more dangerous than I had imagined?

With a deep breath, I stepped away from the crowd, seeking solace in the shadows cast by the grand chandeliers. I needed air, a moment to recalibrate my racing thoughts. Each step echoed in my ears, the thumping of my heart drowning out the laughter and clinking glasses behind me. As I turned a corner into a dimly lit alcove, the atmosphere shifted. The air grew colder, and I felt a prickle at the back of my neck—a sensation that I was not alone.

I pressed my back against the cool wall, the rough texture grounding me in reality, but my mind was still spiraling. I was lost in thoughts of betrayal, of mistrust. Just as I began to wonder if this place held more shadows than light, I caught sight of a figure emerging from the darkness. Panic surged through me, and I instinctively took a step back, ready to flee. But then I recognized him.

"What are you doing here?" I demanded, my voice a mix of anger and relief.

He stepped closer, his expression tense, his brow furrowed as though he were wrestling with the very same doubts that tormented me. "I could ask you the same," he replied, the playful lilt in his voice replaced by a seriousness that pulled at my heart. "You shouldn't be alone."

"Is that what this is?" I challenged, crossing my arms defiantly. "A protective instinct? Or are you just worried about how it looks if I'm caught wandering off alone?"

His eyes darkened, a storm brewing behind them. "You think I care what they think?"

The words hung in the air, thick with unsaid emotions. "Then what do you care about?" I shot back, unable to contain the bitterness creeping into my tone.

In a heartbeat, the tension exploded. He took a step forward, closing the distance between us, his hand reaching out to brush against my arm. The contact sent a jolt through me, igniting a spark that was both infuriating and intoxicating. "I care about you," he said, his voice low and raw, filled with a desperation that matched my own. "But everything is complicated, and I don't want to drag you into my family's mess."

"Too late for that," I replied, my voice shaking, though I couldn't tell if it was from anger or something deeper, something more vulnerable. "You've already dragged me in."

The silence that followed felt charged, each heartbeat echoing the truth we both tried to deny. It was as if the world outside had faded away, leaving just the two of us in this cocoon of uncertainty. And then, against my better judgment, I found myself stepping closer, drawn to him like a moth to a flame.

Before I knew it, the air between us shifted, and in an instant, we were enveloped in an embrace that felt like a surrender. His arms wrapped around me, strong and unyielding, as if to shield me from the chaos outside. I closed my eyes, allowing the warmth of his presence to wash over me, the tumult of our earlier argument fading into the background. In that moment, our fears and desires entwined, creating a tangled web of connection that was both exhilarating and terrifying.

"Do you think we can trust each other?" he whispered, his breath warm against my hair, a gentle reminder of the battle still raging between us.

"I don't know," I admitted, my voice muffled against his shoulder. "But right now, I want to."

The honesty hung between us, a fragile thread that could snap at any moment, yet here we were, clinging to it with desperate hope.

The warmth of his embrace lingered in the air as I pulled away, our moment suspended like a whispered secret in the stillness of the alcove. I could feel the heat radiating from his body, a stark contrast to the cold doubt that had settled in my chest. I searched his face for answers, but the shadows lurking in his eyes only deepened my uncertainty. This wasn't merely a romantic entanglement; it was a tangled web of allegiances, betrayals, and a past that threatened to eclipse everything we could become.

"What are we doing?" I asked, my voice a mere tremor in the otherwise serene space, the soft strains of the quartet continuing to play in the background as if mocking our turmoil.

He ran a hand through his hair, a gesture I had come to recognize as a sign of his agitation. "I'm not sure anymore," he admitted, his tone laced with frustration. "One moment, I think we can figure this out, and the next, I'm terrified I'll lose you."

The vulnerability in his admission struck a chord within me. It mirrored the swirling fears that had taken root in my own heart. I wanted to reach out, to reassure him that I was still here, still willing to fight for whatever we had started. But just beneath the surface, doubts clawed at me, whispering insidious questions. How could I trust someone entwined with a family steeped in secrecy and manipulation?

"What if we're just fooling ourselves?" I countered, the words spilling out before I could stop them. "What if this is all a facade, a fleeting moment between two people too caught up in the thrill of it all?"

His expression hardened, a flash of pain igniting in his eyes. "I'm not a facade, and neither are you. I don't want to pretend. Not with you."

"Then why didn't you tell me the truth from the beginning?" I pressed, the anger returning like a tidal wave. "Why let me get caught up in your world without knowing the real stakes?"

"I was trying to protect you!" he shot back, his voice echoing in the hollow space. "Every decision I made was for you. My family... they're complicated. I didn't want to drag you into their chaos."

"Too late," I replied, the sharpness of my tone surprising even me. "You've already pulled me into this mess, and now I don't know who to trust."

He stepped closer, his eyes searching mine as if he were trying to decipher an intricate puzzle. "Trust takes time. Let me show you I'm more than my family. I want to be better—for you."

I held his gaze, battling the urge to give in, to believe the sincerity in his voice. "And if I find out you're lying again?"

"Then you have every right to walk away," he said, his voice low but firm. "But I need you to give me a chance to prove myself. Can you do that?"

The tension hung in the air, electric and raw. I could feel my heart thundering in my chest, wrestling with the part of me that wanted to believe him against the part that was screaming to protect myself. "What do you propose we do?"

His expression shifted, a hint of a smile breaking through the tension, reminding me of the boyish charm that had first drawn me to him. "Let's start with honesty. I'll tell you everything, no more secrets. But you have to promise to listen without jumping to conclusions."

A reluctant breath escaped me. "Alright. But if you leave anything out..."

"I won't," he interrupted, his voice earnest, almost desperate. "I swear. I'll start from the beginning."

As he began to speak, recounting the tangled history of his family—his father's ambition, his mother's relentless pursuit of power, and the moral compromises made in their pursuit of wealth—my mind raced to keep pace with his words. It was like peeling back layers of an onion, revealing not only the pungent truth of their dealings but also the weight they had placed on his shoulders. Each revelation added complexity to the man standing before me, and the tangled threads of his life began to weave themselves into a larger tapestry.

"I was supposed to be the perfect son, the heir who carried on the legacy," he confessed, his eyes darkening with the weight of his memories. "But I never wanted that life. I wanted to be... me. To make choices that felt right, not just what was expected."

"What does that mean for us?" I asked, the question hanging in the air like a promise yet to be fulfilled.

"It means I'm willing to fight for what I want," he said, determination etching his features. "And I want you in my life, not just as a secret or a trophy. I want us to navigate this chaos together."

Just as the moment started to feel hopeful, a familiar voice sliced through the atmosphere like a blade. "There you are, darling! I've been looking everywhere for you!" A striking woman emerged from the crowd, her presence commanding, the shimmer of her gown accentuating the sharpness of her gaze. My heart sank as I recognized her—his mother.

"Mother, this isn't a good time," he said, the tension in his voice palpable.

"Oh, but it's the perfect time for family!" she cooed, her gaze flicking to me with a cool appraisal that made my skin crawl. "And who is this lovely young woman?"

I straightened, steeling myself against the penetrating scrutiny of the woman who had clearly been waiting for her moment. "I'm—"

"Don't bother," she interjected smoothly, cutting me off. "I'm well aware of who you are. The girl who thinks she can change my son's path. Isn't that adorable?"

The condescension in her tone was infuriating, yet I felt my resolve harden. "I'm not here to change anyone," I replied, my voice steady. "I'm here for him."

Her laughter rang out, brittle and sharp. "How noble of you. But trust me, darling, change doesn't come easily in our world. It's a dance, and you'd do well to learn the steps before you trip over your own ambitions."

The air crackled with tension as she stepped closer, her gaze icy and unwavering. I could feel my heart racing, the weight of the moment pressing down on me. Whatever fragile truce had formed between us moments before felt like it was slipping away, threatened by the specter of his family looming over us.

"You can't protect him from his family," she continued, a smirk playing on her lips. "And sooner or later, you'll realize that."

"Enough," he said, his voice cutting through the tension like a knife. "You don't get to speak for me. I'm done with your games."

The room seemed to hold its breath as the atmosphere shifted, leaving me caught between his resolve and the palpable tension crackling from his mother. I had stepped into a world far more intricate than I had anticipated, and with each passing moment, it became increasingly clear that the battle for our future was just beginning.

The atmosphere in the alcove shifted like a live wire, crackling with unspoken words and unrestrained emotions. His mother's arrival had punctured the fragile bubble we had constructed, and the ensuing tension was almost tangible, curling around us like smoke. I felt a strange mixture of anger and protectiveness surge within me, not just for myself but for him. This wasn't just about our budding romance; it was about claiming our agency amidst a tempest of expectations and manipulations.

"I don't need your approval, Mother," he said, his voice steady, yet I could hear the strain beneath the surface. "You've made your choices. I'm making mine."

"Oh, honey, it's sweet that you think you have a choice." She leaned in slightly, her perfume—a sickly sweet blend of gardenia and something sharper—clung to the air between us. "This isn't a game. You're dealing with a legacy that you can't simply wish away."

"I'm not wishing anything away. I'm choosing to live my life," he retorted, an edge creeping into his voice. "And that includes being with her."

"Her? Do you really think she understands the stakes here?" she sneered, her eyes narrowing as she scrutinized me. "What do you even know about us, darling? About the sacrifices made for this family? You think this is just about love?"

My breath caught in my throat, her condescension a bitter pill to swallow. "I know enough to see through your veiled threats," I shot back, surprising even myself. "You may be his mother, but you don't control his life—or mine."

For a moment, silence reigned, heavy and suffocating. His mother blinked in shock, her carefully composed demeanor cracking ever so slightly. The ballroom beyond us continued to pulse with laughter and music, but here, time seemed suspended as we stood on the precipice of something monumental.

"Do you hear that, sweetheart?" she finally said, her tone syrupy but laced with malice. "The music? It's a reminder of how out of your league you really are."

I felt the weight of her words like stones sinking in my stomach. But as I looked at him, standing resolute beside me, I realized that I wasn't backing down. "Maybe it's you who needs to listen," I challenged, my voice steadying with conviction. "He's not a pawn in your game. You may have raised him, but you don't own him."

"Enough!" he interrupted, stepping in front of me, a shield against the storm. "This isn't about you and me, Mother. It's about what you've done to our family, what you've made us become. I refuse to be a part of it any longer."

Her expression darkened, and for the first time, I saw a flicker of vulnerability beneath her steel facade. "You think you can walk away? You think your little rebellion will change anything? It won't. Our enemies are watching, and they won't hesitate to strike if you turn your back on us."

My heart raced as I grasped the gravity of her words. The very foundation of his family's legacy was crumbling, and we were at the center of it. "What enemies?" I asked, my voice barely above a whisper, anxiety curling around my throat.

"Those who want to see us fail," she said, her gaze shifting between us as if assessing her options. "The alliances we've forged are fragile. They could break at any moment if you continue down this reckless path."

"Stop," he said, cutting her off. "You're using fear to control me. That's not going to work anymore."

"You think you're the first one to stand up to me?" she retorted, her tone sharp as a blade. "You think I'll just let you walk away? You have no idea what you're up against."

Just then, a sudden commotion erupted from the main ballroom, a cacophony of voices rising above the music. My pulse quickened as I turned to see guests parting like the Red Sea, their faces painted with a mix of confusion and concern. I glanced back at him, uncertainty gnawing at my gut. This was becoming something far more perilous than a simple family squabble.

"Stay close," he murmured, his hand finding mine and squeezing tightly, grounding me amidst the chaos unfolding around us. "We need to find out what's happening."

As we moved through the gathering crowd, the air felt thick with anticipation, each heartbeat echoing the anxiety coursing through me. I could hear snippets of conversations, hushed whispers laced with fear, and dread curled in the pit of my stomach.

"What's going on?" I asked, trying to catch glimpses of the unfolding drama.

"Something about a break-in," he replied, his brow furrowing. "We need to get to the bottom of this. If it's connected to my family..."

We pushed through the throng, and I could see the tension rippling through the guests as they exchanged furtive glances. The ornate doors at the far end of the room swung open, and a group of men in dark suits strode in, their expressions grim and urgent. Instinctively, I tightened my grip on his hand, feeling the weight of the moment settle heavily on my shoulders.

"Stay behind me," he ordered softly, his voice low but commanding.

My heart thundered in my chest as we approached the unfolding scene. The men began to address the crowd, their voices cutting through the murmurs like shards of ice. "We need everyone to remain calm," one of them said, his tone clipped and authoritative. "There has been a security breach, and we're currently assessing the situation."

The murmurs grew louder, panic creeping in as people exchanged worried looks. I could feel my heart racing, each beat a reminder of the stakes involved. This wasn't just a gala anymore; it was a battlefield, and we were caught in the crossfire.

"What kind of breach?" I pressed, my voice barely above a whisper, but he shook his head, his eyes darting around the room as if searching for something—or someone.

Before he could respond, a woman burst through the crowd, her eyes wide and frantic. "They've taken someone!" she cried, her voice cracking with fear. "They've taken him!"

The words hit me like a punch to the gut, and I froze, the world around me blurring into a haze of panic. "Who?" I managed to ask, but my voice felt lost amidst the chaos.

"The heir," she gasped, clutching her hands to her chest as if trying to contain the dread swirling around her. "They've taken him, and they're demanding a ransom."

His grip on my hand tightened painfully, and I could feel the tension radiating off him. I had assumed we were discussing his family's politics, but this was a whole new level of danger.

"What do they want?" he asked, his voice barely a whisper, the resolve in his eyes turning into something more desperate.

"They didn't say. Only that they want a meeting. Tonight."

The realization hit me like a jolt, an electric surge of fear and adrenaline. This was no longer just about us; this was about his family, their legacy, and perhaps our lives. "We have to go," I said, urgency propelling my words.

But before we could move, a flash of movement caught my eye from across the room. A figure slipped through the crowd, their intentions hidden behind a mask of shadows. My breath caught in my throat as I recognized the familiar silhouette, the cold fear surging anew.

"Wait!" I shouted, but it was too late. The figure darted toward the exit, leaving behind a trail of uncertainty that coiled around me like a serpent. The gala was unraveling, and in its wake, I felt the ground beneath me shift, threatening to swallow us whole.

With one last glance at the chaos, I turned to him, determination flaring within me. "We can't let them take anyone else," I said, my voice firm despite the uncertainty hanging in the air.

He nodded, his expression resolute. "Let's find out what we're really dealing with."

And as we moved deeper into the throng of chaos, a chilling realization settled over me: in this world of shadows and secrets, nothing was as it seemed, and we were just beginning to unravel the truth.

Chapter 12: A Descent into Darkness

The old estate loomed before us, a grotesque silhouette against the bruised twilight sky. Its once-grand façade was now a canvas of peeling paint and creeping ivy, as if nature conspired to reclaim it. I felt a shiver creep down my spine, not just from the cold that hung in the air like a lingering secret, but from the gnawing apprehension that had settled in my gut ever since we stumbled upon the first clue—an innocuous photograph tucked beneath a floorboard in my grandmother's attic. A photograph that linked our families in ways I had never imagined.

As we stepped through the threshold, the creaking door echoed our hesitation, a dissonant prelude to the chaos that awaited us inside. Dust motes danced in the pale light filtering through grimy windows, and the scent of mildew hung thick, wrapping around me like a shroud. Each step deeper into the estate seemed to amplify the thudding of my heart, a wild drumbeat against the silence. I glanced sideways at Ethan, my companion in this treacherous dance. His brow was furrowed, eyes narrowed, and for a moment, I could almost see the wheels turning in his mind, unraveling the tangled threads of our entwined destinies.

"What are we hoping to find here?" he asked, his voice low, as if the walls themselves might overhear and betray us. The air was dense with unspoken fears, and I could feel my own insecurities bubbling to the surface. We were children playing at detective work, stepping far beyond the bounds of our naïveté, yet here we were—two unlikely allies, united by an insatiable curiosity and a desperate need for answers.

"I don't know," I admitted, the words tumbling out before I could stop them. "Maybe just a glimpse into the truth. Or maybe we're just chasing shadows." I felt a flicker of embarrassment, but Ethan's expression softened, an understanding passing between us. In that moment, I recognized our shared vulnerability—a bond crafted in the crucible of fear. It was comforting yet disconcerting, like standing too close to a fire.

As we navigated the dimly lit corridors, the floorboards protested under our weight, their creaks resonating like whispers in the dark. Each room we passed felt like a time capsule, remnants of lives once lived now dust-covered and forgotten. I caught a glimpse of a grand piano draped in sheets, its keys silent witnesses to the laughter and sorrow that once filled these walls. A flicker of longing pierced my heart. What stories could it tell? What secrets did it hold, just like us?

We paused at a door that appeared slightly ajar, the flickering light beyond beckoning us like a siren. Taking a deep breath, I pushed it open, and we stepped inside. The room was surprisingly intact, adorned with faded portraits that stared down at us, their eyes unblinking, as if guarding the memories trapped within. A heavy desk dominated one corner, papers strewn across it like fallen leaves, bearing names that sent a chill through me—names from both our families. The evidence of our ancestors' lives mingling in this forsaken space was a visceral reminder of how deeply intertwined we had become.

"What the hell?" Ethan whispered, bending closer to the scattered papers. I moved beside him, my stomach knotting at the sight of documents referencing secret meetings and coded messages. It felt like we had cracked open a Pandora's box, and whatever came spilling out would forever change the narrative of our families.

"This...this can't be real," I murmured, picking up a particularly worn sheet. The ink was faded but legible, detailing a transaction that sent my mind racing. "They were involved in something illegal. Drugs? Human trafficking?" The implications of what we were uncovering felt like a heavy weight pressing down on me, threatening to crush me under its enormity.

Ethan's expression darkened, the playful spark that usually danced in his eyes extinguished. "We need to leave," he said, his voice steady yet urgent. But I found myself rooted in place, a morbid curiosity anchoring me to the spot. What if we were the only ones who could bring this to light? The thought pulsed through my veins, igniting a fierce determination within me.

"No," I insisted, shaking my head. "We can't just walk away. Not now. Not when we've come this far." The resolve in my voice surprised even me, but the thought of letting this opportunity slip through my fingers was unbearable. Ethan's eyes widened, a mixture of admiration and concern flickering in his gaze.

"Okay," he relented, a reluctant smile breaking through his worry. "But we do this together. No more playing hero." The weight of our unspoken agreement hung heavy in the air, and I felt an unexpected thrill course through me. We were embarking on a dangerous path, one that could either shatter everything we knew or forge a new beginning from the ashes.

As we sifted through the papers, piecing together the tangled threads of our families' legacies, I couldn't shake the feeling that we were being watched. A shiver skated across my skin, a primal instinct warning me of impending danger. The shadows in the corners of the room seemed to deepen, coalescing into a lurking presence that was all too aware of our intrusion.

"Did you hear that?" I whispered, my voice barely a breath, as the floorboards creaked ominously behind us. Ethan tensed, his expression hardening as he turned toward the door. The air crackled with tension, the thrill of discovery now mingling with an undercurrent of dread. Whatever darkness lay hidden in this estate, it was awakening, and we had stirred it from its slumber.

The door swung open with a reluctant groan, revealing the narrow hallway beyond. I held my breath, feeling the hair on the back of my neck rise as the air thickened with an ominous weight.

The shadows stretched toward us, dark tendrils that threatened to wrap around our ankles, pulling us back into the depths of this forgotten estate. Ethan's eyes darted toward the end of the corridor, where flickers of movement teased our senses, weaving a tapestry of uncertainty and unease.

"We might not be alone," he whispered, a thread of urgency lacing his words. I couldn't tell if it was fear or excitement that made my pulse quicken, but I stepped forward nonetheless, the promise of truth compelling me onward. If we were about to confront the ghosts of our pasts, I'd prefer to face them head-on.

"Great. Just what I needed. A ghostly audience for our little investigation," I replied, trying to lighten the moment. Ethan shot me a glance that mingled exasperation with a hint of admiration, but he didn't retort. Instead, he followed my lead, his resolve anchoring me as we navigated the murky unknown together.

As we crept along the hallway, I noticed the walls were adorned with peeling wallpaper, revealing layers of decay beneath. Each step we took seemed to echo through the house, a cacophony of sound that amplified our heartbeats. The scents of dampness and old wood mingled in the air, heavy and cloying. I could almost taste the history clinging to the walls, like an old tale waiting to be unraveled.

We reached a room at the end of the hall, the door slightly ajar. My curiosity piqued, I peered inside. The space was a study, the remnants of a life once vibrant scattered across the furniture. Bookshelves lined the walls, their spines cracked and faded, while a massive oak desk stood at the center, littered with papers, ink stains, and an old lamp that cast a warm, inviting glow. It was almost comforting, like an oasis amidst the desolation.

"Wow, this place really knows how to keep its secrets," I murmured, stepping inside. I was immediately drawn to a faded leather-bound book on the desk, its pages yellowed with age. "Look at this." I flipped it open, revealing meticulous handwriting and strange symbols that danced across the pages like a secret language begging to be decoded.

Ethan leaned over my shoulder, the warmth of his body a steady presence. "What do you think it is?" His voice was a hushed reverence, as if we were intruding on something sacred. I shrugged, flipping through the pages, my fingers brushing the fragile paper.

"Looks like some sort of ledger. It might be a record of transactions, or…" My voice trailed off as I came upon a page marked with a large, red circle. The ink was still bold, the words written with a frantic energy that made my skin prickle. "Ethan, this looks important."

"What does it say?" he asked, peering closer. I felt the heat of his breath on my neck, an unexpected rush of warmth that ignited a spark of something unnameable.

"It mentions a meeting, some sort of trade happening tonight," I replied, excitement bubbling within me. "And it's not just any trade—it involves both our families." The words hung in the air like a dire warning, electrifying our surroundings. The implications were staggering, weaving a thread that bound us tighter than I had ever anticipated.

"Tonight? As in, we might be in the right place at the wrong time?" Ethan's eyes widened, and I could see the gears turning in his mind, strategizing our next move. "We need to leave. Now."

"Not yet," I countered, my voice steadier than I felt. "What if this is our chance? What if we can uncover something that explains all this mess?" The urgency in his expression made my heart race, but I couldn't let fear dictate our actions. The mysteries of our past beckoned, and I was unwilling to retreat.

Before Ethan could respond, a sound shattered the stillness—footsteps echoing through the hall. My breath hitched in my throat, and I motioned for silence. The footsteps grew louder, and I could feel the tension crackling in the air like static electricity before a storm. I quickly shoved the book into my bag, the weight of our discoveries pressing against me, a reminder of the stakes we were playing for.

Ethan grabbed my arm, his grip firm yet reassuring. "What do we do?" he asked, urgency dripping from his tone. We shared a moment of quiet understanding, a flicker of determination igniting in our gazes. There was no turning back now.

"Hide," I whispered, my heart pounding against my ribcage. Without another word, we slipped behind the desk, crouching low. The shadows enveloped us, a sanctuary in the midst of uncertainty. My mind raced as I listened intently to the footsteps approaching, each echo amplifying the adrenaline coursing through my veins.

Through the narrow gap between the desk and the wall, I caught a glimpse of a figure in the doorway—tall, imposing, with a sharp silhouette that sent chills racing down my spine. He stepped into the room, his presence commanding, and I could feel Ethan's breath quicken beside me. I bit my lip, trying to suppress a gasp as the man surveyed the study, his eyes scanning the room with a predatory intensity.

"Is anyone here?" he called out, his voice low and gravelly, like stones scraping against one another. The air crackled with tension as I held my breath, praying he wouldn't look our way. My heart pounded in rhythm with the impending dread, a countdown to disaster.

The man stepped further inside, his gaze sweeping over the desk, the papers, and the scattered remnants of lives lived in this forgotten space. "I know you're here," he said, a sly smile creeping across his lips as if he relished the thrill of the hunt. "Come out, come out, wherever you are."

My pulse raced as Ethan and I exchanged panicked glances. What kind of danger had we stumbled into? The man moved closer, his footsteps echoing like a death knell, and I felt a wave of panic wash over me. In that moment, I realized that this estate was more than just a relic of our pasts; it was a battleground of secrets and lies that could consume us if we weren't careful.

"We need to make a run for it," Ethan whispered urgently, his eyes darting toward the door, weighing our options. But just as we began to inch away from our hiding spot, the man's gaze locked onto the space where we had been crouching. My breath caught in my throat, and for a heartbeat, time seemed to freeze. We were no longer mere investigators; we had become pawns in a dangerous game, with shadows and whispers closing in around us.

The man in the doorway didn't move, his gaze piercing through the dim light, as if he were testing the very fabric of the shadows for any signs of life. My heart raced, a wild drum in my chest, drowning out the soft whispers of our collective breaths. The tension hung thick in the air, a palpable force that threatened to suffocate us. Ethan's fingers tightened around my wrist, his touch both a warning and a promise that we were in this together.

"We can't stay here," I hissed, a desperate urgency creeping into my voice. I could feel my instincts screaming at me to run, to escape the predator lurking in the room. The walls felt like they were closing in, and I needed to make a move before the silence betrayed us.

With a silent nod, Ethan and I began to inch back, the old desk creaking ominously beneath our weight. Every sound seemed amplified, echoing off the walls like a warning bell. I couldn't shake the feeling that the man was toying with us, a cat poised over its cornered mouse, reveling in the suspense of the moment. I glanced back at him, just in time to catch the hint of a smirk playing on his lips.

"Too late for that," he said smoothly, his voice low and almost mocking. "You think I don't know how to find you? You've walked right into my trap."

Ethan and I froze, the color draining from my face. This was no simple intruder; he was a predator, and we had blundered into his den of secrets. "What do you want?" I managed to croak, my voice barely above a whisper, panic threatening to choke me.

His smirk widened, revealing a glimmer of teeth in the darkness. "Let's just say I'm very interested in the family connections you've been digging into. You have no idea how deep the roots of this corruption go." His eyes glinted with a predatory light, and a cold shiver skated down my spine.

Ethan's hand tightened around mine, and I could feel the pulse of determination in his grip. "We're not here to play your games," he shot back, a defiance in his voice that surprised me. I felt a rush of warmth at his bravery, even as my mind spun with thoughts of how precarious our situation had become. We were outnumbered and outmatched, caught in the web of a man who likely knew more than we ever could.

"Games? Oh, darling, this isn't a game. This is life and death. And right now, you're both in over your heads." He took a step forward, the light catching his features, revealing a face that was both handsome and unsettling. "Now, I can make this easy for you—or I can make it very difficult."

"Easy sounds nice, how about you let us leave?" I quipped, attempting to inject humor into a situation that felt increasingly dire. But I was met with a cool chuckle that sent a chill racing down my back.

"Cute, but I'm afraid that's not how this works. You see, your families have been playing their parts in this sordid little drama for too long. It's time for a reckoning." His voice dripped with an eerie calmness, as though he were announcing the arrival of dessert rather than a threat.

Ethan moved subtly, shifting his weight as if plotting an escape route. I knew that look; it was the same one he wore when he was about to dive headfirst into trouble—his eyes sparkling with mischief even in the face of danger. "If you're going to kill us, can we at least have some say in the matter?" he retorted, a wry smile creeping onto his face.

"Ah, feisty. I like that." The man leaned closer, the stench of stale cigarettes wafting over us, almost suffocating. "But this isn't about killing you. Not yet, anyway. I need you both to understand the stakes."

Before I could respond, the sound of heavy footsteps echoed outside the door. My stomach sank as I realized we weren't alone anymore. The man's demeanor shifted instantly, his smile evaporating into a look of keen interest.

"Looks like my guests are arriving sooner than expected," he said, the glimmer in his eyes intensifying. "And you two will play a very important role."

Panic surged within me, my instincts flaring. "Ethan, we have to go!" I urged, my voice urgent. But as I spoke, the door swung open to reveal two men, faces obscured by shadows, their postures rigid and threatening.

"Get them," the man ordered, his voice low and authoritative.

Adrenaline shot through me, a primal instinct for survival kicking in. "Run!" I shouted, grabbing Ethan's arm and pulling him toward the nearest window, desperate for an escape. But just as we turned, one of the newcomers lunged for us, grabbing Ethan's shoulder and spinning him around.

"No!" I screamed, the sound tearing from my throat, panic and fear igniting a fire in my chest. I felt like I was moving in slow motion, every second stretching into eternity as Ethan's eyes locked onto mine—his expression a mix of determination and fear.

"Go!" he shouted, and with a surge of strength, he broke free from the man's grasp. The moment felt electric, charged with the unspoken promise of survival. But I hesitated, torn between the instinct to flee and the need to protect the bond we had forged in darkness.

I turned and sprinted toward the window, adrenaline coursing through my veins. The heavy glass loomed before me, and I could hear the chaos erupting behind us, the sound of footsteps pounding against the wooden floors like a heartbeat quickening in tempo.

As I reached the window, I felt a hand on my arm, strong and unyielding. "We have to—" I started, but my words were cut short by a sharp pain slicing through my side. I glanced down, horror flooding through me as I realized I had been caught—an unforgiving grip that yanked me back into the room.

The men were closing in, shadows converging as I struggled against the weight of the darkness that threatened to consume us. Just as I felt the cold fingers of despair clutching at my throat, I caught sight of Ethan, his expression fierce and defiant as he hurled himself at the nearest man.

"Let her go!" he roared, but before I could scream his name, the world spiraled into chaos—a cacophony of shouts and the clatter of bodies colliding, and all I could do was watch as the shadows engulfed him.

In that moment, time froze, a breath caught between fear and resolve, leaving me teetering on the precipice of despair. I knew this was a fight we could not afford to lose, but as the darkness closed in, a chilling realization dawned upon me. We were not just pawns in this game; we had become players in a deadly encounter, and the stakes had never been higher.

Chapter 13: The Heart's Reckoning

The forest loomed around us, a tapestry of shadows and silvery moonlight woven through the leaves, transforming the ordinary into a realm of magic. The air was thick with the scent of pine and damp earth, mingling with the heady fragrance of blooming wildflowers that dared to thrive in this secluded sanctuary. I could hear the rhythmic whisper of the wind, a soft serenade that accompanied the thudding of my heart, a metronome marking time in a world that felt suspended between chaos and calm. He stood there, just a breath away, his gaze locked onto mine with an intensity that both thrilled and terrified me.

"Do you think we'll ever really escape this?" I asked, my voice barely above a whisper, each word laden with the weight of our shared fears and unspoken desires. I had often felt that our lives were a series of narrow escapes, each one leaving us breathless and scarred, yet alive against all odds.

"Escape?" He chuckled softly, the sound a warm embrace in the cool night. "I don't know. But if we do, I'd rather do it with you than alone." There was a lightness in his tone, an echo of hope that flickered like a candle fighting against the wind. I could see the lines of worry etched into his forehead, but in this moment, he chose to look beyond them, daring to dream of something brighter.

As I gazed into his eyes, I felt the carefully constructed walls I had built around my heart begin to crumble, brick by brick. It was maddening how quickly the tide of my emotions had shifted. Just days ago, we were adversaries, tangled in a web of distrust and disdain. Now, here we were, standing on the cusp of something profound, a fragile bridge spanning the chasm of our tumultuous past.

"I've hated you for so long," I confessed, the words slipping out before I could catch them. "It's maddening how easy it is to fall into this… this… whatever it is between us." The admission felt freeing, yet terrifying. I half expected him to laugh, to dismiss my feelings as mere folly in the face of danger. But instead, he took a step closer, our breaths mingling, a tangible connection that sparked electricity between us.

"I never hated you," he replied, sincerity woven through every syllable. "I was angry, yes, but hate? That was never it. I was just too stubborn to admit how much you meant to me."

His honesty struck me like a bolt of lightning, illuminating the shadowy corners of my heart that I had thought were forever shrouded in darkness. In that fleeting moment, we were stripped bare, our defenses laid down like discarded armor. The laughter and barbs that had once filled our exchanges fell away, replaced by something far more vulnerable and beautiful.

"Maybe we're just two broken people trying to mend our pieces together," I mused, my fingers grazing his arm, feeling the warmth radiating from his skin. I was caught in the kaleidoscope of his gaze, swirling with every color of emotion, a reflection of my own confusion and longing.

"I like that," he said, a slow smile creeping across his face, and suddenly, the tension of the moment morphed into something light, something buoyant that lifted my spirits higher than I thought possible. "Let's mend each other, then."

And in that heartbeat, the world around us faded into a hushed whisper as I leaned in, instinctively drawn to him, the distance between us evaporating. My lips brushed against his, tentative at first, like a hesitant dancer on the edge of the stage, afraid to step into the spotlight. But the moment our mouths met, the spark ignited into a blaze of warmth and fervor. It was intoxicating, a whirlpool of passion that threatened to consume us whole.

Just as I surrendered to the sweetness of the kiss, a sound sliced through the night like a knife, shattering the delicate spell we had woven. A sharp crack echoed through the trees, followed by a low growl that sent chills racing down my spine. The warmth that had enveloped us dissipated, replaced by an icy grip of fear that seized my heart.

I pulled back, our foreheads still touching, our breaths mingling, but the urgency of the moment crashed down upon us. "What was that?" I whispered, the words barely escaping my lips as dread clawed at my throat.

"Stay behind me," he commanded, his voice a low rumble, the playful banter replaced by an edge of seriousness that sent a shiver of awareness through me. The shadows deepened, swirling like dark tendrils reaching for us as we both turned, straining to pierce the gloom.

The world that had felt so safe mere moments ago now morphed into an arena of uncertainty, and my heart raced with a primal instinct to flee. But rooted in place, I couldn't help but steal another glance at him, the silhouette of the man I had begun to trust—who had unexpectedly become my ally in a battle far larger than either of us had anticipated.

A rustle in the underbrush made my pulse quicken. I grasped his arm, the muscle taut beneath my fingers, a reminder that we were not alone, and whatever was lurking in the dark was drawn to us. My instincts screamed at me to run, but a flicker of defiance ignited within. Whatever came next, I would stand my ground, side by side with him.

"Together?" I murmured, the resolve in my voice surprising even me.

"Always," he affirmed, his eyes glinting with determination, even as danger drew closer, a shadow poised to pounce. In that moment, I knew we were bound together, not just by the remnants of our rivalry, but by a fierce love that could not only survive the storm but thrive within it.

The darkness closed in, but I was ready to face it head-on, armed with the strength of our connection and the undeniable truth that love, no matter how fragile, was worth fighting for.

The rustle in the underbrush snapped me back to reality, a stark reminder that danger was not a mere figment of our imaginations. It was real, palpable, and closing in. A thick tension settled between us, palpable enough to slice through the humid air, and I instinctively took a step closer to him. The warmth radiating from his body was my only anchor amidst the uncertainty that swirled around us like a thick fog.

"What do you think it is?" I asked, my voice steady despite the tremors of fear reverberating within. My heart pounded, each beat a drum echoing the primal instinct to survive.

"Let's hope it's just a rabbit," he replied, a half-smile dancing at the corners of his mouth. The bravado in his voice didn't quite mask the tension in his posture. He shifted his weight, a primal readiness glimmering in his gaze. "But I wouldn't bet my life on it."

Before I could respond, the bushes parted with a loud crack, and my breath hitched in my throat. Out of the shadows emerged a figure, not the fluffy creature I had hoped for but a towering silhouette cloaked in darkness. My pulse raced as it stepped into the moonlight, revealing itself to be a tall man, his features obscured by a hood that cast a veil of mystery over him.

"Who are you?" I demanded, summoning the courage that simmered beneath my fear. The moment felt surreal, as if we had stumbled into the pages of a thriller novel, the kind I'd once devoured with a cup of tea and a blanket pulled tight around my shoulders.

"Just a traveler passing through," he replied, his voice low and smooth like velvet. But the glint in his eyes told another story, one fraught with secrets and intentions that simmered just below the surface. "Though it seems I've stumbled into something far more interesting."

"Interesting? Is that what you call it?" I shot back, crossing my arms defensively. "Because it feels more like a nightmare."

The man chuckled softly, and the sound sent a shiver down my spine. "You'd be surprised how many nightmares can turn into delightful surprises."

I shared a quick glance with him beside me, his eyes wide with caution. There was something in the stranger's demeanor that set my instincts on high alert, a dangerous allure that pulled at my curiosity even as it pushed my sense of self-preservation into overdrive.

"Perhaps you'd like to share your delightful surprises elsewhere," my companion interjected, stepping slightly in front of me, his body a shield against the unknown. The protective gesture sent a rush of warmth through me, even as my heart raced with the realization that we were very much in a precarious situation.

"Very noble of you," the man replied, a smirk playing on his lips. "But I think I'll linger for a moment longer. After all, the night is young, and the company is… intriguing."

"Intriguing? That's one way to describe impending doom," I muttered under my breath, feeling the tension creep back in.

"Tell me, what are two bright souls like yourselves doing in a place like this? Isn't it dangerous?" he continued, his gaze flickering between us, a predator sizing up its prey.

"We're just looking for a little peace," my companion answered, his voice even and unyielding. "But it seems you're not here to facilitate that."

The man chuckled again, and I couldn't shake the sense that he was enjoying our discomfort. "Peace is overrated. I'm here for adventure."

"Adventure?" I echoed, skepticism lacing my tone. "Is that what you call lurking in the woods at night?"

"Lurking?" he scoffed, feigning offense. "I prefer to think of it as exploring. The forest has many secrets, you know. Some are worth uncovering."

"Or avoiding," I shot back, irritation prickling at my nerves. "What secrets are you after?"

He leaned closer, the moonlight glinting off his eyes, revealing a flicker of something dangerous—a hunger, perhaps, or a desperation I couldn't quite place. "Rumors of lost treasure, hidden deep within these woods. They say it's guarded by a force so fierce that only the bravest would dare to seek it."

"Treasure?" I said, incredulous. "In a place like this? You can't be serious."

"I assure you, I'm as serious as they come." He smiled, and for a moment, I was taken aback by the charm that seeped through his menacing facade. "But I suppose you wouldn't be interested in something so... daring."

"Daring is one word for it," my companion interjected, his voice steady. "We're more interested in staying alive right now."

"Alive?" The man laughed, a deep, resonant sound that echoed through the trees. "Ah, but what's life without a little risk? Without stepping outside your comfort zone?"

"I think I'd prefer the comfort of my own home, thanks," I retorted, crossing my arms tightly against my chest.

The man's expression shifted, the playful glint in his eyes replaced by something sharper, more focused. "Tell me, what are you two really running from?"

My heart dropped. The question sliced through the bravado I had carefully constructed, exposing the raw, jagged edges of my vulnerability. I met my companion's gaze, and for a fleeting moment, we were two souls adrift in a sea of uncertainty, tethered only by the thin thread of trust we had begun to weave.

"Nothing that concerns you," he said, a protective edge lacing his voice.

"Ah, but it does concern me," the stranger replied smoothly. "In fact, it concerns everyone who crosses my path. You see, danger isn't just lurking in the woods. It's everywhere, hidden behind smiles and polite conversations."

"What do you know about danger?" I asked, my voice low and fierce, the remnants of fear igniting a spark of defiance. "You're just a man hiding in the shadows."

"Aren't we all?" he countered, his tone suddenly grave. "But let me offer you a piece of advice: sometimes, it's the shadows that hold the most power."

A gust of wind swept through the trees, carrying with it a sense of foreboding that settled deep in my bones. As I turned my gaze from the stranger back to my companion, I sensed that we were at a crossroads—a choice lay before us, heavy with the weight of uncertainty. We could either stand our ground against this enigmatic figure or turn and run, retreating into the darkness that threatened to consume us.

"What do you want from us?" I demanded, my voice steady despite the tremor of uncertainty lingering in my chest.

"I want nothing," he replied, the smile returning to his face, though it did little to ease the tension in the air. "I simply wanted to remind you that the night is filled with possibilities. Sometimes, those possibilities can lead to... unexpected adventures."

"And sometimes they lead to danger," my companion added, his gaze unwavering, a wall of strength beside me.

"Ah, but isn't that what makes life interesting?" The man tilted his head, as if weighing our responses. "Consider this: every choice you make in this moment could change the course of your lives forever."

The shadows danced around us, and the silence that followed his words was deafening. My heart raced with the realization that the choice was ours to make, and the weight of that realization both thrilled and terrified me.

I could feel the weight of the man's gaze as it bore down upon us, sharp and invasive, as if he were peeling back layers of my carefully constructed defenses. The tension in the air thickened, a palpable barrier that held us all captive. The woods, once a sanctuary, now felt like a living entity, alive with unseen eyes and whispered secrets, every rustle a reminder of our precarious situation.

"What's it going to be, then?" he asked, a playful smirk tugging at the corners of his mouth. "Are you two going to stand there and let fear dictate your choices, or will you seize this moment and run with it?"

"Run with what?" I shot back, a mix of defiance and curiosity fueling my words. "A treasure hunt in the middle of the night? Sounds like a recipe for disaster."

"Or an exhilarating escape," he countered, his eyes glinting with mischief. "Sometimes, the scariest paths lead to the most rewarding destinations."

"And sometimes they lead to a dead end," my companion interjected, arms crossed, his posture a barrier against the stranger's charm. "You're just a voice in the dark. We don't even know if we can trust you."

"I like to think of myself as more than a mere voice," the man replied, a mocking tone lacing his words. "But trust is a fragile thing, isn't it? Easily broken, yet so hard to rebuild."

I couldn't shake the nagging feeling that beneath his bravado lay a truth wrapped in layers of deception. "So, what's your angle? You come here with a tale of hidden treasure and dangerous adventures, but all we've seen is you lurking like a shadow."

He stepped closer, the moonlight catching the sharp angles of his face, revealing a fleeting vulnerability beneath the bravado. "Perhaps I was looking for companionship. Or perhaps I just enjoy stirring the pot. Life is far too mundane without a little excitement, don't you think?"

"Excitement is one thing; recklessness is another," I replied, unable to quell the unease coiling within me.

"Ah, but is it reckless to live? To seek what others won't?" He leaned back, regarding us as if we were the puzzle pieces he needed to fit into his grand scheme. "I can promise you this: the path I'm offering is not for the faint of heart, but it is one that could change everything for both of you."

My heart raced, caught between the allure of adventure and the safety of the known. "And what exactly do you want in return for this grand adventure?"

"Just a bit of your time. Nothing so sinister." His smile was disarming, yet there was a glimmer in his eyes that spoke of hidden agendas. "The choice, as they say, is yours. Stand and face the night—or step forward into the unknown."

The forest seemed to hold its breath as I exchanged a glance with my companion. It was a moment rife with unspoken words, a shared understanding of the risks we were weighing. The adrenaline coursed through my veins, blurring the edges of my rational thoughts. Was it worth it? Did we dare to step into the depths of uncertainty, or was the safety of retreat too enticing to ignore?

"Let's say we entertain this idea of yours," my companion finally spoke, his voice measured, as if he were weighing each word like a precious stone. "What do we have to lose?"

The stranger's smile widened, a flash of triumph sparking in his gaze. "Ah, now we're talking! Follow me, and I promise, you won't regret it. You'll see the world in ways you never imagined."

With a resigned sigh, I took a step forward, emboldened by the thrill of possibility. "Lead the way, then."

As the man turned, the shadows danced behind him, whispering secrets as he stepped into the darkness. My heart fluttered with a mix of excitement and dread. I cast a sideways glance at my companion, who gave me a nod, his expression a blend of skepticism and resolve. Together, we plunged into the unknown, every step echoing with uncertainty.

The path twisted through the trees, the underbrush thick with the scent of moss and earth, creating a natural labyrinth that seemed to pulse with life. I could feel the cool night air against my skin, a stark contrast to the warmth of the moment we had shared before our sanctuary was invaded.

"Do you think he's telling the truth?" I whispered to my companion as we followed closely behind the stranger, who moved with an unsettling confidence through the gloom.

"Truth is a slippery thing," he replied, his voice low but steady. "Sometimes it's easier to believe a lie than face the uncomfortable realities."

As we wound deeper into the woods, I tried to shake the feeling of being watched. The trees loomed overhead like sentinels, their branches weaving a tapestry of shadows that shifted with every gust of wind. The quiet was almost too loud, punctuated only by the distant call of an owl and the rustling of leaves, as if nature itself were holding its breath.

"Do you hear that?" I asked suddenly, stopping short.

"Hear what?" my companion responded, scanning the darkness with narrowed eyes.

"It sounds like... voices."

The stranger turned, his expression shifting from amusement to something darker. "Ah, yes. The forest has many voices. Some are just echoes of your own fears."

"Or perhaps it's the spirits of those who ventured too far," I added, my heart racing. "Do you often hear them on your treasure hunts?"

He chuckled, though the sound lacked genuine mirth. "Only when they wish to be heard."

Before I could press further, a flash of movement caught my eye. I turned, peering into the depths of the trees, where the darkness seemed to pulse with an otherworldly energy. The feeling of being watched intensified, and I felt a chill run down my spine.

"Keep moving," my companion urged, urgency creeping into his voice.

As we pressed forward, the air thickened, and the very shadows seemed to shift around us. Then, like a crack of thunder in an otherwise calm sky, a shrill scream erupted from the depths of the forest, shattering the fragile tension.

My heart leapt into my throat as panic surged through me. "What was that?"

The stranger's demeanor shifted, the playful arrogance replaced by a steely focus. "We need to hurry. We're not alone."

The words hung in the air like a death knell, and suddenly the thrill of adventure felt more like a desperate flight from something we could not see. My instincts screamed at me to turn back, but before I could voice my fears, the trees around us began to tremble, as if responding to the unspeakable terror that loomed just beyond our sight.

And then, the darkness erupted into chaos. A shadow lunged forward, breaking through the veil of trees, revealing a creature of nightmares—its eyes glinting with malice, its growl a low rumble that sent a jolt of pure adrenaline through my veins.

"Run!" my companion shouted, grabbing my arm and pulling me back, but it was too late. The creature surged forward, its maw open wide, revealing a row of jagged teeth that gleamed under the moonlight.

The world around us dissolved into a cacophony of fear and instinct, the forest turning into a blur of shadows and terror as I grasped my companion's hand, our fates intertwined in a desperate attempt to escape. The thrill of adventure had turned into a fight for survival, and the darkness that had once whispered promises of possibility now threatened to consume us whole.

Chapter 14: Whispers of Fear

The moon hung low in the sky, casting a silver sheen over the cobbled streets of Millstone, where the scent of damp earth mingled with the whispers of the past. Every corner seemed alive, shadowy figures dancing in the dim light as I darted through the alleyway beside the old tavern, its weathered sign creaking in the chilly night air. I had always loved the way this place felt, a tapestry of stories woven into its very fabric, but now, the atmosphere crackled with tension, like the prelude to a storm.

"Did you hear that?" I paused, my heart racing, the soft rustle of leaves setting every nerve on edge. I glanced over my shoulder, half-expecting to find a pair of eyes watching me from the gloom. But only the lingering fog answered, swirling lazily around my feet as if it were playing a game of hide-and-seek.

Beside me, Jake let out a breath, a low rumble of irritation. "What's with you and the jumpiness? This isn't a horror film; it's just a walk through town."

I shot him a look, one that said I wasn't about to let him off that easily. "It's not just a walk, Jake. We're not exactly in the safest of neighborhoods, especially not with everything that's been happening."

He rolled his eyes, but I could see the tension in his jaw. "Right, like anyone's going to come after us in the middle of the night. Besides, we've got a plan. The only thing we need to worry about is executing it without losing our heads."

"A plan," I muttered, the word tasting bitter on my tongue. Plans had a way of unraveling, leaving chaos in their wake. "You mean your plan to confront Tamsin? Just a little friendly chat about the mysterious disappearances in Millstone?"

He smirked, his playful demeanor a welcome distraction. "Exactly. We knock on her door, offer her a cup of tea, and then ask about all those missing people. What could go wrong?"

I snorted, my nerves easing just a fraction. "Oh, I don't know—perhaps she'll just invite us in for cookies and tell us all her darkest secrets."

Jake chuckled, the sound breaking the tension like a brittle twig snapping underfoot. "See? You're getting into the spirit of things."

Yet, as we continued down the narrow path, the shadows deepened, stretching into eerie shapes that clawed at my imagination. Each crackle of twigs or distant murmur only served to amplify my unease. This was a game we were playing, but the stakes felt impossibly high.

Millstone had always been a town steeped in mystery, a place where stories mingled with reality until they were indistinguishable. But lately, it had become a theatre for something darker. Disappearances had risen like an insatiable tide, drawing whispers from the corners of taverns and the depths of homes. Something was lurking in the shadows, something that sent shivers down my spine.

As we approached Tamsin's house, a dilapidated Victorian that loomed ominously against the backdrop of the night sky, I felt a chill that had nothing to do with the air temperature. "You sure about this?" I asked, my voice barely above a whisper.

Jake's confident facade flickered, just for a moment. "We have to be. We need answers."

We stepped onto the creaking porch, and I knocked, the sound echoing through the stillness like a gunshot. The door swung open, revealing Tamsin, her expression a mixture of surprise and guarded curiosity. Her hair, a cascade of silver, framed a face that held secrets older than time itself.

"Ah, it's you two," she said, her voice smooth like honey yet edged with an unspoken warning. "What brings you to my door at this hour?"

"Just thought we'd drop by for a chat," Jake said, his bravado barely concealing the nervous energy swirling around us. "Mind if we come in?"

Tamsin hesitated, her gaze flickering over my shoulder as if sensing the unseen shadows lurking behind us. "I suppose a short conversation wouldn't hurt. Come in, but be quick about it."

We stepped inside, the warmth of her home enveloping us like a blanket. The scent of herbs and something sweet wafted from the kitchen, creating an unsettling contrast to the cold reality of our mission. I couldn't shake the feeling that the house was watching us, every trinket and shadow bearing witness to our intrusion.

"Nice place," Jake remarked, attempting to lighten the mood as he wandered toward a table laden with peculiar artifacts. "You collect this stuff?"

Tamsin arched an eyebrow, a playful smile tugging at the corners of her lips. "You could say that. Each piece tells a story, much like people do. You just need to know how to listen."

"Is that what you do? Listen to your treasures?" I asked, half-joking.

Her laughter was light but held an undertone that sent a shiver down my spine. "Oh, dear, if only it were that simple. The real treasures are often hidden beneath layers of fear and silence."

I felt Jake stiffen beside me, the room closing in as we navigated the delicate balance of trust and suspicion.

"Speaking of fear," Jake began, his tone shifting, "we wanted to ask about the disappearances. They've been troubling the town. Do you know anything?"

Tamsin's expression hardened, the flicker of amusement extinguished like a snuffed candle. "Some questions are better left unasked, my dear. The answers can be... perilous."

I exchanged a glance with Jake, and the unspoken understanding crackled between us. Here we were, standing on the precipice of a truth that could either save us or plunge us into darkness. My heart raced, a wild drumbeat against the silence as I braced myself for what came next.

"Perilous?" I echoed, the word tasting bitter on my tongue. "What do you mean?"

Tamsin stepped closer, her voice dropping to a conspiratorial whisper. "In this town, secrets are currency, and the truth can cost you dearly."

As the weight of her words settled over me, I realized that the shadows had teeth, and we were in a world where nothing was as it seemed. Trust was a fickle thing, and I couldn't shake the sense that we were being hunted, the predator closing in with every heartbeat.

The room felt stifling, the air thick with unspoken fears as Tamsin's gaze bore into me. I shifted under her scrutiny, trying to project confidence I didn't feel. "Perilous how?" I asked, my voice steadier than my insides. "You're telling us there's danger in uncovering what's happening in Millstone?"

A flicker of something—was it regret or fear?—crossed Tamsin's features before she masked it with a thin smile. "Knowledge is a burden, my dear. The more you know, the more you wish you didn't. Secrets have a way of twisting themselves, especially in a place like this."

I glanced at Jake, who was now perched on the edge of his seat, fingers drumming restlessly against the table. "We need to know, Tamsin. We've seen the effects of those secrets. People are suffering."

With a resigned sigh, she retreated to the counter, pouring two steaming mugs of tea that filled the room with the heady aroma of spices. "Sometimes, what you see isn't the entire picture," she said as she placed the cups in front of us. "What appears to be the threat might only be a shadow of something much larger."

I took a tentative sip, the warmth flooding my senses, but the taste was overshadowed by the chill of her words. "Larger? Are you suggesting there's something more at play here?"

Tamsin leaned back against the counter, her eyes narrowing. "It's not just the disappearances, dear. There are forces at work in Millstone that predate even me. Old grudges, buried secrets. They rise up, pulling unsuspecting souls into the depths."

"Do you believe it's someone in the town?" Jake interjected, his curiosity piqued despite the tension coiling around us like a serpent.

"Or perhaps someone outside," she mused, her gaze drifting toward the window where shadows flickered in the faint light. "You must tread carefully. Sometimes the monsters hide behind familiar faces."

A chill ran down my spine, and I instinctively glanced toward the door, half-expecting someone to burst through with accusations or worse. "So, you're saying we shouldn't trust anyone?"

"Trust is a luxury," Tamsin replied softly, "and one that can lead to ruin if misplaced. You two seem close, but be wary—intimacy can be a mask for deception."

Jake's eyes flicked to me, and for a heartbeat, I felt the weight of her words settle between us like an icy fog. "I appreciate the warning, Tamsin," I said, my voice firming with resolve, "but we can't live in fear of shadows. We need to act."

"Then you must be prepared for the consequences."

As she spoke, I felt a strange unease creeping in, one that gnawed at my confidence. Jake shifted beside me, his bravado crumbling beneath the gravity of the moment. "We're ready," he declared, though even I could hear the uncertainty lacing his words.

"Ready to chase a ghost?" Tamsin countered, raising an eyebrow. "Perhaps you should consider what you're really asking for."

I met her gaze, determination igniting in my chest. "We can't back down. Not now. We owe it to the people who've vanished, to those who are too scared to speak up."

Tamsin's expression softened, and for a fleeting moment, I thought I saw a glimmer of respect in her eyes. "Very well. But if you choose to pursue this path, remember: the truth doesn't always set you free. Sometimes, it locks you in a cage of your own making."

With that cryptic warning hanging in the air, we left Tamsin's house, stepping back into the night, the cool air invigorating yet fraught with tension. The cobblestone streets were bathed in silvery light, but they felt unwelcoming, as if they were aware of the secrets we sought to unravel.

Jake fell into step beside me, his shoulders tense. "What do you think she meant by 'forces at work'?"

"Something more than just random disappearances," I replied, rubbing my arms against the chill. "It feels like we're dealing with a web of lies, not just individuals making bad choices."

He nodded, the wheels in his mind clearly turning. "You think someone's orchestrating all this?"

"I wouldn't be surprised," I said, my mind racing. "What if the disappearances are linked to something bigger, a power struggle or a cult? We need to dig deeper."

He chuckled darkly, a sound that sent an uneasy flutter through me. "Great, just what we need—a mystery steeped in drama. Like we're in one of those old movies where everyone's a suspect."

"Let's hope it's not that bad," I said, a grin playing at my lips despite the rising tension. "Though I do expect a dramatic showdown. Maybe with some dramatic music playing in the background?"

"Only if I get to be the hero," he shot back, feigning a heroic pose as we approached the town square.

But beneath our light-hearted banter lay an unspoken truth: we were walking into the unknown, a labyrinth of secrets where trust was scarce. I glanced at him, my heart a strange mixture of hope and dread. "What if we can't find the truth?"

"We will," he said, his confidence wavering only slightly. "We'll make it through this. Together."

As we entered the square, I stopped short, the sight before us bringing my heart to a halt. Figures lingered in the shadows—faces familiar yet distorted by the dim light. It was a gathering, an air of tension crackling like static, the kind that made the hair on my arms stand on end.

"Who are they?" I whispered, my breath hitching in my throat.

"Friends or foes?" Jake murmured, scanning the crowd. "This feels like a secret meeting."

The night suddenly seemed alive with whispers, the air thick with anticipation. Every instinct in me screamed to turn and run, but curiosity and a deeper sense of duty rooted me to the spot. We needed answers, and this was the first lead we'd stumbled upon.

"Ready?" Jake asked, determination lighting his eyes.

"Let's find out what they're hiding," I replied, steeling myself.

With hesitant steps, we approached the gathering, the shadows embracing us like old friends. We were about to plunge into a world of whispers and fear, and I could feel the thrilling, dangerous pulse of possibility thrumming in my veins.

The air crackled with an electric tension as we approached the gathering, each step feeling heavier than the last. Shadows loomed over the town square, wrapping around the figures gathered like a thick fog. Their murmurs created an unsettling symphony, a mix of urgency and fear that prickled at my skin. It was impossible to ignore the unease curling in my stomach, but curiosity propelled me forward, a moth drawn to the flickering flame of truth.

"Are we sure we want to get closer?" Jake whispered, scanning the crowd with a blend of excitement and apprehension. "I mean, what if this is some sort of secret society? Do we need to worry about cult rituals?"

I laughed softly, though the tension gnawed at my insides. "Unless they're sacrificing goats, I think we're safe for now. Just remember, we're not here to join a club. We're here for answers."

We maneuvered our way through the throng, weaving past faces that appeared simultaneously familiar and foreign. As we got closer, I noticed they were huddled in groups, their voices lowered to hushed whispers that barely penetrated the night air. The flicker of lantern light cast eerie shadows on their faces, illuminating eyes wide with fear or fury. It was a community on edge, and the weight of their collective anxiety settled heavily on my shoulders.

"Do you recognize anyone?" Jake murmured, his eyes scanning the crowd like a hawk.

"Not really," I replied, but then I spotted Mrs. Eldridge, the owner of the local bookstore, her usual demeanor of warmth replaced by a fierce intensity. "Wait, is that Mrs. Eldridge? What's she doing here?"

As if sensing our gaze, she looked up, locking eyes with me for just a heartbeat before turning away, her expression shadowed by concern. "Maybe she knows something," I whispered, already feeling a tug of urgency. "Let's talk to her."

Before I could take a step, a figure pushed through the crowd, a tall silhouette that made my heart skip a beat. It was Tamsin, her silver hair catching the lantern light like a beacon in the dark. She moved with purpose, her sharp eyes scanning the gathering, and I couldn't shake the feeling that she was more than just an observer.

"What do you think she's doing here?" Jake asked, his voice barely above a whisper.

"Maybe she's the puppet master," I quipped, though I felt a flicker of anxiety beneath my words. "We need to find out."

Before we could make our move, the crowd began to shift, like leaves rustling in a sudden wind. A man stepped into the center, his voice booming with a charisma that pulled every eye toward him. "We cannot remain silent any longer!" he declared, his presence magnetic and commanding. "Our town is plagued by fear and uncertainty, and it is time we stand up for ourselves!"

The air crackled with energy, and I could feel the collective heartbeat of the crowd thrumming with his words. "It's time to take back what's ours! We will not let the shadows dictate our lives!"

His fervor ignited something in the crowd, murmurs of agreement rippling through the masses. Jake's brow furrowed in concern. "He's got them riled up. This could turn into a mob mentality very quickly."

I nodded, unable to tear my eyes away from the man, whose passion seemed genuine yet dangerously potent. "What if he's right? What if we're dealing with something bigger than we imagined?"

"Or what if he's the one stirring the pot?" Jake countered, his skepticism still firmly in place.

Just then, Mrs. Eldridge stepped forward, her voice shaky yet resolute. "We need to be careful, everyone. We don't know who's behind these disappearances, or what they truly want from us."

The man shot her a withering glance. "And what would you have us do, sit idly by while our friends vanish into the night? If we don't act, we may become the next victims!"

The crowd roared in response, their energy electric and frightening. I could see the fear blending with a rising tide of anger, and I felt the urgent need to step in before things spiraled out of control.

"Jake," I whispered urgently, "we can't let this go on. We need to talk to her. Now."

Without waiting for his response, I slipped through the crowd, feeling Jake's hand grip my arm, pulling me back for a moment. "Be careful," he murmured, his eyes reflecting the swirling chaos around us.

"Always," I replied, offering him a small smile before moving forward, determination propelling me through the sea of faces.

Mrs. Eldridge stood a few paces away, and I approached her cautiously, the din of the crowd fading into a dull roar as I focused on her. "Mrs. Eldridge!" I called out, trying to pierce the veil of noise.

She turned to me, her features softening for just a moment before worry washed over her face. "Oh, dear, you shouldn't be here. It's not safe."

"I know, but we need to talk," I insisted, glancing back at the man who was still rallying the crowd, his voice growing louder, more impassioned. "Do you know anything about what's happening?"

Mrs. Eldridge hesitated, glancing around as if the shadows themselves were listening. "There are whispers, my dear. Whispers of a group that operates in the dark, pulling strings and influencing those in power. I thought it was just talk, but..."

"But now you're not so sure?" I pressed, my heart racing.

Just as she was about to answer, a loud crash interrupted us. The crowd fell silent, all heads turning toward the source of the noise. A figure stumbled from the edge of the gathering, eyes wild with panic. "They're coming! We need to get out of here!"

Chaos erupted. The man in the center shouted for order, but the crowd was in a frenzy, fear spiraling out of control. I grabbed Mrs. Eldridge's arm, pulling her closer as the crowd surged, panic taking root.

"Who's coming?" I yelled above the din, my heart pounding against my ribcage.

"The shadows! They're watching us!" the figure screamed, his voice a raw edge of terror. "We're not safe!"

In that moment, everything shifted. The crowd erupted into chaos, people shouting and scrambling in every direction. My pulse quickened as I turned to find Jake, but the throng swallowed him whole.

"Jake!" I shouted, panic flaring. I reached out to the tumultuous sea of bodies, desperate for a glimpse of him, but he was lost in the chaos.

And then, just as suddenly as it began, the commotion paused. A deep, unnatural silence enveloped the square, broken only by the soft rustling of leaves.

In the eerie quiet, I caught sight of Tamsin, standing at the edge of the square, her expression unreadable. A chill ran down my spine as I noticed the shadows coiling around her feet, thick and menacing, as if they were alive.

"What have you done?" she murmured, more to herself than to anyone else.

I felt a cold wave of dread wash over me as the whispers began again, but this time, they weren't just in the crowd. They echoed in my mind, swirling with the uncertainty of everything I had just witnessed. I turned to face the man who had stirred the crowd, now standing frozen as if the life had been sucked from him, a look of horror plastered on his face.

And then, in the blink of an eye, the darkness surged. The shadows pooled and twisted, taking shape, and I could see figures emerging from the gloom, their intentions unreadable. My breath caught in my throat as I realized the danger was no longer abstract.

I was no longer just a bystander in this fight; I was ensnared in the very web of secrets we had come to uncover, and as the figures stepped forward, the last thing I heard before everything plunged into chaos was a single voice, sharp and cold, slicing through the silence: "You should have stayed away."

Chapter 15: The Unraveling

The air crackled with tension as I approached the crumbling façade of the old mill, its once-vibrant colors now faded and peeling. Sunlight fought to pierce through the heavy clouds gathering above, casting ominous shadows that flickered across the moss-covered stones. I could feel the weight of history in those walls—decades of whispered secrets and unspoken truths lay heavy in the atmosphere. Each step closer sent a shiver down my spine, a mixture of anticipation and dread intertwining like the roots of the gnarled trees encircling the property.

This was the last place I wanted to be, yet here I was, clutching a weathered piece of paper in my hand that had led me here. The scrawled name of our family's former groundskeeper, Oliver, was etched into my mind like a warning. He had been a fixture in my childhood, a quiet, unassuming presence in our lives, always tending to the gardens and mending the fences. But the more I thought about it, the more I realized how little I really knew about him. Was he still the gentle soul I remembered, or had time twisted him into something darker, something unrecognizable?

As I stepped onto the porch, the wood creaked beneath my weight, echoing like a mournful sigh. I hesitated, glancing around at the wildflowers that had reclaimed their territory, bursting through the cracks in the stone path. Nature had a way of reclaiming what was once lost, much like I hoped to reclaim the truth buried beneath layers of deception. I knocked, the sound reverberating in the stillness, and waited, my heart racing as I prepared to confront the ghosts of my past.

The door swung open slowly, revealing Oliver's lined face, framed by a mess of silver hair that danced in the slight breeze. His eyes, a deep shade of brown, held a glimmer of recognition before a wall of caution descended over them. "Isabel," he said, his voice gravelly yet tinged with warmth. "It's been a long time."

"Too long," I replied, trying to mask the tremor in my voice. "I need your help."

He stepped aside, allowing me into the dimly lit room that smelled faintly of cedar and old books. The space was cluttered, remnants of his life strewn about—photographs, tools, and jars filled with herbs that spoke of his former life as both caretaker and keeper of secrets. I took a deep breath, the air thick with nostalgia, and sat on a worn chair that creaked under my weight.

"I'm not sure what I can offer you," Oliver said, his gaze shifting to the window, where the sky had begun to darken ominously. "There are things best left forgotten."

"Maybe," I countered, leaning forward, my voice steady despite the storm brewing inside me. "But I need to understand what happened. My family... there are whispers of something sinister, and I believe you hold the key."

He studied me for a long moment, the silence heavy with unspoken thoughts. Finally, he sighed, running a hand through his hair. "You should know, Isabel, that the truth isn't always pretty. Sometimes it's more than we can bear."

I flinched at his words, feeling the weight of my own secrets pressing down on me. "I've faced my demons," I said, surprising even myself with the resolve in my voice. "I'm ready for whatever you have to say."

Oliver finally settled into the chair across from me, the corners of his mouth twitching as if he were caught between a smile and a frown. "All right, then. But you should understand, it's not just your family's history we're dealing with. The past has a way of intertwining lives in unexpected ways." He leaned closer, the warmth of his presence grounding me as I prepared for the deluge of memories that would follow.

"Your father and I were close once. He had ambitions that went beyond this town, dreams that danced on the edge of reality. He was involved in things that weren't quite right, not in the eyes of those who watched closely. And I... I was his right hand, blinded by loyalty." He paused, his brow furrowing in regret.

"Blinded?" I echoed, sensing the weight of betrayal in his words. "What do you mean?"

"There were deals made, promises exchanged in the shadows. I thought I was helping to build something beautiful, but it turned out to be a façade, hiding corruption and greed beneath. Your father..." His voice trailed off, leaving an uneasy silence in its wake.

My heart raced. "What happened?"

"Things went south. A betrayal from within. Your father lost everything, and in the aftermath, I was left to pick up the pieces. I had to disappear, to shield myself from the consequences of our actions. But you—your family—was never meant to be a part of it."

Each revelation felt like a knife twisting in my gut, drawing out a painful truth I had never wanted to confront. "And you think that's why they're coming after me now?"

"I don't know who 'they' are," he admitted, his eyes narrowing with concern. "But I suspect they're still watching, waiting for the right moment to strike. The past doesn't die easily, Isabel. It lingers like a ghost, haunting those who dare to dig too deep."

His words sent a chill racing through me, and I felt the weight of my own fears bubbling to the surface. "I can't just stand by and let them destroy my family's legacy," I said, my voice cracking slightly. "I have to fight back."

Oliver nodded, a deep sense of understanding passing between us. "Then we'll fight together. But first, you need to be ready for the truth. You need to understand what you're up against, and it's not just the past. It's the choices we make now that will define us."

In that moment of shared vulnerability, I felt a spark of connection ignite between us—a fragile bond forged in the fires of our shared histories. As the storm outside rumbled, I knew we were on the brink of something monumental, a convergence of paths that would lead us to the heart of a conspiracy darker than I had ever imagined. I took a deep breath, steeling myself for the unraveling that lay ahead, determined to face whatever storm awaited us with courage and conviction.

As I sat in the dim light of Oliver's cluttered room, the air between us thick with unsaid words, I could feel the foundations of my world shifting. His revelations spun around me like a tempest, and I struggled to find solid ground in the chaos. "You don't know what they want from me," I said, my voice steadying as I searched his eyes for answers. "But I can't let fear dictate my life any longer."

Oliver leaned back, his brow furrowed, studying me as if trying to uncover the layers hidden beneath my bravado. "Fear can be a powerful motivator, Isabel. It can either paralyze you or propel you into action. What do you want to do?"

I hesitated, considering my response. In that moment, I realized the truth had transformed me; it was no longer just about unearthing the past, but rather seizing the future. "I want to take control. I want to uncover the truth, not just for my family but for myself. No more running."

"Then we'll start tonight." He rose, a spark igniting in his eyes. "There are records in the old archives behind the mill—documents that may hold the answers you seek. If the rumors are true, they've been hidden for years, waiting for someone brave enough to dig them out."

Bravery felt like a cloak I could scarcely wear, but something in his conviction pulled me along. We stepped outside, the storm brewing ominously above us, the sky darkening as if it sensed our resolve. The wind picked up, swirling leaves around our feet like spirits gathering for a dance. My heart raced, not from fear but from the thrill of the unknown.

As we approached the archives, a structure I had never noticed despite countless childhood visits, the atmosphere shifted. It loomed over us, a decrepit edifice with shattered windows that seemed to stare down at us like watchful eyes. "This place gives me the creeps," I admitted, shivering despite the warmth of my coat. "It looks like it's been waiting to collapse since the dawn of time."

"Or perhaps it's just waiting for the right person to uncover its secrets," Oliver replied with a grin, his voice lightening the mood as he pushed open the heavy door. It creaked open, revealing a dusty interior filled with shelves that towered precariously, laden with old boxes and forgotten memories.

The air inside was stale, the scent of mildew mingling with the faintest hint of lavender. As I stepped inside, the darkness enveloped me, and I felt the pulse of history beneath my fingertips. "Where do we start?" I asked, my voice barely above a whisper.

Oliver motioned toward a far corner, where a large, ornately carved wooden desk stood. "That's where your father used to work when he wanted to be alone with his thoughts. I suspect there's more than just old papers lying around."

We made our way to the desk, dust swirling like tiny galaxies in the beams of light streaming through the broken windows. I opened a drawer, and my heart raced at the sight of faded documents stacked haphazardly. "These could be it," I murmured, sorting through the papers as my pulse quickened with anticipation.

Hours slipped by as we sifted through the records, the world outside forgotten in the pursuit of truth. I stumbled upon letters—some in my father's handwriting, others from unfamiliar names—each one revealing a tangled web of connections and betrayals. The revelations unfolded like a dark flower, petals of deception unfurling under the harsh light of scrutiny.

"Look at this," I said, holding up a letter addressed to my father from someone named Margot. "She speaks of a deal gone wrong, something that could ruin everything he built."

Oliver leaned in closer, studying the words as if they were a spell waiting to be deciphered. "Margot was an associate. She had her hands in many pots, and not all of them were savory. If your father was entangled with her, it might explain the fallout."

"Why would he keep this from us?" I whispered, my stomach twisting with betrayal. "What else was he hiding?"

"Fear, perhaps. Fear of what you might uncover, or fear of protecting you from something too deep to understand. Family can be a double-edged sword." His voice softened, and I saw a flicker of empathy in his eyes.

Just then, a noise from the entrance made us both jump. "Who's there?" a voice called, low and menacing. The atmosphere shifted from one of exploration to acute danger. We exchanged panicked glances, and I realized our quest for truth had attracted unwelcome attention.

"Quick, hide!" I whispered, pulling Oliver behind the desk as the footsteps grew louder. My heart thudded in my chest, a war drum announcing our impending doom. As I crouched low, I could see the shadow of a figure moving just outside the door, the outline too familiar for comfort.

"Isabel?" the voice called again, this time more urgent. I barely recognized it at first; it was my brother, Ethan. "Isabel! Are you in there?"

Relief washed over me, but I held my finger to my lips, urging silence. I didn't want him to stumble into whatever trouble we had inadvertently invited. Oliver and I stayed frozen, breaths held, as I watched Ethan peer through the dusty window, searching for signs of life.

"Isabel, please!" he pleaded, worry lacing his tone. "I know you're in there. You need to come home."

His desperation pierced through the tension, and I felt the weight of responsibility settle heavily on my shoulders. "Ethan, I can't. Not yet," I whispered, knowing that my answer would only escalate his anxiety.

Suddenly, Oliver nudged my arm, drawing my attention back to him. His eyes were wide, a hint of panic flashing through them. "What if he's in danger? What if they're looking for him too?"

The thought sent a chill through me. "We can't let them find us here." My voice trembled, and I quickly gestured for Oliver to follow my lead.

Ethan continued to call out, his worry palpable, and I knew that I couldn't let him walk into a trap. With a nod to Oliver, we crept toward the back of the archives, seeking an escape. The building might be old and crumbling, but it still offered passage through a narrow exit that led to the overgrown garden behind the mill.

As we slipped through the door, I could hear the weight of my brother's footsteps growing fainter, and the storm outside roared to life, rain pelting the earth with ferocity. The wind whipped at my hair as I glanced back at Oliver, who wore a look of determination mingled with fear.

"This isn't over," he said, and his voice was strong, steadying me as the storm outside mirrored the turmoil brewing inside. The connection we had forged felt unbreakable, a tether to hold on to amidst the chaos.

"Let's get to safety, and then we'll figure out what to do next," I replied, my resolve hardening as we sprinted into the shadows of the night, two souls united against a world that seemed intent on tearing us apart. The weight of our mission loomed large, but I felt a flicker of hope igniting within me. We would face whatever came next together, ready to confront the storm on the horizon.

The rain fell in sheets as Oliver and I sprinted through the overgrown garden, our footsteps muffled by the soft earth and dense foliage. Each drop felt like a judgment, a reminder of the uncertainty that loomed over us. The night was alive with the sound of the storm, the wind howling like a pack of wolves hungry for secrets. I could feel the weight of our mission pressing down on my shoulders, the truth swirling just out of reach, teasing me like a cruel lover.

"Do you think Ethan will be okay?" I asked, glancing back toward the darkened windows of the mill. My heart raced, torn between the urgency of our escape and the nagging worry for my brother left behind.

Oliver's eyes narrowed, scanning the surrounding trees for signs of movement. "He'll be fine for now. But we can't linger. If whoever was searching for him knows we're here, they won't stop until they find us."

"Right." I nodded, pushing aside the fear that threatened to claw its way back into my mind. "Let's get to my car. We can regroup and figure out our next move from there."

Navigating through the dense underbrush, we stumbled into a small clearing where my old sedan waited, its silver body glinting dully in the intermittent flashes of lightning. I fumbled with my keys, my hands shaking as I glanced nervously at the shadows creeping closer with each heartbeat. The rain drummed relentlessly against the roof, masking any sounds that might betray our presence.

As we climbed inside, the world outside seemed to fade, the car cocooning us in a bubble of relative safety. I turned the key in the ignition, but the engine sputtered and coughed as if reluctant to wake from its slumber. "Come on, come on," I muttered under my breath, the tension in my gut tightening with every failed attempt. The storm raged outside, a perfect reflection of the tempest brewing within me.

"Maybe it's just wet," Oliver suggested, his voice calm despite the chaos outside. "Try again. Give it some gas."

I pressed the accelerator gently, the engine finally roaring to life, and relief washed over me. "Thank you, old girl," I said with a half-hearted laugh. I pulled away from the clearing, heart racing, grateful to be escaping the haunted shadows of the mill.

The roads glistened with rain, reflecting the moonlight like shards of glass. As I drove, the comforting rhythm of the tires on the wet pavement began to ease my anxiety, but the knot in my stomach remained, a reminder of the danger that still lurked.

"Do you have a safe place in mind?" Oliver asked, leaning back in his seat, a weary expression crossing his face.

"Just a small cabin my family owns by the lake," I replied, glancing sideways at him. "It's isolated enough that we should be safe for a while, at least until we can figure out who's after us and what they want."

As I navigated the winding roads, the rain poured down, making visibility a challenge. I turned on the wipers, the blades sweeping furiously against the deluge. "Why did you leave the family's employ, Oliver? You said you were loyal to my father."

He was silent for a moment, his eyes fixed on the landscape flashing by. "Loyalty can turn sour when the people you trust betray you. Your father... he changed after the fallout. He became paranoid, and I couldn't stay in that kind of environment. I thought it best to distance myself."

His words hung in the air, heavy with unspoken regret. "But now you're back. Why?"

"Because some things can't be ignored, Isabel," he replied, his gaze steady and unwavering. "The past always has a way of resurfacing, especially when secrets are involved."

I nodded, the truth of his words settling in the pit of my stomach. The shadows of my family's history were more than just specters; they were living entities, lurking in the corners of my mind. Just as I thought I had put them to rest, they clawed their way back, demanding attention and retribution.

As we neared the cabin, the trees lining the road swayed ominously, branches twisting like skeletal fingers in the wind. I parked the car and glanced around, scanning the darkened landscape for signs of trouble. The cabin stood stoically at the water's edge, a beacon of refuge amid the chaos. But even as I took a deep breath, I felt the familiar knot of unease unfurl within me.

"I'll check the perimeter," Oliver said, breaking the silence as he stepped out into the rain. "Stay here."

"Be careful," I called after him, my heart pounding as I watched him disappear into the darkness. Alone in the car, I felt the silence seep in, wrapping around me like a shroud. My mind raced, contemplating the risks we were taking, the enemies we were unearthing.

Minutes passed like hours, the storm raging outside only heightening my anxiety. I drummed my fingers against the steering wheel, the rhythm frantic and erratic. Just as I began to convince myself that everything was fine, Oliver returned, his expression grave.

"We need to move," he said, urgency lacing his voice. "There's something wrong."

"What do you mean?" My heart sank. "Is someone here?"

"I saw tracks leading away from the cabin—fresh ones. It looks like we're not the only ones who know this place."

Panic surged within me. "What do we do?"

"Get inside and grab whatever you can. We'll figure out our next steps once we're safe." His voice was steady, but I could see the storm brewing behind his eyes.

I nodded, scrambling out of the car and racing toward the cabin. Inside, the familiar scent of cedar and damp wood enveloped me, a stark contrast to the chaos outside. I hurried to gather supplies—flashlights, a first-aid kit, and some clothes. My hands trembled as I stuffed items into a backpack, each second feeling like an eternity.

Oliver moved quickly, his sharp eyes scanning the corners of the room, searching for anything that could be useful. "Do you have a phone?" he asked, glancing over at me.

"Of course, but the signal out here is spotty at best." I tucked my phone into my pocket, wishing it were a more reliable lifeline.

Just then, a loud crash echoed from outside, a sound that sent adrenaline surging through my veins. "What was that?" I gasped, dropping the backpack.

"Stay here," Oliver commanded, his tone brooking no argument. He stepped toward the door, opening it just enough to peek out into the storm.

I felt a wave of panic wash over me, but I swallowed it down. "No, I'm coming with you." I couldn't let him face whatever was out there alone, not when the shadows of betrayal had already haunted us too long.

As I stepped outside, the rain battered against us, soaking us instantly. "What do you see?" I asked, squinting into the darkness, but all I could make out were shapes swirling in the downpour.

"Nothing yet, but we can't take chances." His voice was low, a warning that sent shivers down my spine.

Before I could respond, a figure emerged from the trees, cloaked in shadow, gliding toward us with an unsettling grace. My breath caught in my throat as the figure stepped into the feeble light of the cabin's porch, revealing a familiar face framed by the darkness.

"Hello, Isabel. I've been looking for you."

My heart dropped, recognition flooding my senses, and the storm around us seemed to still, leaving an eerie silence in its wake. The past had come rushing back, clawing its way into the present with an undeniable force, and as I stood frozen in shock, the realization hit me like a punch to the gut. I was not as safe as I had hoped.

Chapter 16: Flames of Reckoning

The air was thick with the scent of burning cedar and damp earth as we stood at the edge of the secluded clearing. The trees loomed like silent sentinels, their branches swaying gently, whispering secrets I dared not decipher. My heart raced, each pulse a reminder of what was at stake—of the confrontation looming just ahead. The sun dipped low, casting long shadows that danced along the ground, as if urging us to flee, to escape the reckoning that awaited. But there was no turning back; we had come too far, and the truth was a flame we could no longer ignore.

Ethan stood beside me, his jaw set with determination, eyes reflecting the fiery hues of the sunset. His presence was both a comfort and a source of dread. There was an unspoken bond between us, one forged in shared trials and whispered dreams, yet it was tangled in the chaos that had upended our lives. I had always admired his strength, the way he navigated the world with an unwavering sense of purpose. But now, as we prepared to face the architect of our troubles, I could see the flicker of uncertainty behind his bravado, and it ignited a spark of fear within me.

"Are you ready for this?" he asked, his voice a low rumble that blended with the distant sound of a rushing stream. It felt like the world held its breath, waiting for my response. I glanced at him, his dark hair tousled by the evening breeze, the sharp lines of his face softened by the golden light. There was something fiercely protective about him, but it was tinged with an intensity that hinted at the tempest brewing beneath the surface.

"I have to be," I replied, the words tumbling out, buoyed by a surge of resolve. "For us. For everyone we love." I took a deep breath, letting the crisp air fill my lungs, the coolness a stark contrast to the fire igniting in my chest. My hands trembled slightly as I clutched the small pendant that hung around my neck—a token of my past, a reminder of everything I had fought to protect.

The pendant was a simple silver charm, etched with the symbol of our family, but its weight felt like a promise of the legacy I carried. My ancestors had faced their demons, and now it was my turn. Yet, beneath that resolve was a flicker of doubt. Would we emerge from this unscathed, or would the shadows of our families' pasts consume us whole?

The silence between us was heavy, thick with the weight of unspoken fears. Ethan reached for my hand, his fingers brushing against mine in a tender yet possessive gesture. "Whatever happens, we face it together," he said, his gaze steady, anchoring me in a turbulent sea of uncertainty. I nodded, though the knot in my stomach tightened. Love was a powerful force, but so too was the darkness we were about to confront.

As we moved deeper into the clearing, the flicker of a fire came into view, illuminating the figure that stood at its center. A silhouette framed by flames, it was as if the very darkness had materialized into a person. My heart raced, recognizing the familiar stance, the confidence that exuded from the figure before us. Lucas. The very embodiment of chaos, my once-beloved brother, now a puppet master pulling the strings of our lives.

"Welcome," he said, his voice smooth like silk, yet laced with venom. The fire crackled ominously behind him, casting eerie shadows that danced like specters at the edge of my vision. "I've been waiting for you two. I knew you would come."

"Why, Lucas?" I shouted, rage and sorrow intertwining within me. "Why did you do this? You had everything! A family, a life... why destroy us?"

He smiled, a predatory grin that made my skin crawl. "Because I was tired of living in the shadow of a legacy that didn't belong to me.

I wanted to create my own destiny, and this"—he gestured around him—"is just the beginning."

Ethan stepped forward, anger radiating from him. "You think this chaos is freedom? You've torn our lives apart!"

"Freedom is messy," Lucas retorted, eyes gleaming with a madness that sent a shiver down my spine. "And loyalty? It's a weakness. Look where it got you both."

In that moment, I felt the weight of our families' legacies, the entanglements of blood and betrayal threatening to choke the life from us. Lucas had turned loyalty into a weapon, wielding it with a malevolence that echoed through our shared history. But it was not just his betrayal I feared—it was the darkness creeping into my own heart, the unsettling thought that perhaps he was right.

"Your path doesn't have to be ours," I said, my voice trembling but steady. "You can still choose to come back. We can fight this together."

For a brief flicker, doubt crossed his face, vulnerability lurking beneath the bravado. But it vanished as quickly as it appeared, replaced by a hardened resolve that made my blood run cold. "You don't understand. There is no going back. This is where I belong."

The air crackled with tension, the flames behind Lucas licking at the night sky, reaching out as if to engulf us all. And in that moment of defiance, I knew we were standing at a precipice, our fates intertwined in ways we had yet to comprehend. Would I be willing to fight for the love I had known, or would I succumb to the darkness that promised freedom from the burdens of the past?

"Ethan," I whispered, urgency clawing at my throat. "We have to be careful. He's lost. He doesn't know what he's doing."

But as I looked at Lucas, the firelight reflecting off his features, I realized that the greatest threat was not just his descent into madness but the choice I would have to make between love and loyalty. The heat of the flames seemed to swell around us, and in that moment of reckoning, I felt the weight of the world pressing down, the realization that we were standing on the brink of destruction, and only one of us would emerge unscathed.

The flames flickered wildly, casting elongated shadows that danced against the trees, painting a macabre picture of our gathering. Lucas's laughter rang out, a cruel sound that reverberated through the clearing, sending a chill crawling down my spine. His eyes glinted with a feverish light, the heat of the fire reflecting the chaos in his soul. "You really think you can save me?" he taunted, voice dripping with disdain. "You're as naive as you are loyal."

Ethan's grip on my hand tightened, grounding me in the moment even as uncertainty threatened to engulf us. The very essence of who we were hung in the balance. I could feel the air thickening around us, a palpable tension laced with unspoken truths. Every instinct screamed at me to run, to distance myself from this twisted version of my brother, but there was nowhere to hide. The path had been laid out before us, and it was a winding road lined with treachery.

"We're not trying to save you, Lucas," Ethan said, his voice steady yet simmering with restrained fury. "We're trying to stop you. You're hurting people who don't deserve it." His words hung in the air like an accusation, and for a moment, the fire crackled ominously, mirroring the discord brewing between us.

Lucas stepped closer, his expression shifting to something more sinister, as if he enjoyed the power he held. "And what gives you the right to judge me? You've always been the golden boy, haven't you? The dutiful son, the ever-loyal friend. But look where that's gotten you." He glanced at me, and for an instant, I felt the weight of our shared history pressing down upon us. "In love with the enemy."

I recoiled at the accusation, my heart racing. "I'm not your enemy, Lucas. I'm your sister." The word felt heavy, laden with meaning and the pain of loss. "We can end this madness together. We don't have to fight."

His eyes narrowed, the flicker of vulnerability extinguished. "It's too late for that," he said, voice low and dangerous. "You've chosen your side, and I'll show you the true meaning of loyalty." He stepped back, raising his arms as if to command the very flames that swirled behind him.

Before I could respond, a distant sound shattered the tension—an engine roar growing louder, breaking through the stillness of the night. My heart sank. I knew that sound all too well. "More of your followers?" I asked, dread pooling in my stomach.

Lucas grinned, an unsettling mixture of triumph and malice. "More like reinforcements. It's time to show you just how far I'm willing to go." The engine noise escalated into a cacophony of revving motors, and with it came the unmistakable rumble of approaching vehicles.

"Ethan, we need to go," I urged, urgency punctuating my words. The last thing we needed was an army of Lucas's loyalists descending upon us. I could already picture the chaos that would ensue—a stampede of misguided loyalties crashing down on us like a tidal wave.

But Ethan stood firm, his resolve unwavering. "Not without a plan. We can't just abandon this fight. Lucas needs to see the damage he's done." I admired his bravery, yet it felt like we were teetering on the edge of a cliff, and one wrong step would send us plummeting into the abyss.

"Do you think he'll listen?" I shot back, frustration bubbling beneath the surface. "He's not the brother I knew anymore. He's lost in this delusion of power."

"Maybe, but that doesn't mean we should give up on him," Ethan countered, his voice fierce with conviction. "If we can reach him, we might be able to turn this around."

As the headlights of the approaching vehicles pierced the darkness, illuminating the clearing, I could see figures spilling out, the silhouettes of familiar faces twisted with allegiance to a misguided cause. My heart raced as I recognized friends and acquaintances, drawn in by Lucas's intoxicating vision of freedom. It felt like betrayal slicing through my veins.

"Lucas!" I shouted, desperation clawing at my throat. "Look at what you're doing! You're manipulating everyone! This isn't freedom; it's a prison of your own making!" The words rang out into the night, a plea that hung in the air, laden with emotion.

But Lucas's laughter echoed, hollow and cruel. "They're not prisoners; they're my followers. They understand what it means to break free of the shackles of expectation. Unlike you, who cling to your family's name like a lifeline."

I stepped forward, ready to confront the onslaught of feelings crashing over me. "You think freedom means tearing everything down? You're so blinded by your ambition that you can't see the destruction you're causing!"

He held my gaze, and for a moment, I caught a flicker of something—doubt? Regret? But it vanished as quickly as it had come, replaced by the hardened resolve of someone who had made a choice. "You'll see, sister. One day, you'll thank me for this."

With that, the first of his followers stepped forward, the firelight catching on their determined expressions. The air crackled with tension, and I felt Ethan's presence beside me, a solid anchor in the growing storm.

"We need to move," he murmured, and I could sense the urgency in his voice. "If they're here, then we can't let them take us by surprise. We can use the trees as cover."

I nodded, adrenaline coursing through me, spurring me into action. As the figures moved closer, the weight of our family's legacy hung heavily on my shoulders, and I felt the stirrings of a plan begin to coalesce in my mind. We could use the element of surprise, just as Lucas had; we could turn his own tactics against him.

"Stick close," I whispered to Ethan, and he tightened his grip on my hand. Together, we melted into the shadows, moving silently among the trees, the crackling fire fading behind us. My heart raced not just with fear, but with a flicker of hope that maybe, just maybe, we could confront the darkness together. The night was far from over, and the flames of reckoning were only just beginning to burn.

The forest enveloped us in its thick embrace as we slipped between the trees, the muffled sounds of the gathering behind us gradually fading into an eerie silence. Each step felt like a small rebellion, a defiance against the chaos that threatened to consume not only Lucas but everything we had ever held dear. Ethan's presence beside me was both a comfort and a catalyst; together, we were stronger, but with each heartbeat, the weight of uncertainty pressed down, threatening to crush our resolve.

As we maneuvered through the underbrush, I could hear the muffled voices of Lucas's followers—their fervent loyalty was palpable, wrapping around us like a shroud. It stung to realize how easily they had been drawn into his web of deception. "They're not just friends, Ethan," I whispered, a pang of sorrow breaking my voice. "They're family to us, too. How did it come to this?"

Ethan paused, turning to face me, his expression a mixture of determination and compassion. "We can't let their blind loyalty sway us. We have to protect what's left of our family." His words ignited a flame within me, pushing aside my doubts. But the reality of the situation hung over us, threatening to engulf our resolve like the flames behind Lucas.

We crept deeper into the shadows, the vibrant hues of the sunset melting into the indigo of twilight, and as darkness blanketed the clearing, the forest transformed into a labyrinth of uncertainty. I could feel the weight of my pendant against my chest, a talisman of all I had ever known, urging me forward. Every rustle in the underbrush sent adrenaline surging through my veins, heightening my senses and sharpening my focus. We were in enemy territory, and each heartbeat was a reminder of the urgency of our mission.

"Do you remember the old oak tree?" Ethan asked suddenly, breaking the heavy silence. "The one we used to climb as kids? We'd sit up there for hours, plotting our adventures."

A smile tugged at my lips, the nostalgia washing over me like a warm blanket in the midst of the storm. "I remember you nearly fell out once, trying to impress a girl. I thought Mom was going to have a heart attack."

His chuckle was a welcome sound, cutting through the tension. "And you were the one who climbed up after me, all while pretending you weren't terrified."

"Just trying to maintain my reputation as the brave sister," I replied, the playful banter momentarily lifting the veil of dread that loomed over us. But the shadows were closing in, and we both knew that our time was running out.

Suddenly, a flash of light illuminated the path ahead, the headlights of vehicles illuminating the trees in a blinding glare. Panic surged through me, and I pulled Ethan closer to the trunk of a sturdy oak, our bodies pressed against the rough bark. "They're coming," I whispered, my heart racing as the rumble of engines grew louder, reverberating through the ground like an impending earthquake.

We peered through the branches, watching as Lucas's followers streamed into the clearing, their faces aglow with fervor. They looked like a battalion ready for war, unified in their misplaced devotion. The sight filled me with both dread and a fierce desire to fight back. "What do we do?" I asked, my voice barely a whisper.

Ethan's jaw clenched, determination etched on his features. "We need to disrupt their rally before it gains momentum. If we can expose Lucas's lies, maybe we can pull some of them back to reality."

"Expose him how?" I asked, desperation creeping into my voice. "He's the one holding all the cards right now."

"I know," he said, his gaze narrowing as he took a moment to strategize. "We can use the forest to our advantage. We'll create a distraction—draw their attention away from him. Then we can confront Lucas directly."

I nodded, a surge of adrenaline coursing through me. "Let's do it. We can't let this go on."

We slipped deeper into the shadows, moving with a deliberate stealth as we maneuvered through the thick underbrush. With each step, I felt the pulse of the earth beneath my feet, a reminder of the stakes at play. The lives of our friends, our family, hung precariously in the balance, and I was willing to risk everything to bring Lucas back from the brink.

Ethan and I navigated toward a thicket of brambles that bordered the clearing. It was a perfect spot to create chaos without being seen. I rummaged through my bag, fingers brushing against the items inside until I found what I was looking for: a flare gun. A remnant of our childhood camping trips, it now felt like a beacon of hope.

"Perfect," Ethan said, eyes lighting up with a mix of mischief and determination. "Once the flare goes off, it'll grab their attention. We'll use that moment to confront Lucas. It's risky, but it might just work."

With a nod, I took a deep breath, steadying my nerves. I could feel the fire within me rekindle, fueled by the desperation to protect the people I loved. "On three, then?"

"On three," he agreed, and we counted down in unison, anticipation crackling in the air like static electricity. As I raised the flare gun and took aim at the sky, I felt the weight of the moment settle upon me, a culmination of everything that had led us here.

"Now!" Ethan shouted, and I pulled the trigger.

The flare shot into the night sky with a brilliant whoosh, erupting into a cascade of vibrant colors that illuminated the darkness like a phoenix rising from the ashes. Gasps echoed through the clearing, followed by shouts of confusion and alarm as the followers turned their attention skyward, captivated by the unexpected display.

In that moment of distraction, Ethan and I charged toward the chaos, determination fueling our every step. We could see Lucas at the center, his expression shifting from surprise to rage as he realized what was happening.

"Lucas!" I shouted, my voice cutting through the tumult. "This is your last chance! Step back from this madness!"

He turned, eyes blazing, and for a heartbeat, I could see the brother I once knew flickering behind the facade of the madman he had become. But just as quickly, it vanished, replaced by a sneer that twisted his features.

"You think this changes anything? You're a fool to think you can stop me!" His voice boomed, full of confidence, but beneath it lay a tremor that suggested the cracks were beginning to show.

And then, as if conjured by some dark magic, a figure stepped from the shadows behind him—a shadow that seemed to swallow the light, cloaked in darkness and armed with intent. My heart lurched as recognition set in, and I felt the ground shift beneath me.

In an instant, everything spiraled into chaos. As the new figure emerged, the last vestiges of hope flickered and waned. The darkness closed in, and I realized we were not the only ones playing a dangerous game. In that heart-stopping moment, betrayal carved its path into my heart, leaving me with one haunting question: could we truly confront the flames of reckoning, or would they consume us all?

Chapter 17: The Burden of Truth

The air crackled with unspoken words as I stepped into the dimly lit kitchen, where sunlight struggled to filter through the lace curtains, casting intricate shadows that danced on the tiled floor. The scent of brewed coffee hung thick in the air, mingling with the faint sweetness of cinnamon from the sticky rolls cooling on the counter. I glanced at the clock, its hands creeping lazily toward noon, an unforgiving reminder that time, unlike our lives, remained stubbornly linear.

"Are you sure we should be doing this?" Ellie's voice cut through the silence, low and tentative as if afraid to disturb the fragile truce we had forged in the aftermath of revelation. Her dark curls fell around her face, framing her wide eyes that flickered with uncertainty. They were the same eyes that had sparkled with mischief during our carefree childhood, the same ones that now mirrored the weight of our shared legacy.

"We have to," I replied, my tone steadier than I felt. "We owe it to ourselves, to everyone who came before us." The words rolled off my tongue like a mantra, one I hoped would imbue me with the courage I desperately sought. Together, we stood at the precipice of truth, gazing down into the abyss of our parents' tangled histories and secrets.

Ellie bit her lip, glancing at the stacks of faded photographs strewn across the kitchen table, their edges curled and yellowing with age. The images captured moments of laughter and innocence, a stark contrast to the turmoil that had surfaced. Each photograph was a glimpse into the past—a past filled with love and lies, intertwined like vines creeping up a wall. "What if it breaks us?" she whispered, her voice barely above a breath.

I inhaled deeply, savoring the comforting aroma of coffee while wrestling with the knot in my stomach. "Or what if it sets us free?"

My own words surprised me, resonating with a truth I hadn't fully embraced until that moment. The thought of breaking free from the chains of our families' mistakes flickered like a candle in the dark, casting away the shadows that loomed over us. "We need to confront this. Together."

Ellie nodded slowly, her resolve hardening like the crust of the cinnamon rolls we used to bake on lazy Saturday mornings. I could see her gears turning, her mind whirring with possibilities and fears. It was a look I knew well; it was the same expression she wore when we plotted our little rebellions against our mundane small-town lives.

"Okay, then." She squared her shoulders, her chin lifted defiantly. "Let's do it."

We began sorting through the photographs, each image prompting a flood of memories—both cherished and painful. I picked up one depicting a summer barbecue from a decade ago. There was our father, grinning broadly, the sunlight catching the glint of his teeth, while my mother stood beside him, laughter crinkling the corners of her eyes. I swallowed hard, feeling the bittersweet tug of nostalgia. They were our parents, heroes of our childhood, yet beneath their smiles lay a labyrinth of betrayals that could shatter our carefully constructed illusions.

"What do you think they were thinking?" Ellie asked, tracing her finger over the glassy surface of the photo. "Did they even realize what they were doing to us?"

I shook my head, the familiar anger rising within me, swirling with sorrow. "Maybe they didn't care. Or maybe they were just trying to protect us from their mess." The words tasted bitter, but the truth was that their mess had become our own, a legacy we couldn't outrun. "What I do know is that we can't let their choices define us."

As the afternoon sun shifted, casting golden rays through the kitchen, illuminating the clutter, our conversation deepened, becoming a weaving of shared dreams and unspoken fears. Each revelation was a step into the light, a deliberate choice to face the darkness lurking in the corners of our lives. We talked about our plans for the future, dreams we had shelved under the weight of familial expectations.

"What if we start fresh?" Ellie suggested, her eyes sparkling with renewed hope. "What if we move to the city? Just you and me, chasing our dreams?"

The idea flickered like a spark, igniting a yearning deep within me. I could picture it—life in the city, vibrant and chaotic, where we could redefine ourselves beyond the shadows of our past. "I'd love that," I admitted, a smile breaking through my earlier resolve. "But what if we don't have enough money?"

"Money's overrated." She waved a hand dismissively, the warmth of her laughter wrapping around us like a cozy blanket. "We'll figure it out. We always do."

Her words resonated with a truth I had nearly forgotten amidst the turmoil of recent events. Our lives had always been a series of improvisations, moments of serendipity that led us to this point. We had navigated chaos before—this would be no different.

With each picture we sorted through, we wove a tapestry of our dreams, stitching together the threads of our hopes and fears, leaving behind the shadows of our parents' decisions. The weight of the past began to lighten, replaced by the exhilarating prospect of carving our own paths.

As we piled the photographs into neat stacks, I felt a growing sense of purpose blooming within me, like the first daffodils of spring breaking through the winter frost. "Let's promise each other something," I said, my heart pounding in my chest. "No matter what happens, we face it together. No more secrets."

Ellie looked at me, her expression serious yet playful, a glimmer of mischief dancing in her eyes. "Deal. But only if we can keep the cinnamon rolls in the plan. No promises without pastries."

I laughed, the sound bubbling up from somewhere deep inside, lightening the heaviness that had settled over us. "Deal."

And in that moment, surrounded by remnants of our past, I felt the shackles of our parents' legacy begin to loosen, the path ahead shimmering with possibilities as we stepped into our own future, hand in hand.

The evening light spilled through the kitchen window, draping us in a warm, golden glow as we began to tackle the mountain of clutter on the table. In the corners of the room, shadows deepened, creeping across the floorboards like silent witnesses to our unfolding drama. I took a deep breath, inhaling the aroma of freshly baked cinnamon rolls that still clung to the air, mingling with the palpable tension of our conversation. There was something comforting in the sweetness, a stark contrast to the bitterness of our revelations.

"Okay, so what's next on our grand adventure?" Ellie asked, her tone teasing yet laden with genuine curiosity. She leaned back in her chair, her fingers playing absently with a loose thread on her sweater, as if searching for something to hold onto amid the chaos.

I pondered for a moment, the gears of my mind churning as I stared at the disarray before us. "Well, first, we need to organize these photos. I think it might help us understand what we're dealing with," I replied, trying to sound confident even as doubt nagged at the edges of my mind.

"Right. The past is a puzzle we must solve before we can plan our escape," Ellie said, her eyes sparkling with a blend of humor and determination. "I just hope the pieces aren't too jagged."

"Or that we don't end up cutting ourselves in the process," I added, allowing a small smile to break through. Her lightness was infectious, a much-needed balm to the weight we both carried.

As we sorted through the images—our fingers grazing over faces that held so much joy and sorrow—we stumbled upon a photograph that made me catch my breath. It was an old, faded picture of our mothers together, arms linked, grinning broadly against a backdrop of sunflowers that seemed to stretch endlessly toward the horizon. The laughter captured in that moment felt like a relic from a time long forgotten, a testament to their bond that somehow felt both fragile and unbreakable.

"Look at them," I said, holding the photograph aloft. "It's like they were living in a fairytale, blissfully unaware of the storm brewing in the background."

"Or maybe they were just really good at pretending," Ellie murmured, her gaze fixed on the picture. "How did it all go so wrong?"

I let the question hang in the air, heavy with the weight of unspoken truths. "Maybe they thought they were protecting us. But protecting us from what? Their mistakes? Their secrets? We're left to sift through the ashes of their choices."

Ellie shrugged, her expression shifting to one of defiance. "Maybe it's time we stopped being their shadows. We should write our own story, one where we don't repeat their mistakes."

A determined spark ignited within me at her words. "You're right. No more shadows. No more whispers. We take our lives back."

Just as the atmosphere lightened with our shared resolve, a knock at the door shattered the moment. I exchanged a glance with Ellie, her brow furrowed in confusion. "Who could that be?" I asked, a hint of trepidation creeping into my voice.

"I don't know, but it's not like we've been holding a party," she replied, a nervous laugh escaping her lips. "Should we hide the cinnamon rolls? You know, just in case it's the morality police."

I chuckled, but my heart raced as I moved toward the door. Peering through the peephole, I caught a glimpse of an unfamiliar figure—a tall man with tousled dark hair, dressed in a fitted leather jacket that clung to him like a second skin. There was something vaguely familiar about his silhouette, a haunting resemblance that pulled at the edges of my memory.

"Who is it?" Ellie whispered, hovering just behind me, her curiosity piqued.

"I don't know. He looks... like someone I should know," I replied, stepping back and glancing over my shoulder at her. "Should I let him in?"

"Why not? At this point, we've already invited chaos into our lives. What's one more unexpected guest?" she quipped, a playful grin breaking through her apprehension.

With a deep breath, I swung the door open, revealing the stranger standing on the threshold. His eyes, a piercing blue, locked onto mine, and in that instant, the world around us faded into oblivion.

"Lila?" he said, his voice a low rumble that sent a shiver down my spine.

"Who are you?" I asked, my heart racing as confusion and recognition battled for supremacy.

"I'm Noah. We need to talk." His gaze flicked past me, searching the kitchen, and I could almost see the shadows of our past reflected in his eyes.

"Talk? About what?" I replied, crossing my arms defensively as uncertainty washed over me.

"About everything," he said, stepping forward, his demeanor intense. "About your parents, about my mother... and the secrets that connect us."

The air grew heavy with tension, and I could feel the weight of Ellie's scrutiny as she moved to my side, her presence a steady anchor. "Secrets? What kind of secrets?" she asked, her voice barely above a whisper.

Noah hesitated, his expression shifting as if he were weighing the implications of his next words. "The kind that could change everything you thought you knew. We're tangled in a web far more complicated than either of you can imagine."

I glanced at Ellie, whose wide eyes mirrored my own disbelief. "We've been through enough revelations today," I said, my voice firm. "What more could you possibly tell us?"

"More than you'd like to hear, I'm afraid," he said softly, stepping closer, urgency radiating from him. "But if you want the truth, you need to hear it all. It's about your families, their past, and the choices that haunt us all."

The room seemed to close in around us, a perfect storm brewing on the horizon. I sensed a shift, a tide turning that would drag us deeper into a whirlpool of revelations we weren't prepared for. Yet, standing here with Noah—this enigmatic stranger whose presence felt both familiar and unsettling—I realized that maybe the only way to forge our own paths was to confront the tangled roots that held us captive.

"Fine," I said, my heart pounding as the words escaped my lips. "We'll listen. But you better make it worth our while."

Noah nodded, the corners of his mouth lifting in a faint smile. "Trust me, Lila. You have no idea just how worth it this will be."

With a mixture of apprehension and intrigue, I motioned for him to enter, our lives set on a collision course with truths long buried. The shadows deepened, and I couldn't shake the feeling that we were on the brink of something monumental, teetering between revelation and chaos.

Noah stepped inside, the door creaking ominously behind him as he entered our sanctuary. I felt as if the walls themselves were closing in, leaving us vulnerable to the truths he was about to unveil. He scanned the room, absorbing the remnants of our childhood scattered across the kitchen. The tension crackled in the air, thick enough to cut with a knife.

"Your mothers were best friends, but there was more to it," he began, his voice steady yet charged with urgency. "They shared a bond that went beyond friendship, something they never revealed. A secret that has been buried for years."

Ellie and I exchanged glances, skepticism evident in our expressions. "You can't just drop a bombshell like that without some evidence," I replied, crossing my arms defensively. "What do you mean 'more than friendship'?"

He took a deep breath, his gaze drifting to the photographs still scattered on the table. "I don't know the details, but it was something profound. They were involved in something dangerous, something that tied their fates together in ways they couldn't escape."

The words hung in the air, resonating with echoes of our earlier conversations. I had felt the weight of the past pressing on my chest, but this—this was a whole new level of complexity. "Dangerous? How?"

"The kind of dangerous that involves secrets, lies, and people willing to do whatever it takes to keep those secrets hidden," he replied, his tone turning serious. "Your family wasn't just a victim of circumstance; they were players in a game much larger than any of us realized."

"Okay, so they were in a book club gone rogue? Give me a break," Ellie quipped, but her voice trembled slightly, betraying her uncertainty.

Noah met her gaze with unwavering intensity. "This isn't a joke, Ellie. I found out because my mother kept files—documents, photographs, correspondence. It wasn't just idle gossip; they were involved in something that put all of us in danger."

I felt the chill of dread creep into my bones. "What kind of danger are we talking about? And why are you bringing this to us now?"

"Because I believe it's time you knew the truth," he said, his voice low. "Your parents weren't just protecting you from their past; they were trying to shield you from something that could still come back to haunt you."

The pieces of the puzzle began to swirl in my mind, but the picture remained maddeningly incomplete. "Why should we trust you?" I shot back, trying to mask my growing unease.

"Because I have no reason to lie," he said, exasperation tinging his voice. "And because I'm in this too. If there's a threat lurking, it's not just your past I'm trying to protect; it's my own."

Ellie's brow furrowed as she processed this new information. "So you're saying our parents were involved in some secretive, nefarious activities, and now we're at risk because of it? How do we know this isn't some wild goose chase? You could be here to toy with us, to get us riled up over nothing."

"I'd rather be safe than sorry," he replied, meeting her challenging gaze. "The more you know, the better equipped you'll be to protect yourselves. I have leads—names, places. If you're willing to follow me down this rabbit hole, we might find out exactly what our parents were entangled in and how deep the deception goes."

I felt a rush of conflicting emotions. Part of me wanted to slam the door shut, to retreat back into the comfortable cocoon of ignorance. But another part—the part that had been ignited by Ellie's earlier words—craved the truth. "All right," I said slowly, testing the waters. "Let's say we're in. Where do we start?"

Noah stepped forward, his eyes alight with a fierce determination. "We need to start at the beginning. There's an old house just outside of town—my mother's childhood home. It hasn't been lived in for years, but I believe the answers we seek might be hidden inside."

Ellie shook her head, a hint of humor breaking through her unease. "Great. Because nothing says 'let's uncover deep family secrets' like a creepy, abandoned house in the middle of nowhere."

"No sarcasm, please," Noah retorted, a faint smile flickering across his lips. "This is serious."

"Right. Serious business—like a horror movie waiting to happen." She raised an eyebrow, but the bravado was beginning to slip, replaced by a glimmer of genuine curiosity.

"We can't be afraid of the dark anymore," I said, my voice steadying as my resolve solidified. "If there's even a chance that we can piece together our families' truths, we have to take it."

Noah nodded, clearly relieved by our agreement. "I'll drive. Grab whatever you need, and meet me outside in fifteen minutes."

The urgency in his voice snapped us into action. As we hurriedly gathered our things, my heart raced at the prospect of diving headfirst into the unknown. I glanced at the photographs one last time, each face now tinged with the weight of their untold stories.

"Do you really think we'll find something?" Ellie asked, her voice quiet as we moved about the kitchen.

"I have to believe we will," I replied, trying to infuse confidence into my words. "Otherwise, what's the point of all this?"

When we stepped outside, the sky was a deep indigo, punctuated by scattered stars that twinkled like distant dreams. The car's headlights cut through the darkness, illuminating our path ahead. I slipped into the back seat, my thoughts a whirlwind as we drove through familiar streets that now felt alien, transformed by the secrets they harbored.

The ride was charged with anticipation, every minute stretching into eternity as we neared the outskirts of town. The road narrowed, flanked by trees that seemed to whisper dark secrets among themselves. A sense of foreboding settled in the pit of my stomach, tightening with each passing second.

As we pulled up to the old house, the moonlight revealed a dilapidated structure, its once-white paint now peeling and weathered. Shadows loomed large, wrapping around the edges like fingers grasping at the past.

"Welcome to the site of our impending doom," Ellie muttered, eyeing the house with trepidation.

"Or the discovery of a lifetime," Noah countered, his voice laced with excitement and fear.

We stepped out of the car, the crunch of gravel underfoot breaking the silence. I glanced at the imposing silhouette of the house, the air thick with history and unspoken words. "Are we really doing this?" I asked, a mix of anxiety and thrill coursing through me.

"Absolutely," Noah replied, pushing open the creaking front door, the sound echoing into the night. "Let's find out what our families were hiding."

As we entered, the stale air enveloped us, heavy with the scent of mildew and forgotten memories. Dust danced in the beams of moonlight that filtered through grimy windows, and I felt an inexplicable chill creep up my spine.

In that moment, the door slammed shut behind us with a force that rattled the walls, echoing like a finality that left no room for retreat. The world outside faded into silence, and I knew we were no longer just stepping into a house; we were stepping into the heart of a mystery that could change everything we thought we knew.

"No turning back now," Noah said, glancing over his shoulder, a mix of determination and dread in his eyes. The shadows seemed to shift, whispering secrets we were not yet ready to hear.

And just then, a noise echoed from the darkened hallway—a soft, haunting sound that sent a chill racing through me, freezing me in place.

Chapter 18: Into the Lion's Den

The hum of voices swirled around me like a living thing, each laugh and whisper vibrating against the polished marble floor of the grand hall. The air was heavy with the mingling scents of expensive perfume and the savory aroma of hors d'oeuvres, wafting from the glittering trays carried by well-dressed servers. My heels clicked rhythmically against the floor, a sharp counterpoint to the softer murmurs that fluttered through the air like gossiping butterflies. I'd never felt so alive, nor so vulnerable. This was a world of elegance, a masquerade where secrets lay beneath the surface, and I was about to dive into the depths.

The gala was hosted by Ardent Technologies, a name that conjured images of innovation and trust, but behind the gleaming facade lay a network of deceit as intricate as the lace of my dress. I smoothed my hand over the deep blue fabric, the color reflecting the sharpness I needed to embody tonight. I'd spent hours in front of the mirror, working through the myriad of emotions that threatened to spill over. It was not merely a party; it was the battleground where I would confront the puppeteer pulling the strings of our lives, the enigmatic figure known only as "The Architect."

Cameron, my partner in both this chaotic mission and my heart, appeared at my side, his presence grounding me. He wore a tailored black suit that hugged his athletic frame, the silver tie a stark contrast against the deep black. "You look stunning," he said, his voice low and smooth, with just a hint of mischief. "Are you sure you're ready for this?"

"Ready?" I smirked, a bubble of anxiety trying to push its way to the surface. "More like prepared to set fire to this whole charade." I leaned closer, my breath mingling with his, the connection crackling like electricity. "We've come too far to back down now."

The look he shot me was a mix of admiration and concern. "Just remember, we're not just here to expose the truth. We need to stay alive while doing it."

"Always the optimist," I quipped, rolling my eyes even as my heart quickened at the thought of the dangers that lay ahead. We navigated through clusters of elegantly dressed guests, each conversation a delicate dance of flirtation and subtext. I caught snippets of laughter and the clink of champagne glasses, but my focus was drawn to the shadowy corners of the room, where the truth could lurk, hidden in plain sight.

As we approached the grand staircase, I spotted my nemesis across the room. A tall figure dressed in an immaculate white tuxedo stood beneath a glimmering chandelier, a glass of something golden in hand. He exuded an air of confidence and power that sent a chill down my spine. It was Marcus Hale, the CEO of Ardent, and the man rumored to be the puppet master of this twisted game. I could feel the pulse of my heart against my ribcage, each beat a reminder of what was at stake.

"What's our play?" Cameron asked, his voice barely above a whisper.

"We'll blend in," I replied, nodding toward a group of executives laughing heartily at a nearby table. "Just like we practiced. We need to keep our eyes on Marcus and find out who he's talking to."

As we maneuvered through the crowd, I caught sight of the ornate bar, its surface lined with crystal bottles gleaming like jewels. I'd need a drink to steel my nerves, and maybe one to disguise the nervous tremor in my hands. I flagged down a server and took a glass of sparkling water, the bubbles tickling my throat, a brief distraction from the chaos around me.

"Look," Cameron murmured, tilting his head toward Marcus. "He's not alone."

My breath caught as I spotted a familiar face beside him: Claire Winters, a high-ranking official known for her ruthless ambition and chillingly sharp wit. She leaned into Marcus, her laughter echoing with an edge that felt like ice. Their conversation was obscured, but the way Marcus leaned closer, his expression one of feigned charm, made my stomach twist. They were conspiring, no doubt about it.

"We need to get closer," I said, the urgency in my voice rising. "If we can overhear their conversation, it could be the key to unraveling everything."

With determination fueling my steps, we approached the pair, careful to weave through the throng of guests without drawing attention. The ambient music swelled, a lively waltz that felt almost mocking in its cheerfulness.

"Do you think anyone suspects?" Claire asked, her voice smooth yet laced with underlying tension. "The stakes have never been higher."

"Let them come," Marcus replied, a predatory smile curving his lips. "The naïve believe they can play the game without understanding the rules. We hold the cards; they don't even know the game exists."

My heart pounded in my chest, each word a dagger that pierced through my resolve. I glanced at Cameron, who mirrored my unease, the weight of the truth hanging between us like an unsaid promise. This wasn't just about the secrets they were hiding; it was about lives, our lives, caught in the crossfire of their ambitions.

Suddenly, a commotion erupted at the far end of the room, a crash of glass shattering against the floor. Heads turned, and the atmosphere shifted, the air crackling with tension. I seized the moment, nodding to Cameron as we slipped away from the crowd, our eyes fixed on Marcus and Claire, their focus distracted.

"Now's our chance," I whispered, adrenaline surging through my veins. We ducked into the shadows, weaving between the guests, determined to gather the evidence we needed. The stakes had never been higher, but the thought of facing down Marcus filled me with a sense of purpose. Each step closer to the truth was a step away from the darkness that threatened to engulf us.

As we inched nearer, the world around me faded into a blur, every sound sharpening, every heartbeat echoing in my ears. We were no longer just participants in this charade; we were players in a game that could mean the difference between freedom and captivity, truth and lies. With every breath, I reminded myself of the power we wielded, the secrets we were determined to unearth. The lion's den awaited, and I was ready to confront whatever lay within.

The crowd surged around us, a sea of laughter and clinking glasses, yet I felt suspended in my own bubble of intensity. Each laugh seemed to mock our quiet determination, every flutter of silk or satin a reminder of the facade we were upholding. I could see Marcus and Claire from the corner of my eye, their silhouettes stark against the flickering light of the chandelier as they exchanged whispered secrets, unaware of the storm brewing just a few feet away.

"What's the plan?" Cameron murmured, glancing at me as we slipped behind a towering potted palm. The leaves brushed my arm, cool and fragrant, grounding me amidst the tension.

"Listen first, act later," I replied, my eyes fixed on the pair. "We need to hear what they're planning, then we can decide how to play this."

Just as I settled into my resolve, the air shifted again, electrifying with the sudden arrival of another guest. A woman in a deep crimson gown entered the hall, her presence commanding instant attention. With every step, she seemed to weave a spell, heads turning in her wake, conversations momentarily halted as though the air itself held its breath. Her auburn hair cascaded in waves, framing a face that seemed to be carved from marble, striking and formidable.

"Who is that?" I whispered to Cameron, my curiosity piqued.

"Not sure," he replied, his eyes narrowing. "But I don't like the look of her."

As she drew closer to Marcus and Claire, I caught the glint of something in her hand—a small device, glimmering as it caught the light, akin to a miniature weapon or perhaps something more sinister. A knot of apprehension tightened in my stomach.

"Is that what I think it is?" I whispered, feeling the weight of uncertainty press down on me.

"Depends on what you think it is," he replied, his tone laced with humor, even as he shifted to shield me from view.

"Let's just say I'd prefer it not be a detonator," I shot back, trying to keep the edge of panic from my voice. My mind raced through the possibilities, painting vivid images of chaos erupting in this sophisticated setting.

The woman approached Marcus, her voice low and sultry. "I trust you've been keeping an eye on our little friends?"

"Of course," Marcus replied, his smile more predatory than I had seen before. "Their attempts to uncover the truth are amusing, really. But I assure you, they'll be dealt with."

A shiver traveled down my spine. "They?" I echoed softly, sharing a glance with Cameron. The implications were clear. We were in deeper waters than I had anticipated, swimming with sharks who wouldn't hesitate to bite.

"We need to get out of here," I said, urgency clawing at my insides. "If they're onto us—"

"Then we need to act, not flee," Cameron countered, his eyes flashing with determination. "We can't let them intimidate us."

My heart raced, torn between instinct and strategy. "But we need proof first. We can't expose them on a hunch."

Before we could devise our next move, the woman in crimson leaned closer to Marcus, the device glinting ominously between them. "And the plan for the gala? It's time to make a statement. Show them who truly holds the power in this city."

The words hung heavy in the air, suffocating my resolve. I glanced at Cameron, and without needing to say a word, we shifted into motion, moving silently away from the palm, hearts pounding in rhythm with our desperate breaths.

"Where are we going?" he asked, his voice barely a whisper, but laced with a resolve that echoed my own.

"To the bar," I replied, my mind racing as I scanned the room for an escape route. "We can get a better vantage point and keep an eye on them."

We slipped past the cluster of guests, each step purposeful yet cautious. The bar, polished to a gleam, stood as a beacon amidst the chaos, and as we neared it, I could almost taste the tang of adrenaline. I spotted an unoccupied stool at the far end, angled just right for us to observe without being too obvious.

"Two drinks, please," I said to the bartender, my voice steady despite the storm brewing within. "Something strong."

As he poured the drinks, I stole glances at Marcus and Claire, who appeared to be deep in conversation with the woman, now gesturing animatedly with the device. My heart raced; this was a moment of pivotal tension, the calm before the inevitable storm.

"Here's to facing our fears," Cameron said, raising his glass, the light catching the ice cubes and illuminating the dark shadows around us.

"To exposing the truth," I replied, clinking my glass against his. The fizz of the drink mirrored the energy crackling between us, a shared determination radiating like an electric current.

"Ready?" Cameron asked, a playful grin breaking through the tension.

I nodded, locking my gaze on the trio. "Let's see what we can uncover."

As we settled onto the barstools, the chaos of the gala faded slightly, replaced by the intensity of our mission. The conversation between Marcus, Claire, and the mysterious woman took on an urgency that resonated in my bones, and I strained to catch every word.

"Tonight is about more than just a celebration," Marcus said, his voice low, yet it carried through the air like a whispered secret. "It's about asserting dominance over our little problem. Let them think they can unearth the truth; we will bury it first."

I felt a wave of nausea wash over me, the reality of their plans crashing down like a heavy tide. "They're not just playing games. They're preparing for something drastic."

Cameron's hand tightened around his glass, his jaw set. "We need to warn the others. This could escalate quickly."

As if the universe had conspired against us, the room seemed to dim at that moment, the lights flickering ominously. Gasps echoed as laughter faltered, and a momentary hush fell, tension winding like a tightly coiled spring. It was the moment of revelation, where danger danced at the edges of anticipation.

From the corner of my eye, I saw the woman turn, her gaze scanning the crowd with a predatory sharpness. The air vibrated with unease, and I felt Cameron's body tense beside me.

"Stay low," I whispered, a sense of urgency building in my chest. "They might be looking for us."

The flickering lights continued, and I could feel the atmosphere shift, thickening like fog rolling in across the water. The gala was transforming from a celebration into a ticking time bomb, and we were caught right in the middle.

"Do you think they saw us?" Cameron asked, his voice strained yet determined.

"Not yet, but we need to keep it that way," I replied, adrenaline flooding my system. "We're not just up against Marcus now; it's a whole team of them. If they're prepared to take drastic measures, we need to be ready."

As I surveyed the room, my eyes narrowed, strategizing our next move. The stakes were dangerously high, but I was not about to let fear dictate our fate. We would fight, clawing our way toward the truth, together, because that was the only way we could hope to emerge from this tangled web of deception.

The lights flickered again, a fleeting moment of chaos in an otherwise carefully curated scene. The gasps of surprise morphed into murmurs of concern, the guests shifting uneasily in their silken gowns and sharp suits. I could see the threads of tension weaving through the crowd, binding us all in a fragile moment that felt like the calm before a storm.

"They're definitely onto something," I said under my breath, eyes darting toward Marcus and his companions, who remained unperturbed. The woman in red appeared to thrive in the uncertainty, her smile unfaltering, her stance relaxed as if the growing tension were simply a play she enjoyed watching unfold.

"We need to move before they decide to do something reckless," Cameron replied, his tone urgent yet cool, betraying a confidence that steadied me. "Any ideas?"

A flurry of thoughts raced through my mind, each one more implausible than the last. The gala had transformed into a minefield of potential danger, and I was acutely aware that one misstep could be catastrophic. "What if we—"

Before I could finish, the lights plunged into darkness, plunging us into an abyss of uncertainty. A collective gasp echoed through the hall, followed by a chorus of anxious chatter that crescendoed into a symphony of confusion. The brief silence that preceded the chaos felt as fragile as a soap bubble, shimmering yet destined to pop.

"Stick close to me," Cameron said, his grip tightening around my waist, pulling me closer as if to shield me from the encroaching shadows. I could feel his body tense against mine, a taut line of determination ready to snap into action.

As my eyes adjusted, I could make out shapes moving in the darkness, the flickering emergency lights beginning to illuminate the scene in eerie flashes. The glow danced across the floor like specters revealing their true forms, and I felt a surge of adrenaline rush through me. "We need to find a way to the exits," I said, my voice barely above a whisper. "We can't stay here."

Cameron nodded, his eyes scanning the room, assessing the risks. "There's an emergency exit near the kitchen," he suggested, pointing to a faint outline of a door. "But we'll have to get through the main crowd."

Just as we prepared to move, a sudden burst of light flared from the chandelier overhead, momentarily blinding us. It illuminated Marcus, who stood defiantly, raising his hands as though conducting an orchestra of panic. "Ladies and gentlemen!" he called out, his voice booming, commanding attention like a king addressing his subjects. "Please remain calm. We are merely experiencing a minor inconvenience."

The laughter that followed was nervous, the guests exchanging glances filled with uncertainty. Claire and the woman in crimson remained near Marcus, their expressions unreadable, but their body language betrayed an unsettling calmness that hinted at a hidden agenda.

"A minor inconvenience?" I scoffed quietly, shaking my head. "This is not just a blackout; something is brewing."

Cameron's gaze sharpened. "Exactly. They're using this chaos to cover their plans. We can't afford to be caught in the middle of it."

We edged through the crowd, weaving between startled guests who whispered frantically, their elegant facades cracking under the pressure. The tension was palpable, each breath filled with a cocktail of fear and excitement that intoxicated me more than the drinks floating around the room.

Suddenly, a loud crash erupted from the far end of the hall, causing the remaining guests to jump, their chatter escalating into a frenzied clamor. "What was that?" I exclaimed, instinctively clutching Cameron's arm.

"Stay close!" he urged, pulling me into the dim light that flickered sporadically. We ducked low, moving toward the kitchen exit, each step a calculated risk. Just as we neared the door, a figure appeared, silhouetted against the chaos.

"Get down!" Cameron shouted, shoving me behind a nearby table just as the figure unleashed a burst of fire into the air. The crack of a gunshot echoed, followed by the shouts of terrified guests scrambling for cover.

"Who the hell is that?" I gasped, my heart racing as I pressed against the table, adrenaline coursing through my veins.

Cameron's expression hardened. "No idea, but they're not here for a chat."

The figure—clad in black from head to toe—stepped into the light, revealing a mask obscuring their face. They moved with a fluidity that was almost mesmerizing, each motion deliberate and calculated. I couldn't help but wonder if they were part of Marcus's game or a wildcard in this high-stakes poker match.

"Cameron, what do we do?" I whispered urgently, my pulse thrumming in my ears.

"Wait for my signal," he replied, his voice steady as he peered around the table, assessing the chaos unfolding. "We need to make a distraction."

Suddenly, the masked figure fired again, the shot ricocheting off a nearby chandelier, sending a cascade of glass raining down like deadly confetti. Guests screamed and ducked, a wave of panic surging through the crowd, and in that moment, I felt the world shift beneath my feet.

"We can't wait any longer," I said, adrenaline coursing through me. "We need to act now!"

With a swift motion, I grabbed a nearby champagne bottle from a discarded tray, its contents still sparkling, and without thinking, hurled it toward the figure. It shattered against the floor, the glass exploding into a million fragments, drawing the attention of the masked assailant.

"What are you doing?" Cameron hissed, incredulous.

"Distracting!" I shot back, scrambling to my feet. The masked figure turned, startled, their weapon wavering as they assessed the source of the noise.

"Let's go!" Cameron seized my wrist, pulling me toward the exit as we raced toward the door. The chaos around us surged, the sounds of shouts and gunfire melding into a symphony of bedlam that fueled my determination.

But as we reached the kitchen entrance, a metallic clang echoed, the sound reverberating through the air like a death knell. I glanced back just in time to see Marcus's gleeful grin piercing through the darkness, his eyes sparkling with a dangerous delight.

"You really thought you could escape that easily?" he called, his voice laced with mocking laughter.

Panic flooded through me as I realized we were cornered, trapped in a web spun of deceit and danger. "Cameron, they're blocking us!" I shouted, the weight of dread sinking in.

"Not for long," he replied, determination igniting in his gaze. "Follow my lead!"

In that moment, as we prepared to make our last stand against the forces arrayed against us, I felt a rush of defiance. We had come too far to back down now, but as I turned to face our pursuers, the world around us erupted into chaos, and the weight of uncertainty hung heavy in the air, teetering on the brink of catastrophe.

Chapter 19: The Heart of Deceit

The gala was a tapestry of extravagance, a grand affair where shimmering chandeliers dripped crystal light upon elegantly clad guests swirling about the marble floors. I floated among them, my fingers brushing against the silky fabric of my gown, which hugged my curves in all the right places. The scent of jasmine and sandalwood wafted through the air, mingling with laughter and whispered secrets, creating a heady atmosphere that intoxicated the senses. My heart raced, but not just from the opulence surrounding me; it was the thrill of the chase, the uncertainty lurking beneath the surface of this gilded paradise that both frightened and exhilarated me.

I had come to uncover the truth, to peel back the layers of deceit that cloaked this evening in a veneer of celebration. Yet, every glance I stole at him, the enigmatic figure in the crowd, sent my resolve spiraling. His deep blue eyes sparkled like the ocean beneath a moonlit sky, drawing me in like a siren's song. We had a mission—our lives depended on it—but the air between us crackled with an energy that was equally dangerous.

"Isn't it just breathtaking?" a voice chimed beside me, and I turned to see Clara, her auburn hair cascading like a waterfall over her shoulder. She tugged at my sleeve, pulling my attention away from him momentarily. "They say the diamonds on Lady Wexley's tiara are worth more than a small fortune. And the food! You simply must try the truffle risotto."

"Truffle risotto?" I replied, forcing a smile, though my thoughts were still on the mysterious man who seemed to orbit my consciousness like a planet caught in gravitational pull. "I suppose I should be grateful for the distraction."

Clara's brow furrowed, her eyes scanning the room, and for a moment, I feared she sensed my distraction was more than mere curiosity about the menu. "Are you feeling alright? You seem... elsewhere."

"I'm fine," I insisted, though I was anything but. The crowd ebbed and flowed like the tide, and I lost sight of him, the pull of his presence eclipsed by an unsettling stillness that settled over the gala. It was as if the very air thickened, a warning that something was off. Panic clawed at my chest as I moved through the throng, each step a silent prayer that I'd find him before the dark clouds of danger closed in.

I pressed through clusters of guests, each face a mask of laughter and sophistication, blissfully unaware of the tension that hummed beneath our polished veneer. My heart thudded louder, drowning out the music and laughter, as I called his name silently in my head, a mantra of urgency that echoed in the corners of my mind.

Just as despair began to wrap its icy fingers around my heart, I spotted him at the far end of the hall. He stood there, bathed in the soft glow of the golden light, a striking figure against the backdrop of swirling colors. Relief washed over me like a cool breeze on a stifling day. I navigated through the crowd, my pace quickening until I was almost running.

But as I drew closer, I noticed a shift in the atmosphere. The laughter faded, replaced by a low hum of murmured conversations. Shadows seemed to flicker at the edges of the room, and a chill coursed through me. I reached for him, and our eyes locked in a moment of shared urgency that transcended words.

"What's wrong?" I whispered, barely audible above the clink of glasses and the rustle of silk. He stepped closer, his breath warm against my ear, sending shivers down my spine.

"Stay close," he murmured, his voice low and urgent. "I think we've been compromised."

Before I could respond, a sudden explosion of laughter erupted nearby, and in that moment of distraction, I lost him again. The crowd had shifted like quicksand, swallowing him whole, and I felt the walls close in. The panic surged anew, and I pushed through the throng, my heart racing as I searched for him, the sense of danger becoming palpable with each passing second.

The atmosphere thickened, the celebration now a deceptive façade concealing something far more sinister. My eyes darted across the room, searching for any sign of him. And then, in the midst of the swirling chaos, I found him again—his posture tense, his jaw set in determination as he scanned the room with an intensity that sent a jolt of recognition through me. I rushed toward him, and without thinking, I reached for his hand, intertwining our fingers like a lifeline.

His eyes softened for a brief moment, and as if the world around us vanished, we leaned into each other. Our lips met in a hurried kiss, electric and urgent, a collision of fears and hopes that both anchored and liberated me. It was a kiss that spoke volumes, reminding me why we were here, why we had fought so hard. But as our lips parted, reality crashed back in, a reminder that the darkness was still lurking, waiting for an opportunity to strike.

"We need to move," he said, his voice a mix of urgency and resolve. The heat of his body against mine was comforting, yet I could feel the tension rippling through him. "They're onto us."

The unspoken bond between us tightened, a thread woven from shared fears and desires. I nodded, my heart racing with both exhilaration and dread, as we slipped through the crowd, blending in yet feeling distinctly apart. Each moment pulsed with uncertainty, our mission drawing us deeper into the labyrinth of deceit that threatened to swallow us whole. The taste of danger lingered in the air, but so did the promise of connection—a reminder that in this world of chaos, we had each other. And that, perhaps, was the most powerful weapon of all.

The pulsating energy of the gala had shifted from celebration to something much darker, an undercurrent of danger that rippled through the air like static electricity. As we slipped away from the throng, I could feel the tension coiling around us, thick as fog. My hand remained entwined with his, a lifeline that felt both reassuring and perilously frail. The glint of jewels and the soft rustle of silk surrounded us, but my focus sharpened on the dimly lit corridor leading away from the main ballroom.

"Where are we going?" I whispered, my voice barely above the hum of distant laughter and clinking glasses. The walls felt like they were closing in, pressing me against the urgency of our predicament.

"To a place where we can think," he replied, his gaze scanning the area like a hawk on the hunt. There was a gravity in his expression, a fierce determination that made my heart flutter with a mix of fear and exhilaration.

As we moved deeper into the shadows, the opulence faded, replaced by the sterile whiteness of the hallways lined with abstract art that seemed to mock our stealth. The bold strokes and chaotic splashes of color felt alive, swirling around us as if trying to escape the tightening grip of secrecy that had enveloped the night. My mind raced with questions, the whirlwind of the gala still fresh, but I forced myself to focus on the moment.

"Do you think they've figured it out?" I asked, stealing a glance at him. There was something comforting in the way he held himself, each step purposeful, as if he were guiding us through the storm rather than running from it.

"I hope not," he said, pausing for just a heartbeat to meet my gaze. "But I can't shake the feeling that we're being watched. We need to be careful."

A shiver danced down my spine at the thought. The thrill of our kiss lingered like a sweet melody, yet the harsh reality of our situation threatened to drown it out. "Great. I always wanted to feel like a character in a spy novel. Just missing the high-tech gadgets and the obligatory villain in a top hat."

He smirked, a flash of amusement cutting through the tension. "I could make a hat if you want. Maybe something with a secret compartment for your snacks?"

I laughed, the sound lightening the mood between us. "As if I'd share my snacks with anyone, especially not a villain. But perhaps I'll consider it for a future date. You know, the kind where we aren't hiding from our lives being ruined?"

His smile faded slightly, replaced by a look of concentration as we rounded a corner into a narrow alcove. "Look," he said, his voice low. "This area seems deserted. We might be able to catch our breath and regroup."

The alcove was dim, lit only by a flickering chandelier that cast playful shadows on the walls. The air was cooler here, tinged with the faint scent of polished wood and something floral, possibly the remnants of a forgotten arrangement. I leaned against the wall, trying to shake the adrenaline coursing through me.

"What do we do next?" I asked, trying to keep my voice steady. "Do we confront whoever is behind this? Or do we gather more information first?"

"Confronting might be a bit premature," he replied, leaning closer, his breath warm against my ear. "But gathering intel could lead us to the truth. And with the stakes as high as they are, we can't afford any mistakes."

Just as I opened my mouth to respond, the sudden sound of footsteps echoed down the corridor, each step like thunder against the stillness. I stiffened, my heart racing. "What if it's them?" I whispered, a chill creeping into my voice.

"Then we need to be quick." His fingers tightened around mine, and without a second thought, he pulled me further into the alcove, pressing our bodies together in the narrow space. The proximity was intoxicating, the warmth radiating from him igniting a fire within me even as danger loomed.

We held our breath, straining to listen as the footsteps grew closer, the voices now distinct. They were deep and male, laced with authority, exchanging hushed words that carried a weight I could not ignore.

"...if we don't act now, everything we've worked for could unravel," one voice warned, tinged with frustration. "The gala was the perfect distraction, and yet here we are, standing in shadows."

"Patience," the other replied. "We have to wait for the right moment. If we're too hasty, we'll lose everything."

My stomach twisted as the implications sank in. They were talking about us—or, more precisely, about the very mission that had brought us to this glittering yet treacherous gala. Panic surged again, but I forced myself to remain still, to breathe.

"Do you think they're talking about the plan?" I whispered, my voice barely more than a breath.

"Absolutely," he said, his eyes darting toward the edge of the alcove. "We need to know who they are and what they know."

The footsteps paused just outside our hiding spot, and I could feel the tension in the air thickening, pressing in on us like a vice. "What do we do if they come in here?" I whispered, my heart pounding in my chest.

"Just trust me," he murmured, his gaze unwavering, filled with a mixture of determination and something deeper—something I dared not explore just yet.

The voices began to fade, and I felt a rush of relief mixed with urgency. "Let's follow them," I suggested, breaking the silence. "We need to find out where they're going."

He hesitated for a fraction of a second, weighing the risk, and then nodded. "Stay close."

We crept out of the alcove, careful to remain silent, our hearts pounding in sync as we navigated the hallway, following the distant voices. Each step was a delicate balance of caution and anticipation, the thrill of danger swirling around us like the heady perfume of the gala.

As we approached a door slightly ajar, I caught sight of a lavishly furnished room bathed in dim light, where the two men stood discussing something that sent my mind racing. Their silhouettes were sharp against the glow, their expressions grave. I glanced at him, a question in my eyes, and he nodded, a silent agreement that we would get closer.

Just then, the door creaked slightly, and I froze, heart in my throat. But before I could retreat, he took a decisive step forward, and I followed, adrenaline fueling my resolve as we edged closer to uncover the secrets that could unravel everything we held dear. The night was far from over, and with each heartbeat, the stakes grew higher.

The whispers from the room seeped into the air like poison, thick with secrets that threatened to unravel everything we'd worked for. Each syllable wrapped around my mind, pulling me deeper into a web of intrigue that danced just out of reach. As we crouched in the shadow of the door, I could feel his breath against my cheek, warm and steady, grounding me amidst the chaos.

"Do you think we're about to stumble upon a nefarious plot?" I murmured, my heart racing. The thrill of danger was intoxicating, a rush that pulsed through my veins. I had always been drawn to adventure, but this—this was a different breed altogether.

"More like a dinner party gone wrong," he quipped under his breath, a playful glint in his eyes despite the tension coiling around us. "At least they didn't serve the truffle risotto. I have a feeling it would taste better than what they're plotting."

I stifled a laugh, the absurdity of the situation striking me as comically surreal. Just as I was beginning to relax into the moment, one of the men shifted, stepping closer to the door, and my stomach dropped. We were too exposed. I could see the outline of a sleek glass bottle in his hand, glinting ominously in the low light.

"Keep your voice down," he whispered urgently, his eyes narrowing. "We need to hear what they're saying."

The men continued their conversation, the cadence of their voices laced with tension. "I don't care how much they want to pay us," one of them said, his tone clipped. "This is a risk we can't afford to take. If we're caught, it's over."

"Over for us, maybe," the other replied, a hint of arrogance in his voice. "But think of the power we'll have. We're on the verge of something monumental. We just need to execute flawlessly."

My heart thundered in my chest as the implications of their words sank in. They were discussing something dangerous, something that could change everything. I leaned closer, desperate to catch every word.

"What exactly are you proposing?" the first man asked, skepticism threading through his tone.

"The gala is the perfect distraction. While everyone is busy celebrating, we can move in undetected. The package is secure, and once we have it, we'll control everything. The city, the businesses—everyone will answer to us."

The "package." My mind raced, trying to piece together the fragments of their plan. What did they want? Who were they working for?

Just then, the door creaked under the pressure of a sudden gust of air, and I froze, holding my breath. The men turned, their eyes narrowing as they caught a glimpse of something just outside the doorway. My heart sank.

"We should check it out," the second man suggested, taking a step forward. My instincts screamed at me to retreat, but there was nowhere to go.

"Stay put," the first man commanded, his voice low but firm. "If they're here, we can't let them see us."

Without thinking, I grabbed his hand, pulling him back deeper into the shadows as the men approached the door. Our bodies pressed together, the warmth radiating from him a stark contrast to the cold fear threading through my veins. I could feel his heartbeat, steady and calm, against my palm, reminding me that I wasn't alone in this precarious moment.

"Do you have a plan?" I whispered, panic rising like bile in my throat.

"Improvise," he replied with a quick grin, though his eyes betrayed the seriousness of our situation. "It's worked for us before."

The footsteps stopped just inches from our hiding place, the tension in the air thick enough to slice through. I could see the first man peering into the hallway, suspicion etched across his features. Time seemed to stretch infinitely as I held my breath, praying that we wouldn't be discovered.

"Nothing," he said finally, stepping back with a scowl. "Just the wind. Let's get back to the plan."

As they retreated, I released the breath I hadn't realized I was holding, and we slipped back into our previous positions, pressing our backs against the wall. The thrill of narrowly escaping detection washed over me, but the urgency of the moment snapped me back to reality.

"We need to find out what that package is," I said, my voice steady now with determination. "Whatever it is, it's vital."

He nodded, his expression serious as he looked me in the eye. "But first, we need to get a better vantage point. We can't just eavesdrop on these guys forever."

"Agreed," I replied, a plan beginning to form in my mind. "There's got to be a way to follow them without getting caught."

Just then, the distant sound of laughter and clinking glasses from the gala drew my attention, a stark reminder of the world outside our hidden bubble. I glanced at him, determination sparking in my chest. "If we can blend back into the crowd, we can follow them discreetly."

"Right," he said, his expression softening for a brief moment. "You're brilliant. Let's go before we lose them again."

We slipped back through the door and into the opulence of the gala, the lights blinding after the darkness of the alcove. The lively chatter and festive atmosphere felt almost jarring, a reminder that behind the masks of joy lay a treacherous game being played out.

Scanning the room, I caught sight of the two men, their backs turned to us as they made their way toward a staircase leading up to the second level. My heart raced with a mix of fear and exhilaration. "There!" I pointed subtly, and he nodded, slipping into step beside me as we maneuvered through the crowd.

"Just act normal," he murmured, the edge of a smile tugging at his lips. "If you can manage that in this chaos."

"Normal is overrated," I shot back, my tone light, though I could feel the tension creeping back in. "Let's just keep our eyes on the prize."

As we made our way toward the staircase, I felt a sense of urgency building within me, each step echoing my heartbeat. We rounded a corner, and the men vanished through a set of heavy double doors at the top of the staircase.

"Now or never," he said, and we pressed forward, the ornate doors looming before us like a gateway to unknown dangers.

"Just remember," I said, my voice low, "we can't let them see us."

With a deep breath, we stepped through the doors, and the world shifted yet again. The atmosphere was thick with anticipation, the air buzzing with the energy of possibilities. Before us lay a dimly lit hallway adorned with portraits of stern-looking figures whose eyes seemed to follow our every move.

"Look at this place," he said, glancing at the walls. "Talk about intimidating."

"More like an old-school horror movie set," I replied, my pulse quickening as we continued forward. The walls were lined with velvet, and every creak of the floorboards felt like a shout in the silence.

Suddenly, the sound of hurried footsteps approached from the far end of the hall, and panic surged again. "They're coming!" I whispered urgently, my heart pounding in my chest.

"Quick! Hide!" he ordered, and we ducked into a side room just as the figures rounded the corner.

Inside, darkness enveloped us, and I pressed my back against the wall, barely breathing as we waited. The voices grew louder, and I strained to hear through the door.

"They can't get away," one of the men said, his voice dripping with urgency. "Not now, not when we're so close."

"Then we find them. No more mistakes." The second voice was filled with menace, making the hair on my arms stand on end.

Just as I thought we might be able to slip away unnoticed, I heard a loud crash echo through the hallway, followed by shouts of alarm.

"Get them!" someone yelled, the sound reverberating through the air like thunder.

"We need to move!" he urged, grabbing my hand and pulling me deeper into the darkness of the room.

Before I could respond, the door swung open, and the silhouette of a man loomed before us, his eyes glinting like a predator's in the dim light.

"Found you," he growled, and the world tilted on its axis as everything around me shattered into chaos.

Chapter 20: A Tipping Point

The sun dipped low on the horizon, casting long shadows across the cracked pavement of our small town. A vibrant mix of oranges and purples smeared the sky, but all I could see were the swirling doubts and fears that clouded my mind. I stood in the middle of the street, the air heavy with a tension that felt palpable, as if the universe itself was holding its breath, waiting for the moment I would finally confront the truth buried deep within my heart. My pulse raced, echoing the distant rumble of thunder, the storm inside me more tempestuous than the brewing clouds above.

This was it. The tipping point. The culmination of every whispered secret, every sideways glance exchanged at family gatherings, every moment when my heart hesitated, caught between loyalty and love. The confrontation I had dreaded for so long was upon me, and my feet felt like lead, refusing to budge from the spot where I'd found myself, staring down the man who had both intrigued and terrified me. Ethan stood a few paces away, his expression a blend of determination and uncertainty, just as torn as I was. The gentle breeze tousled his dark hair, the fading light illuminating the worry lines etched on his forehead.

"Are you sure about this?" he asked, his voice low and steady, betraying none of the chaos I felt swirling in my chest. The earnestness in his eyes felt like a lifeline, yet the pull of the past was a shadow that loomed large, threatening to engulf us both.

"I have to be," I replied, the weight of the words heavier than I anticipated. Each syllable seemed to hang in the air, an anchor tethering me to a truth I had avoided for too long. I took a deep breath, inhaling the scent of impending rain mingled with the bittersweet aroma of fallen leaves. "If we don't confront this now, it'll haunt us forever. We can't run from what's been set in motion."

Ethan's jaw tightened, the storm of emotions reflected in his gaze. I could see the conflict brewing within him—a battle between the heart he had entrusted to me and the heritage that threatened to tear us apart. "You know what's at stake," he said, his voice barely above a whisper. "This isn't just about us. It's about our families, the history that binds us, and the legacies we carry."

Those words echoed in my mind, a haunting reminder of the ties that chained us to a past riddled with animosity. Our families had been at odds for generations, a feud steeped in misunderstandings and old wounds that never healed. The night my mother revealed the secrets of our lineage felt like a death sentence, an unshakable curse that loomed over me. I could see the specter of my father's disapproval, hear the echo of my mother's warnings about Ethan's family, the very people I had come to care for.

"Do you think I chose this?" I shot back, my frustration spilling over. "Do you think I wanted to fall for you, knowing everything that's happened between our families? But I can't deny how I feel about you, Ethan. I won't."

The silence that followed was thick, heavy, as if the very air we breathed had become suffocating with the weight of unspoken words. I could see the muscles in his jaw flex as he processed my admission, and I could feel the divide widening between us, a chasm formed by centuries of bitterness.

Just as I thought we were on the verge of a breakthrough, a figure emerged from the shadows—my brother, Caleb, his presence as unwelcome as a storm cloud on a sunny day. He sauntered toward us, hands shoved deep into his pockets, the casual bravado of his demeanor starkly contrasting with the tension that enveloped me. "What's this? A little family reunion?" he quipped, a sardonic smile playing on his lips.

"Caleb, not now," I snapped, irritation slicing through my nerves like a sharpened knife. His arrival was like a wet blanket on a fire, dousing the flicker of hope I had kindled within myself.

"Right, because it's a great time for deep talks about love and legacy," he retorted, arching an eyebrow. "You both think you can just ignore what's looming over us? You really believe that whatever bond you have can withstand the storm?"

Ethan's gaze flickered to me, a silent plea for understanding. I could sense the storm of conflict brewing in the space between my brother's words and Ethan's heart, a clash of ideals threatening to spill over. "This isn't just about our feelings, Caleb," Ethan interjected, his voice rising with unexpected intensity. "This is about breaking the cycle. About choosing something different."

Caleb's laughter was cold, a sound devoid of warmth. "Break the cycle? You think that's possible? The blood that runs in our veins is laced with the bitterness of our ancestors. You both can pretend all you want, but this—" he gestured broadly, indicating the town that felt more like a prison than a sanctuary, "—this will always pull you back."

"Enough!" I shouted, the weight of my frustration surging to the surface. "You're not hearing us! We want to find a way to heal the past, to reconcile these differences. But we can't do it if you keep throwing up walls. Don't you want to stop the fighting? To break free from this?"

Caleb's expression shifted, confusion etching lines into his youthful features. For a moment, the bravado cracked, revealing the boy who had been my protector, my confidant, before the shadows of our families' disputes had turned us into adversaries. "You really believe that's possible?" he asked softly, vulnerability seeping through the cracks of his bravado.

"Yes," I replied, my heart racing with a fierce determination. "And I believe in us—Ethan and me. We can find a way. But you need to let go of this anger. We can't face our greatest enemy if we're fighting amongst ourselves."

The storm was no longer just outside; it was raging within me, churning with fears and hopes. I felt the weight of the choices before us, the looming shadows of our legacies, and the sheer enormity of what it meant to stand against our families' histories. But in that moment, I knew one truth: I was ready to face whatever came next.

The silence that followed my outburst was a brittle thing, hanging in the air like the thin fog that clung to the early mornings of fall. I could see the wheels turning in Caleb's mind, the way his brow furrowed with confusion and uncertainty. I had always admired his steadfastness, the way he had shielded me from the harsh realities of our family's tumultuous past. But now, his silence felt like a gaping chasm, a rift that could swallow us whole if I didn't bridge it quickly.

"You think you're going to change anything by standing here, all lovey-dovey with him?" Caleb finally replied, his voice laced with incredulity. "You're just asking for trouble. Look at where we are." He gestured to the cracked pavement and the shadows stretching long behind us, the dying light revealing a town steeped in memories, most of them painful.

I turned to Ethan, whose expression mirrored the turmoil within me, and we both instinctively took a step closer to each other. "We're not pretending," I said, my voice firmer now, a hint of resolve igniting the embers of our shared determination. "This isn't about avoiding trouble. It's about facing it together. I won't let fear dictate my choices anymore."

Caleb's laugh was sharp and devoid of humor. "And what if facing it means putting your life in danger? What if that means getting hurt? Do you think I'm going to just stand by while you play house with the enemy?"

"Stop calling him that!" I shot back, the frustration bubbling over. "Ethan isn't the enemy. Our families are the ones who've dragged us into this ridiculous feud! This isn't a game of sides. We can't change history, but we can decide how we move forward."

For a fleeting moment, I saw something shift in Caleb's eyes—a glimmer of understanding, perhaps a flicker of hope. "You really think we can rewrite the narrative?" he asked, his voice softer now, more open.

"Absolutely," I said, my heart racing with a mix of fear and exhilaration. "We have to start somewhere, Caleb. It begins with us."

Before he could respond, a low rumble of thunder echoed in the distance, and I could almost feel the ground shift beneath us. The storm was drawing closer, much like the storm of emotions swirling around us. A flicker of lightning illuminated the sky, briefly casting us in stark relief against the encroaching darkness. I shivered as the chill in the air whispered of impending change, a reminder that we were standing on the precipice of something monumental.

"Look, I know this is messy," Ethan interjected, his voice steady but laced with urgency. "But we're talking about breaking a cycle. If we don't try, we'll always be prisoners of our family's past."

Caleb's expression hardened again, the walls I thought we had started to dismantle reassembling with every word. "And what if it costs you everything? What if you end up losing each other?" His gaze darted between us, filled with a mixture of anger and concern.

"Then it'll be a risk worth taking," I replied, my voice rising above the gusting wind that had started to swirl around us, bringing with it the scent of rain and the promise of change. "I refuse to live my life in fear. If we have to fight for what's right, then so be it. Together, we're stronger."

The wind howled, almost as if it were responding to my declaration. The trees around us rustled violently, their leaves whispering secrets, urging me on. But in the distance, I could see dark figures approaching, shrouded in the mist and fog of the gathering storm. A familiar knot twisted in my stomach, not just from the fear of who might be coming but from the realization that time was slipping away, and our moment of truth was drawing near.

"Speak of the devil," Caleb muttered under his breath, his gaze locking on the figures as they emerged from the shadows.

I followed his gaze and felt a jolt of panic. The air crackled with electricity, a warning of the confrontation that was imminent. Ethan stepped protectively closer to me, his arm brushing against mine, grounding me in the chaos of the moment. The figures resolved into sharp relief, and my heart sank as I recognized the unmistakable faces of my parents, flanked by a couple of Ethan's family members, all of whom looked ready to ignite a firestorm.

"We should leave," Ethan said, urgency creeping into his tone as he took my hand, attempting to pull me away from the impending confrontation.

But my feet felt rooted to the ground, my heart thudding heavily in my chest. "No, we can't run. We need to stand our ground." I was astonished at the strength in my own voice, the confidence that had sprung from a place I didn't know existed within me.

"Stand your ground?" Caleb echoed, incredulity in his voice. "You're not serious! They'll tear you apart!"

"They might try," I countered, determination burning in my chest. "But I refuse to be scared of them anymore. I'm tired of running, Caleb. If this is how it ends, then let it be here, on our terms."

As they approached, the air thickened with hostility, and my parents' faces were storm clouds brewing with disapproval and fear. My mother's expression was a mix of anger and disbelief, her eyes narrowing as they fell on Ethan and me. "What is going on here?" she demanded, her voice cutting through the charged atmosphere like a blade.

"We were just talking," I said, a fierce protectiveness surging within me. "About our future, and the possibility of breaking free from the past."

"Talking?" my father scoffed, his tone laced with disdain. "This is not the time for discussions that threaten our family's honor!"

Caleb stepped forward, an unexpected ally in this moment of conflict. "And what if it's our honor that needs redefining? You can't keep dragging us into this feud. It's time to stop the fighting."

The tension in the air shifted, coiling tighter as my parents exchanged glances, uncertain of how to respond to Caleb's challenge. For a moment, the world fell silent, and I could feel the weight of every choice we had made hanging in the balance. I held my breath, waiting for the storm to break.

"Enough!" my mother said, her voice rising above the wind, a sharp crack that demanded attention. "You have no idea what you're playing with. The consequences of this foolishness will haunt you all."

With those words, I felt the ground shift beneath my feet, the reality of our families' legacies crashing down upon us like an avalanche, threatening to bury us in its weight. The storm was here, both in the sky and within us, and I could only hope that amidst the chaos, we would find the strength to confront our greatest fears together.

The air felt electric, charged with an intensity that sent shivers down my spine as I faced the growing storm of our families' combined wrath. The standoff was like standing on the edge of a precipice, the wind howling around us, threatening to sweep us into the abyss. My heart pounded in rhythm with the thunder that echoed ominously in the distance. As my mother's words hung in the air, their gravity was impossible to ignore. This was no longer just a matter of personal choice; it was a family legacy on the line, and the stakes had never been higher.

"Mom, this isn't about honor," I said, my voice trembling slightly but laced with determination. "It's about breaking free from a cycle that has chained us for far too long. You and Dad taught me that love is stronger than hatred. So why can't we put this behind us?"

My father's face contorted in disbelief, as though my words were a foreign language he couldn't quite grasp. "You think you can just rewrite history? Our families have been enemies for generations! Do you think Ethan's family will suddenly decide to embrace you because you have a crush on their son?"

"Crush?" Ethan shot back, indignation flaring in his eyes. "You think this is some fleeting infatuation? I'm here because I care about her, and I believe we can do better than what our families have given us."

"Care?" my mother scoffed. "You don't know what it means to care. You're blinded by emotions that could lead to destruction."

"Blinded? Or perhaps seeing clearly for the first time?" I retorted, a mix of frustration and hope surging within me. "You both taught me that love is worth fighting for. Why can't we do that for ourselves?" The words spilled from me like an overflowing dam, fueled by a newfound resolve that felt both exhilarating and terrifying.

The gusts of wind picked up, swirling around us, as if the elements themselves were caught in our emotional tempest. I could see Caleb shifting uneasily, caught in the crossfire, his loyalty torn between his family and his sister. He opened his mouth to speak, but the thunder roared overhead, drowning out his words.

My mother stepped forward, her gaze piercing, her voice low and dangerous. "You think this is a game? You don't understand the consequences of your actions. If you pursue this path, you will not only bring ruin upon yourself but on our entire family."

Ethan's grip on my hand tightened, his resolve matching mine. "If we allow fear to dictate our choices, we'll lose ourselves. Isn't that what you're afraid of? Losing the very people you claim to protect?"

A flicker of uncertainty crossed my father's face, but it vanished as quickly as it came. "You're too young to understand the depths of this conflict. You're idealizing something that doesn't exist."

"Or maybe I'm realizing that you've been the ones trapped in the past, not me," I said, a flash of rebellion igniting my words. "I refuse to let your bitterness decide my future."

At that moment, I saw the crack in my parents' armor. The storm around us seemed to hold its breath, the sky darkening ominously. I could feel the weight of my words settle heavily among us, as if the universe itself was weighing the truth of what I had said.

A sudden bolt of lightning illuminated the scene, casting stark shadows across our faces. In that brief flash, I caught a glimpse of something deep within my mother's eyes—a flicker of fear mingled with concern. Just then, a shrill voice broke the charged silence, slicing through the air like glass shattering.

"Is this a family reunion or a melodrama?" The voice belonged to my cousin, Clara, who had approached with a group of friends, her perfectly manicured nails tapping impatiently on her phone. "You all look like you're auditioning for a soap opera. What's the crisis this time?"

Clara's casual demeanor contrasted sharply with the tumult of emotions swirling around us. My mother's expression soured as she recognized her daughter's intrusion, while my father struggled to maintain his stern façade.

"Clara, this is not the time," my mother snapped, her tone sharp enough to cut.

"Oh please, I just came to see if we were finally going to get some excitement around here," Clara quipped, her eyes gleaming with mischief. "But it looks like you're just talking in circles. If you want to have a real fight, at least make it interesting."

I felt a surge of annoyance wash over me. "This isn't a game, Clara. You wouldn't understand what's at stake here."

"Maybe not," she retorted, a playful smirk forming on her lips. "But you're all acting like you're in some sort of epic showdown. Who knew family drama could be so entertaining? Just think of the ratings!"

Ethan stifled a laugh, but it broke through the tension like a ray of sunlight piercing dark clouds. "You should consider a career in theater," he said, a teasing glint in his eyes. "You've got the flair for it."

Clara tossed her hair over her shoulder, unbothered by the growing hostility. "Thanks, Ethan! But seriously, are we just going to stand here like this, or are we going to figure out what's going on?"

"Enough!" My mother's voice sliced through the banter, returning us to the storm of emotions swirling between our families. "This is not the time for jokes. You need to leave, Clara. This is a matter for the adults."

Caleb, sensing the shifting tides, took a step forward. "If we're all adults here, then maybe we should start acting like it." His gaze darted between Ethan and me. "Maybe we should find a way to resolve this without tearing each other apart."

A low rumble of thunder echoed overhead, as if nature itself echoed my brother's plea. "And how do you propose we do that?" my father asked, skepticism heavy in his voice. "Do you really think any of this will change just because you want it to?"

"I don't just want it," I said, raising my voice to cut through the doubt that lingered. "I need it. We need it. If we can't overcome our differences, we'll be left with nothing but ashes."

Just as I thought we might make a breakthrough, the ground beneath us began to tremble slightly, a warning that something was approaching, something more dangerous than the storm looming above.

Caleb's eyes widened, and the look of concern on his face ignited my own anxiety. "What now?" he muttered, glancing around as if expecting the earth itself to swallow us whole.

And then, from the depths of the gathering darkness, a low growl echoed, deep and menacing. The sound reverberated through my bones, freezing me in place. A creature emerged, shadows stretching across the ground as it stepped into the dim light, revealing itself in stark detail. My heart raced as the realization washed over me—this was no mere storm; it was a harbinger of chaos.

Ethan pulled me closer, his expression shifting from determination to sheer dread as the creature advanced, its eyes glinting with a hunger that sent a chill racing up my spine. "What is that?" he breathed, the air thick with a mix of fear and disbelief.

The growl intensified, echoing off the trees as if the very fabric of our world had begun to tear apart at the seams. My family, once embroiled in our own battles, now faced a new, monstrous threat that demanded our united strength.

And as the storm raged overhead, I realized with dawning horror that this confrontation would be unlike any we had faced before—one that could unravel the very bonds we fought so hard to forge.

Chapter 21: Shadows at Dusk

The sun dipped low on the horizon, casting long shadows that danced across the cobblestone streets of Eldermere. As I stood at the edge of the town square, the weight of our recent battle settled heavily on my shoulders. The scent of damp earth mingled with the sweetness of late blooms, yet the beauty felt like a cruel joke against the chaos we had just endured. A week had passed since the confrontation that had altered the course of our lives, and I still felt the chill of its aftermath, wrapping around me like a shroud.

I took a deep breath, inhaling the mingled aromas of fresh pastries wafting from Clara's bakery, my favorite place in town. The promise of warmth and sugar tugged at my senses, a brief escape from the tempest of emotions swirling within. I pushed open the door, the familiar chime welcoming me with a comforting jingle. Inside, the soft glow of fairy lights strung haphazardly overhead created a cocoon of warmth, casting a golden hue on the cheerful decor. Clara, with her ever-present apron dusted in flour, looked up and offered a smile that felt like a balm on my troubled heart.

"Just in time! I made your favorite," she called, her voice bright with genuine enthusiasm. I found solace in her uncomplicated joy, a stark contrast to the shadows lurking at the edges of my mind. I stepped forward, the wooden floor creaking beneath my feet as I approached the counter where a plate piled high with cinnamon rolls awaited me, their sticky sweetness glistening like a promise of comfort.

"Do you ever tire of spoiling me?" I teased, unable to hide the smile creeping onto my lips. Clara rolled her eyes playfully, brushing a stray lock of hair behind her ear.

"Never. You're my best customer. Besides, I need to keep you plump and happy if you're going to help me fend off the competition." Her laughter rang out, light and melodic, but the truth of my heart lay just beneath the surface, ready to break free.

I accepted the warm roll, the dough soft against my fingers, and took a bite. The sweetness melted on my tongue, a reminder of simpler times when worries felt far away. But the momentary reprieve shattered as thoughts of him invaded my mind—him, with his dark eyes that sparkled like the midnight sky, holding secrets and shadows. Each smile he offered felt like a sword that cut deeper into my doubts.

"Where's Aidan?" I asked, glancing around as if his presence might magically materialize amid the flour and sugar. Clara's expression shifted, her brow furrowing slightly as she stepped back to prepare a fresh pot of coffee.

"He's been... preoccupied," she said, the hesitance in her voice echoing my own uncertainty. "You know how he is when things get heavy. He likes to retreat into that broody shell of his." Her eyes softened, a mixture of concern and understanding dancing within them.

I nodded, pushing down the flicker of unease that ignited at the thought of his solitude. Aidan had always been the strong one, the beacon that guided me through the darkness. But even beacons could flicker, and I feared that the weight of our shared past might snuff out his light completely.

"Maybe I should go find him," I mused aloud, though my heart pounded at the prospect. Clara's hand gently squeezed my shoulder, a silent encouragement that rooted me in place.

"Give him time," she urged softly. "You've both been through so much. Sometimes, it helps to let the dust settle." I appreciated her perspective, but the unsettling feeling within me remained, clawing at my insides like a restless beast.

I finished my roll in silence, savoring the last sweet morsel, but my thoughts drifted to the shadows that loomed in our lives. We were rebuilding, yes, but each brick felt precarious, a balancing act teetering on the edge of uncertainty. The scars we bore were not just from the fight; they were etched into our souls, whispered reminders of what we had lost and the fragility of what remained.

As I stepped back outside, the fading light cast a surreal glow over the square, the twilight deepening the colors and enhancing the warmth of the buildings surrounding me. I hesitated, drawn between the safety of Clara's world and the call of the unknown beyond. Aidan had taken to wandering the woods since that fateful day, seeking solace among the trees, and a part of me knew I couldn't let him face those shadows alone.

I made my way to the edge of the forest, where the path twisted and turned, leading into the depths of the trees. Each step resonated with the echo of my heartbeat, a reminder of the uncertainty I felt. The soft rustle of leaves underfoot filled the air, mingling with the distant call of night creatures awakening from their daytime slumber.

"Aidan!" I called, my voice trembling slightly in the cool evening air. The sound seemed to dissolve into the shadows, swallowed by the encroaching night. I pressed on, determined, my senses heightened. The forest felt alive, each whisper of wind a secret carried just out of reach, teasing me with the promise of understanding.

And then, like a ghost rising from the depths of my fears, he appeared. Aidan stood just beyond a cluster of trees, his back turned to me, shoulders tense under the weight of his thoughts. The moonlight caught the contours of his silhouette, transforming him into a figure of stark beauty, yet I could feel the distance stretching between us, a chasm filled with unspoken words and lingering pain.

"Aidan," I breathed, my heart racing as I approached. He turned slowly, his eyes reflecting a myriad of emotions, all swirling in the depths of that dark gaze. I yearned to bridge the gap, to reach out and pull him back into the warmth of the light we had once shared, but I hesitated, unsure if he would welcome me or push me away.

"Why are you here?" he asked, his voice a low rumble, both welcoming and guarded. It was the question I had anticipated, yet I felt as though the weight of my response could tip the balance of everything we had fought for.

"Why are you here?" Aidan's voice pulled me back from the edge of my swirling thoughts. His gaze was a storm of emotions—part guarded, part desperate, but always piercing. I could feel the cool air pressing in around us, wrapping the moment in a delicate tension that crackled like static electricity before a storm.

"I came to find you," I replied, trying to keep my voice steady as I stepped closer. The gap between us felt insurmountable, yet the urgency of the moment pushed me forward, my heart beating wildly against my ribs. "You've been gone for days. I thought... I thought you might need company."

"Company," he echoed, the word laced with a hint of bitterness that stung like a bee. "Or distraction? I know you don't want to face what happened." His eyes narrowed slightly, a flicker of vulnerability hidden behind that mask of indifference. I wanted to reach out, to cup his cheek in my palm and remind him that he didn't have to shoulder this burden alone. But the distance he maintained was a fortress, built from fear and pain, and I felt like an outsider trying to breach the walls.

"Are you really going to pretend that nothing has changed?" I shot back, my frustration bubbling to the surface. "We almost lost everything, Aidan. You think I can just gloss over that?"

The muscles in his jaw tightened, the tension radiating from him like heat waves. "I'm not pretending," he said, his tone low but sharp. "I'm just trying to process it all. And I don't want you caught up in my storm."

"Too late," I retorted, crossing my arms defiantly. "I'm already drenched, thank you very much." The corner of his mouth quirked up, a brief flash of amusement that momentarily broke through the heavy air. It felt like a crack in the armor he had built around himself, and I seized the opportunity. "Look, we can't keep avoiding this. If we want to rebuild, we need to talk. Really talk."

He glanced away, his gaze drifting toward the treetops where the last remnants of daylight flickered like dying embers. "You don't understand," he murmured, almost to himself. "This isn't something that can just be talked out. I can't let you be pulled into my darkness."

"Then let me pull you into the light," I urged, my voice softer, a plea woven through the strength of my words. "Aidan, we fought for each other. We can't just abandon that now, not when it's needed most."

Silence stretched between us, thick and heavy, the kind that could suffocate or set you free, depending on how you approached it. I took a step closer, and the tension seemed to shift, swirling like leaves caught in a gust of wind. "You're not alone, you know. I'm right here, even if it feels like the world is collapsing around you."

His expression softened, the tension in his shoulders easing just a fraction. "I don't want to drag you down with me," he said, almost in a whisper, his eyes searching mine for the truth of my words. "You deserve so much more than this."

"Don't you dare tell me what I deserve," I shot back, an unexpected fire igniting within me. "You think I'm some delicate flower that will wilt at the first sign of trouble? I'm right here, standing in front of you, ready to fight. Together."

He exhaled a breath he'd been holding, the tension flickering like a candle's flame in a draft. "Together," he repeated, the word tasting foreign yet familiar on his lips. "That's the thing. Together means sharing burdens, and mine feels like it might crush us both."

"Then let's figure it out," I replied, my resolve firm. "What happened wasn't just your fight. It was ours. And I won't let you carry that alone."

Aidan shifted his weight, his posture slowly transforming from defensive to contemplative. He studied me for a moment, as if weighing the depth of my resolve against the weight of his burdens. I could feel the air around us thickening, heavy with unsaid words and shared pain.

"Okay," he finally said, his voice steadying. "But promise me you'll be honest. This isn't going to be easy."

"Since when has anything between us been easy?" I countered with a smirk, trying to lighten the mood, even as my heart fluttered with apprehension. "Let's dive into the messy, shall we?"

His lips curled into a reluctant smile, a flicker of the warmth I had missed. "Alright then, let's start with the fact that I nearly lost my head back there. I can still hear their voices echoing in my mind, the taunts and threats, the darkness closing in."

I stepped closer, my heart racing as I placed a hand on his arm. "It's okay to be scared. I am too. But we survived, Aidan. That means something."

"Does it?" he asked, his gaze drifting to the ground. "I keep wondering if we made the right choices, if any of this will haunt us forever."

"I don't have all the answers," I admitted, feeling the truth of my words resonate between us. "But I do know this—whatever we faced, we did it together. That counts for something, doesn't it?"

His gaze met mine, and in that moment, the distance between us began to dissolve, replaced by something more tangible. "You're right," he conceded, the weight of his anguish lifting just slightly. "We're stronger together, even if it means facing the shadows."

"Then let's confront them," I encouraged, my voice steady. "You don't have to face this darkness alone, and I won't allow you to push me away again."

With a deep breath, Aidan squared his shoulders, a flicker of determination igniting in his eyes. "Okay. Let's do this. But first, can we at least move a little closer to the fire?"

"Fire?" I raised an eyebrow, surprised. "I was thinking more along the lines of hot cocoa and blankets, but sure, let's face the fire if that's what you want."

"Now you're talking," he replied, the corners of his mouth twitching upward.

As we turned back toward the heart of the forest, the shadows receded, giving way to the flickering light of a small campfire crackling in the distance. The warmth promised a sanctuary against the chill of the encroaching night. The flames danced, mirroring the rise and fall of our emotions as we stepped closer, hand in hand, ready to confront whatever lay ahead. The shadows might linger, but together, we could carve out a path through the darkness.

The fire crackled to life, sending sparks spiraling into the night like miniature stars rebelling against the darkness. I sank onto a log beside Aidan, feeling the heat radiate against my skin, its warmth a sharp contrast to the cool evening air. The glow flickered across his face, illuminating the lines of worry etched there. It was comforting and terrifying all at once—the light could reveal our truths or cast us into deeper shadows.

"What now?" he asked, leaning forward slightly, his gaze fixed on the flames. "Do we just sit here and pretend that everything's fine?"

"Pretending is not exactly my forte," I replied, a smile creeping onto my lips despite the heaviness in my chest. "So, no, I won't pretend. We both know we have a lot to unpack."

He nodded, still staring into the fire, and I could almost see the gears turning in his mind. "Where do we start?"

"Let's talk about what's haunting you." I hesitated, my own heart beating faster at the thought of his pain. "I mean, we can't just let it fester like an old wound, right? It's better to rip off the Band-Aid."

"Did you just compare my emotional trauma to a bandage?" he shot back, a half-smile breaking through his serious demeanor.

"I think it's an apt metaphor," I quipped, feigning innocence. "Nothing like a little humor to lighten the mood."

His laughter echoed against the trees, rich and deep, momentarily drowning out the crackling of the fire. It felt good, as if we were pushing back against the shadows, if only for a moment. But as the laughter faded, the tension returned, heavy as a storm cloud.

"I guess it's time to confront the mess," Aidan said, his smile slipping as he turned serious once more. "What I faced out there—it wasn't just physical. It's everything. The fear of losing you, the shadows that seem to linger even in daylight."

My heart ached at his admission. "You're not going to lose me," I reassured him, leaning closer, the warmth of his body seeping into my own. "We're stronger than this. Remember? Together."

"Together," he repeated, but I could hear the doubt lingering in his voice like a ghost haunting a forgotten house. "What if I can't keep it together? What if I become a liability?"

"Then we'll figure it out," I said, determination igniting within me. "We'll create a new plan, a new path. You're not a liability; you're my partner. And partners don't bail at the first sign of trouble."

"Speaking of trouble," Aidan said, shifting his weight, his expression shifting as he glanced back toward the dark forest. "What if the shadows come looking for us?"

My heart skipped a beat at the thought, a chill creeping up my spine despite the fire's heat. "We'll be ready for them," I replied, though uncertainty gnawed at the edges of my confidence. "We can't let fear dictate our choices. We need to stand our ground."

Aidan studied me, his gaze piercing, and I could see the flicker of doubt beginning to fade. "You're right. We've come too far to let it all slip away. But I need to know you're sure about this."

"Absolutely," I affirmed, leaning in, our foreheads nearly touching. "You're stuck with me, Aidan. I'm not going anywhere. Even if it means fighting against the shadows together."

He let out a breath he hadn't realized he was holding, the tension easing ever so slightly between us. "Alright then. Let's make a pact. No secrets. No hiding. We face whatever comes together."

"Deal," I replied, a fierce light igniting in my chest. "Now, about those shadows..."

Before Aidan could respond, a rustle came from the edge of the woods. We both froze, the warmth of our moment dissipating as quickly as the smoke rising from the fire. The dark trees loomed ominously, their branches swaying as if whispering secrets to one another.

"Aidan?" I whispered, my voice barely above a breath. "Did you hear that?"

"Yeah," he replied, shifting into a more defensive posture. "Stay behind me."

I wanted to argue, to insist that I could hold my own, but the moment demanded seriousness. We both peered into the darkness, straining our ears to catch any further sounds. The forest was alive with the gentle rustling of leaves and distant calls of night creatures, but the unsettling feeling lingered, a thick, cloying presence that felt all too familiar.

"Maybe it's just a deer," I offered, trying to lighten the mood, though my heart raced with trepidation.

"Or maybe it's something worse," Aidan countered, his voice low and tense. He turned slightly, scanning the perimeter, and I caught a glimpse of his worry flaring back into life. "We should prepare for anything."

I nodded, adrenaline surging through my veins, heightening my senses. "What do you want to do?"

"Grab a few sticks," he instructed, his voice steady as he reached for a nearby fallen branch. "We can use them to defend ourselves if we need to. Just in case."

The crack of twigs beneath my fingers felt oddly reassuring as I collected makeshift weapons, the firelight casting an eerie glow on the dark forest beyond. My heart raced not just from fear, but from a flicker of excitement; the adrenaline was intoxicating, pulling me closer to Aidan as we prepared to face whatever awaited us.

Suddenly, a figure emerged from the trees, stepping into the light. My breath caught in my throat, and I clutched my makeshift weapon tightly, heart hammering wildly. It was a woman, her silhouette cloaked in shadows, her features obscured by the night.

"Who goes there?" Aidan shouted, stepping in front of me protectively, his branch raised like a sword.

The woman raised her hands in a gesture of peace, but the tension in the air was palpable. "I'm not here to fight," she said, her voice steady and calm, a stark contrast to our panicked hearts. "I came to warn you."

Aidan and I exchanged glances, a mix of confusion and curiosity swirling between us. "Warn us about what?" I asked, stepping closer, ready to hear what she had to say but fully aware of the danger that lingered in the darkness behind her.

"There are forces at play, shadows gathering, and they're looking for you," she replied, her eyes glinting with an intensity that sent a shiver down my spine.

"Looking for us?" Aidan echoed, his grip tightening on the branch, the protective instinct flaring anew. "Why?"

She stepped closer, her expression grave, the firelight revealing hints of urgency in her demeanor. "Because you've something they want—something powerful that you don't yet understand."

I exchanged a wary glance with Aidan, my heart pounding in my chest. "What are you talking about?"

Before she could respond, a loud rustling erupted from the woods behind her, followed by a guttural growl that echoed ominously through the trees.

"We need to move," she urged, her voice rising above the cacophony. "Now."

The night had grown darker, the shadows swirling closer, and with it, an undeniable sense of dread filled the air. I glanced at Aidan, his expression mirroring my own fear, and in that moment, we both realized that the true battle was only just beginning.

Chapter 22: The Edge of Tomorrow

The sun hung low in the sky, casting an amber glow that bathed the world in a warm embrace, as if nature itself conspired to soften the harsh edges of our impending confrontation. I stood at the threshold of our family home, the weathered front door creaking slightly as I pushed it open, a sound reminiscent of the whispers and secrets that had seeped into the walls over the years. Each step inside felt like stepping into a time capsule, the scent of vanilla and aging wood wrapping around me like a comforting shawl, even as the anxiety coiled tightly in my stomach.

"Are you ready for this?" My sister Lila's voice broke through my reverie, laced with a mix of concern and a touch of defiance. She stood beside me, arms crossed, her dark hair pulled back into a fierce ponytail that matched the fire in her eyes. Lila had always been my fiercest ally, but today, as we prepared to confront our parents, the weight of the moment pressed heavily upon us both.

"I was born ready," I replied, forcing a confident grin, though I could feel the tremor beneath my bravado. The walls felt alive, as if they were eavesdropping on the generations of unspoken grievances that had accumulated here. The dust motes floated lazily in the golden light, but the tension in the air was palpable, charged with the electricity of unsaid words.

With a deep breath, we stepped into the heart of our home. The living room was a tapestry of faded photographs and mismatched furniture, each piece holding its own story, a record of family gatherings and moments of laughter that had dimmed under the weight of betrayal. I could see my mother's prized ceramic vase perched precariously on the mantel, a relic from happier times, when family dinners didn't feel like a battlefield.

As if sensing our arrival, the kitchen door swung open, and my mother stepped in, her hands floury from kneading dough, her apron speckled with remnants of whatever she had been baking. She looked up, her expression shifting from surprise to cautious warmth, as if trying to decipher our intent before the words even left our mouths. "Girls! I didn't expect you two to drop by. Are you hungry? I just made cookies."

"Not hungry for cookies, Mom. We need to talk," I said, the resolve in my voice surprising even me. Lila's presence beside me bolstered my courage, and I felt the warmth of our shared history wrap around me, giving me the strength I needed.

My mother's brow furrowed, a look of confusion washing over her features. "Can it wait? I've had a long day." Her words hung in the air, a dismissal that sent a ripple of frustration through me.

"No, it can't wait. We need to discuss what happened with Dad and the... the lies," I pressed, each syllable steeped in the tension that had simmered for too long. The mention of our father's deceit was like throwing a match into a pool of gasoline, igniting a firestorm of emotion.

At the sound of our father's name, the kitchen fell silent. My mother's hands trembled slightly as she set the dough down, and I saw the flash of something—fear, perhaps—cross her face. "Your father has had his challenges," she began, her voice low and defensive, but I interrupted her.

"Challenges? Mom, he lied to us. He's been lying to everyone for years. How can we just brush that aside?" The words spilled out before I could contain them, the urgency clawing at my throat.

Lila stepped forward, her eyes fierce. "We deserve the truth. We're tired of living in a shadow. It's time to shed light on the darkness."

A silence stretched between us, heavy and suffocating. My mother's face, usually so composed, crumpled under the weight of our accusations. "You don't understand the full story," she whispered, and I could see her struggle, caught between the love for her husband and the reality of his actions.

"No, we don't. And that's the problem," I retorted, a sharp edge to my voice that felt both empowering and regretful. "We've been kept in the dark long enough. You need to tell us everything."

Her gaze dropped to the floor, and I watched as she wrestled with her silence, as if unearthing memories buried beneath layers of denial and protection. Finally, she spoke, her voice trembling. "Your father had his reasons—reasons I hoped you would never need to know."

I stepped closer, my heart pounding in my chest. "What reasons could possibly justify deceit? What reasons could explain the pain he's caused us?"

My mother looked up, her eyes glistening with unshed tears. "He wanted to protect you. From the truth, from the hurt."

"But it's our hurt, isn't it?" Lila's voice was steady, unwavering. "We can handle the truth. What we can't handle is being treated like children who can't bear the burden of reality."

The air crackled with the unspoken tension, and I could feel the weight of the moment pressing down on all of us. My mother took a deep breath, her shoulders lifting as she straightened. "Alright," she said softly, the fight fading from her posture. "If you truly want to know, I will tell you."

As the words hung in the air, a sudden rustle came from the hallway, and my father appeared, wiping his hands on a kitchen towel, a look of apprehension etched on his face. The atmosphere shifted, thickening with unresolved issues and past grievances, and I felt the walls of the house seem to close in around us, a claustrophobic echo of the life we'd built within it.

"Is everything alright?" he asked, his voice laden with a mix of concern and feigned nonchalance.

"Not yet," I muttered under my breath, preparing myself for the storm that was about to break. The moment had arrived, and there would be no turning back. As we stood on the precipice of revelations, I realized that this was more than just a confrontation; it was a chance to reshape our future, to redefine what family meant in the wake of betrayal. The stakes had never been higher, and I was determined to see it through.

In the hushed corners of the old family estate, the air was thick with the scent of polished wood and hidden grievances. As I stepped into the drawing room, I could feel the weight of history pressing down on us, a tangible reminder of all that had been swept under the ornate carpets. My heart raced—not just with the anticipation of what lay ahead, but with the understanding that today marked a pivotal moment for all of us. My family, a tapestry of secrets woven tightly over generations, needed to unravel, and I was determined to wield the scissors of truth.

"Can we just skip the pleasantries?" I blurted out, my voice surprisingly steady in the face of the impending storm. The room fell silent, eyes darting among one another as if weighing the gravity of my words. My mother, ever the diplomat, cast me a sharp look, her brow arched in that familiar way that suggested I was on the verge of mischief. "This isn't the time for theatrics, darling," she chided, smoothing her blouse with a practiced elegance.

But theatrics were the least of our worries. I could feel the restless energy buzzing like electricity as we gathered—each person a thundercloud ready to burst. "The theatrics ended when the last skeleton fell out of the closet, didn't they?" I shot back, my wit more a shield than a weapon. "Let's get to the heart of the matter." The tension crackled in the air, the kind of tension that feels like a live wire—dangerous yet exhilarating.

My uncle, the family's self-appointed arbiter of decorum, cleared his throat. "What is this really about?" he asked, his tone a mix of curiosity and irritation. "Are we going to air our dirty laundry in front of the entire clan?" He gestured vaguely to the others gathered—my cousins, my aunts, all of them perched on the edges of their seats, like birds ready to take flight.

"Air it? I'd prefer to wash it clean," I replied, the defiance surging within me like a tide. "I'm done pretending everything is fine while we all walk around in our perfectly curated facades. We need to confront what we've been avoiding."

"Such dramatic flair for a Tuesday," one of my cousins murmured, half-smirking, half-sympathetic. She always had a talent for cutting through the tension with a quip, and despite the gravity of the moment, her comment coaxed a reluctant smile from me. Humor was a rare gem in the rubble of our family dynamics.

"Dramatic flair is what's going to save us," I countered, locking eyes with my mother, who appeared to be weighing her options. "If we don't talk about our issues, they'll suffocate us. Isn't that what this gathering is about? To finally acknowledge that we're not just a family—we're a collective of unresolved issues?"

"Unresolved? Try a mountain of festering resentment," my uncle scoffed, crossing his arms. "You think we can just wipe the slate clean?"

"Yes," I replied, my voice steady. "I do. But it starts with accountability. Each of us has a role in this mess, and we all need to admit it."

Suddenly, the door swung open, and my brother stepped inside, his casual demeanor a stark contrast to the intensity of the conversation. "Hey, what did I miss?" he asked, plopping down on a plush chair with an easy grin, oblivious to the charged atmosphere.

"Only the fate of our family legacy," I said, raising an eyebrow.

He leaned back, folding his arms behind his head, as if preparing to hear a particularly engaging story. "In that case, I'm all ears."

I gestured him to join the fray, knowing that his laid-back attitude would either diffuse the situation or ignite it further. "We're discussing how to liberate ourselves from this suffocating web of secrets," I explained, watching as his grin faded into a more serious expression.

"Secrets? Those are the best parts of any family. Like the time Aunt Doris set the kitchen on fire during Thanksgiving," he quipped, but the seriousness of my expression urged him to reconsider. "Okay, okay. I see what you mean. But, how do we begin?"

"We start by acknowledging what's been hidden," I replied, my gaze sweeping the room. "What's that one thing each of us has kept under wraps, thinking it would protect the family? Let's unravel it."

The murmurs of uncertainty began to ripple through the group, a collective hesitation echoing my own internal turmoil. It was clear we all feared the fallout. But beneath that fear lay a flicker of hope—the possibility of a lighter burden, the chance for renewal.

"Let's not get too hasty," my mother interjected, her voice steady but laced with a hint of urgency. "We can't just bring everything to light without considering the consequences. Some secrets are meant to stay buried."

"But some secrets have been choking us for too long," I argued, leaning forward, my pulse racing. "Imagine what we could be if we weren't weighed down by the past."

An uneasy silence settled over the room, but beneath it, I sensed a shift. The tides of emotion began to ebb and flow, and I could almost see the collective resolve coalescing. "Fine," my uncle relented, his expression hardening. "Let's see where this leads us. But remember, some truths can be sharper than knives."

"Then let's wield them wisely," I said, emboldened by his acceptance. "Because the truth might hurt, but it can also heal."

As the conversation unfolded, we began to unearth our buried truths, revealing not just our mistakes but the moments of vulnerability that had shaped us. Each revelation was a jagged piece of a puzzle—painful, yet necessary. What emerged was not just a tapestry of secrets but a portrait of resilience. And in that moment, as the sun dipped below the horizon outside, I felt the weight of generations shift ever so slightly, a promise of change fluttering in the air like the leaves caught in a gentle breeze.

The night wore on, filled with laughter and tears, a chaotic blend of emotions that, against all odds, began to stitch us back together. With each story shared, each hidden facet brought to light, I could sense the strength of our bond growing anew. Perhaps this was the beginning of a new legacy—a family willing to confront their shadows rather than flee from them. The edge of tomorrow beckoned, and I was ready to step forward into the unknown.

With the tension of earlier conversations still crackling in the air, the atmosphere in the drawing room had shifted, transforming into something unexpectedly vibrant. Each person seemed to carry the weight of unspoken truths, their expressions wavering between defiance and vulnerability. I could almost hear the clamor of thoughts colliding, battling against the long-standing traditions that had held us captive for far too long.

"I suppose we should start with the big one," I suggested, leaning back in my chair as if preparing for a thrilling dive into deep waters. "What's the most shocking secret you've kept from us?"

My mother's eyes darted around the room, her discomfort palpable. "Oh, dear. This sounds like a game of charades gone horribly wrong," she remarked, half-joking, but the gravity in her voice betrayed her attempt at humor.

"More like a family therapy session without the awkward couches," I retorted, my resolve firm. "But hey, no one said healing had to be comfortable."

Uncle Gerald shifted in his seat, his brow furrowed as he contemplated the weight of my suggestion. "I suppose I can start," he said slowly, his voice low and measured. "I once borrowed a significant sum of money from your grandfather and never paid him back. I thought it was just for a couple of months, but...well, time slipped by."

A ripple of murmurs washed over the room, shock painting every face. "That's quite a revelation, Uncle," I said, half-suppressing a laugh. "Did you think he wouldn't notice?"

"Of course he noticed!" Gerald's cheeks flushed crimson. "But he loved to play the benevolent patriarch, showering us with gifts while quietly resenting the favors he never received. I didn't want to hurt him, so I let it slide."

"And that's the crux of our family, isn't it?" I leaned forward, eager to peel back more layers. "Always avoiding confrontation, letting resentments fester until they explode. Who's next?"

Aunt Flora cleared her throat, her delicate fingers twisting the silver ring on her finger. "Fine, I'll go," she declared, her voice quivering slightly. "You all deserve to know that I have never truly forgiven your mother for that time she accused me of stealing her boyfriend in high school. It was all a misunderstanding, but she made it seem like I was a homewrecker."

Gasps filled the room, and my mother's face fell, the color draining from her cheeks. "Flora, that was decades ago!" she protested, her indignation barely masking the guilt that bubbled to the surface.

"Doesn't matter," Flora replied, her eyes glistening. "You may have moved on, but that moment shaped my whole life. I lost friendships, trust—"

"Enough!" My brother interrupted, slamming his palm on the table. "This isn't a courtroom drama, but it sure feels like one. We're supposed to be healing, not digging up every painful moment."

The tension swelled, thickening the air until it felt nearly suffocating. "Healing means addressing the wounds, not just bandaging them," I shot back. "What's the point of pretending we're perfect when the truth is so much messier?"

As we continued this delicate dance of revelations, the room became a cacophony of emotions—sorrow, laughter, regret. It was cathartic and exhausting. When it finally quieted, it was my cousin, Mel, who spoke next. "Alright, I'll throw my hat in the ring," she said, leaning forward, her fiery spirit sparking like a match. "You want the truth? I'm the one who caused the car accident last summer that left Grandma's car in a ditch."

Gasps erupted once more, and I caught the frantic glances exchanged between my family members. "But that's not all," she continued, undeterred by the shockwaves she was sending through the room. "I didn't tell anyone because I thought it was my fault. I was speeding, lost control, and she was lucky to walk away. I didn't want anyone to look at me like I was a reckless fool."

"Why wouldn't you tell us?" my mother asked, voice wavering with hurt. "We could have helped you."

"Helped me?" Mel shot back, her eyes narrowing. "You would have thrown me under the bus to save face, like you always do! That's the real issue here, isn't it? We're more concerned with appearances than the people we actually are."

Silence blanketed us, thick and heavy. It was in that moment I realized we were all tethered together by not just blood, but our unshakeable failures and fears. "We've let our insecurities dictate our relationships," I said softly, breaking the standoff. "We've all suffered, and it's time to lay it bare. No more hiding. No more pretending."

As I scanned the room, seeking signs of agreement, the atmosphere shifted again, and a sudden knock on the door shattered our moment of fragile connection. The sound reverberated ominously, a stark contrast to the intimate confessions we'd just shared.

"Who could that be?" my mother whispered, her eyes wide with a mixture of curiosity and dread. The soft murmurs that had filled the room fell to a hush, replaced by a palpable tension, as if we all instinctively sensed that this interruption was more than mere chance.

"I'll check," I volunteered, my heart racing for reasons beyond mere apprehension. I walked to the door, every step feeling heavier than the last. With a deep breath, I turned the handle and pulled it open.

Standing on the threshold was a figure cloaked in shadows, features obscured by the dim light. The air turned electric as the stranger's eyes locked onto mine, a glint of something fierce flickering within them. "We need to talk," they said, voice low yet commanding, slicing through the uneasy silence like a knife.

"Who are you?" I managed, the question tumbling from my lips as if grasping for something solid in this sea of chaos.

But before they could respond, a flicker of recognition ignited in my brother's eyes, and a shadow of dread passed over his face. "No," he murmured, taking a step back, as if the figure standing before us was a specter of our past—someone who could unravel everything we had just begun to mend.

"What do you want?" I asked, the words barely escaping my throat, the reality of our family's fragile peace hanging in the balance. The air crackled with anticipation, and in that moment, it felt like the ground beneath us had shifted irrevocably.

Chapter 23: Healing Wounds

The sun hung low in the sky, spilling its golden warmth over the small town of Willow Creek, where the air smelled faintly of pine and the last hints of summer clung stubbornly to the edges of autumn. The rustle of leaves echoed the whispers of a changing season, and I reveled in the delicate balance of beauty and turmoil that life had become. Each step I took along the familiar path felt like a journey back to myself, a route lined with memories that beckoned with both joy and sorrow.

It was on this afternoon, draped in a light shawl of nostalgia, that I found myself wandering into Gilly's Café, a quaint little spot that had always felt like home. The walls were painted in warm hues, adorned with local art, each piece telling a story I longed to hear. The aroma of freshly brewed coffee swirled around me, mingling with the sweet scent of cinnamon rolls cooling on the counter. I could hear the gentle clinking of cups and the laughter of patrons; it was a comforting symphony of everyday life.

"Hey, Willow!" called Gilly, the café's owner, a sprightly woman with curly hair that danced around her shoulders. She wiped her hands on her apron and flashed a grin that could light up the dreariest of days. "What'll it be today? Your usual?"

I grinned back, my heart lifting at the sight of her. "You know me too well. I'll take a large black coffee and one of those cinnamon rolls. They smell like heaven."

As I settled into my usual corner, a cozy nook bathed in sunlight, I allowed myself a moment to breathe. The chatter around me faded into a gentle hum, and I closed my eyes, soaking in the warmth of the sun on my skin, letting the world slip away for just a heartbeat. It was during these small moments of solitude that I could feel the remnants of my past flicker like fading embers. My relationship with Jake was still healing, each day a new chapter we navigated together, and while I often stumbled through the complexities of our shared history, I also felt the unmistakable thrill of newfound hope.

Just as I began to sip my coffee, relishing its rich bitterness, the bell above the door chimed. I turned, and there he was—Jake. He looked just as I remembered, with tousled dark hair that seemed to defy gravity and an easy smile that could melt glaciers. My heart raced unexpectedly, fluttering like a wayward bird.

"Fancy seeing you here," he said, his voice smooth and teasing as he sauntered over to my table. He pulled out a chair and plopped down without waiting for an invitation, a grin playing on his lips. "I thought you'd be off wrestling with your latest design."

I rolled my eyes playfully. "You know how it is. Sometimes, a girl needs a break from the chaos of fabric swatches and design plans." I couldn't help but smile back at him, feeling the tension from the week dissolve in the presence of his playful banter.

"I get it," he said, leaning back with a relaxed confidence that made the space between us feel electric. "A little coffee therapy never hurt anyone."

"Especially when it's paired with Gilly's cinnamon rolls," I replied, gesturing toward the plate piled high with the sweet, sticky pastries. "Care to join?"

He raised an eyebrow, a hint of mischief dancing in his gaze. "Only if you promise not to steal all the icing this time."

I laughed, a genuine sound that echoed through the café. "No promises there, buddy."

As we chatted, the conversation flowed effortlessly, a familiar rhythm that felt both comforting and exciting. We discussed everything from the quirks of the townsfolk to our dreams of the future. I watched as he animatedly recounted a recent mishap at the hardware store involving an errant can of paint and a very startled cat, and my heart swelled with affection for the man across from me.

There was something invigorating about seeing him laugh, the way his eyes sparkled with mischief.

But beneath the laughter, I sensed the shadows of our past lingering, always threatening to intrude. The wounds of our previous conflicts had not completely healed; they were merely scabs, not yet forgotten. The mention of my father's lingering disapproval or Jake's family troubles had the potential to darken the moment, and I could feel the weight of those conversations hovering like clouds on the horizon.

"Willow," Jake said, his tone shifting slightly as he leaned closer, the warmth of his presence making my heart flutter. "I've been thinking about us... about everything. You know I'd do anything to make this work."

My heart clenched at the vulnerability in his voice. I wanted to reassure him, to remind him of the strides we had made, but a part of me hesitated. The thought of laying bare my own fears felt daunting. "I know, Jake. But we can't ignore the challenges we still face."

His expression softened, a mix of determination and tenderness. "I'm not asking you to. I just want us to tackle it together, you and me, like we always said we would."

In that moment, I felt an undeniable connection—a tether between us forged through shared experiences, laughter, and pain. The journey to healing wasn't going to be easy, but with him by my side, I was beginning to believe it might be possible. As we talked, the café buzzed around us, but it felt like we were in our own world, a bubble of warmth and potential that I never wanted to burst.

"Then let's do it," I finally said, my voice steady. "Let's face everything together. No more running away."

He nodded, his gaze locked onto mine, the weight of unspoken promises hanging in the air. "Together, then," he echoed, and in that simple exchange, I felt a flicker of hope ignite, illuminating the shadows that had once loomed so heavily over us.

The warmth of his hand brushed against mine, a spark of electricity that sent shivers up my arm, grounding me in this moment. As I looked into his eyes, I saw a future filled with laughter, adventure, and the potential for something deeper than I had ever imagined. In the vibrant tapestry of our lives, I knew we could stitch together a new narrative—one rich with color, complexity, and, most importantly, love.

The sun dipped below the horizon, casting a warm amber glow that wrapped around Willow Creek like a comforting embrace. The café was slowly emptying as patrons drifted off to their evening routines, but Jake and I remained at our table, lost in the ebb and flow of conversation. The air thick with laughter, we ventured into deeper territory, weaving through the delicate intricacies of our lives, uncovering layers long buried beneath old wounds and misunderstandings.

"Okay, I have to know," Jake said, leaning forward with a conspiratorial grin. "If you could redesign your life like one of those home makeover shows, what's the first thing you'd change?"

I chuckled, toying with the sugar packet in front of me. "Honestly? I'd probably knock down the wall between my work and my personal life. Just a total demolition. Bring in all the light!"

He laughed, the sound rich and infectious. "Good plan! Then you could just throw out the stress with a sledgehammer. Or maybe even a wrecking ball."

"Exactly!" I grinned back, feeling the ease between us. "And let's not forget an open concept for all my brilliant ideas—something like a sunroom where creativity can just flow freely."

Jake raised an eyebrow, teasing me with a smirk. "I can already see it now. Willow's Ideas Unleashed: an exhibit of crazy sketches and questionable color choices."

"Hey, those questionable color choices are part of my charm," I shot back, pretending to be affronted. "What's your first change, then? A full remodel of the Jake library?"

He laughed, and I watched the shadows dance across his face as he considered. "I think I'd turn my garage into an art studio. You know, a place where I could unleash my inner Picasso."

I snorted, leaning back in my chair. "Right! I can see it now: all those abstract paintings, a splash of color here, a catastrophe there."

He raised his glass of water, feigning a toast. "To chaos! It's where the magic happens."

Just then, the door swung open, and in walked Sylvia, the town's self-proclaimed 'Queen of Gossip.' With her perfectly coiffed hair and an air of dramatic flair, she was impossible to miss. I felt a rush of anxiety ripple through me. Sylvia's gaze swept the room, landing directly on us, and I braced myself.

"Willow, darling!" she exclaimed, her voice dripping with sweetness that masked her sharp tongue. "How lovely to see you here with... oh, Jake! How interesting."

Jake straightened in his seat, a hint of amusement in his eyes, while I forced a smile, feeling the tension in my shoulders rise. "Hi, Sylvia. We're just catching up."

"Catching up, indeed!" She leaned closer, an eager spark in her eyes. "I hear whispers of romance blooming in the air. Care to share any juicy details?"

I shot Jake a glance, and he raised an eyebrow, an expression that suggested we were in for a rollercoaster of a conversation. "Well, it's not a scandalous affair if that's what you're hoping for," I said lightly, trying to steer the conversation into safer waters. "Just two friends enjoying some coffee."

"Friends?" Sylvia's voice was laced with disbelief. "Oh, sweetheart, I know what I see! You two have that spark—the kind that can ignite a wildfire!"

Before I could respond, Jake leaned back in his chair, a playful grin spreading across his face. "Well, if we're igniting wildfires, Sylvia, I hope you're ready with the fire extinguisher."

"Touché," she replied, feigning shock. "But seriously, Willow, you should be careful. You know how quickly things can change around here. One day you're the town darling, and the next... well, let's not delve into that. Just promise me you'll keep your wits about you."

As she turned to leave, I felt a mix of relief and annoyance. "Thanks, Sylvia, always a pleasure," I muttered, shaking my head as she sashayed out, leaving a trail of perfume in her wake.

Jake let out a chuckle, and I couldn't help but join him. "She certainly knows how to make an entrance," I said, rolling my eyes. "And exit."

"I think she just gave us our first unsolicited relationship advice," Jake replied, leaning forward with a teasing glint in his eyes. "What do you think? Should we take her sage wisdom to heart?"

"Oh, definitely. Maybe we should start a 'Willow and Jake's Relationship Survival Guide' complete with tips from Sylvia," I quipped, crossing my arms. "I can already see the cover: a picture of us running from the flaming chaos she's likely predicting."

"Sounds like a bestseller," he said, his laughter melding with mine, easing the tension that had started to creep in. "But seriously, Willow, are you okay with all this... attention?"

I took a moment, considering his question. "I'm learning to be okay with it. The truth is, I don't know what this is—what we are—most days. But I do know that I want to keep exploring it with you. Even if Sylvia thinks it's a wildfire waiting to happen."

His gaze softened, a mixture of admiration and understanding radiating from him. "I want to explore it too. Just promise me that if it ever feels like too much, we talk. No more running."

"I promise," I replied, my heart swelling with gratitude for his openness. "But we both know talking can get tricky."

"Only if we let it." His voice was steady, and I couldn't help but feel the unspoken connection between us deepen.

As the café lights dimmed, I glanced out the window to see the first stars beginning to twinkle in the twilight sky. The world outside was painted in soft blues and purples, and I felt a rush of hope sweep over me. This moment, the laughter we shared, the possibility of what lay ahead, felt like the beginnings of something beautiful.

We lingered a little longer, sharing stories, dreams, and silly anecdotes, our banter punctuated by comfortable silences. Each laugh we exchanged chipped away at the remnants of doubt lingering in the corners of my mind. It was a tentative dance, but with every step, I felt the strength of our bond growing, like roots intertwining beneath the surface.

As we left the café, the cool evening air kissed my skin, invigorating my senses. "What's next?" Jake asked, his hands sliding into his pockets as we walked side by side, our footsteps synchronizing on the quiet street.

"Let's go see the stars," I suggested, pointing toward the open field just beyond the town, where the sky stretched endlessly above, dotted with pinpricks of light.

"Sounds perfect," he said, the warmth in his voice igniting a spark of excitement within me. And so, hand in hand, we ventured into the night, ready to embrace whatever came our way—each star a reminder of the journey ahead, luminous and filled with potential.

The field stretched out before us, a canvas of shimmering grass illuminated by the moon's gentle glow. I could hear the soft rustle of leaves whispering secrets in the cool night air as we walked side by side, the weight of our earlier conversation slowly melting away. Jake's presence beside me felt like an anchor, grounding me in a world that often swirled with uncertainty.

"Do you ever think about what it would be like to just... leave it all behind?" he asked, breaking the comfortable silence that had settled between us. "Pack up and hit the road?"

I turned to look at him, surprised. "You mean like a modern-day Bonnie and Clyde? I'm not sure I'm ready to rob banks just yet."

He laughed, a sound that lit up the night. "Okay, maybe not that. But imagine the freedom! No one telling us what to do or where to go. Just the open road and whatever adventures await."

"It sounds tempting," I admitted, glancing up at the stars that twinkled like scattered diamonds across a deep velvet sky. "But I think I'd miss the little things. Like Gilly's cinnamon rolls. Or this." I gestured to the vastness of the night, the chill in the air a refreshing reminder of life's simplicity.

His eyes sparkled with mischief as he nudged me playfully. "Okay, so we can take Gilly with us. A portable café on wheels! Problem solved."

"Now you're just being ridiculous," I said, shaking my head, unable to suppress a grin. "But if we did have Gilly's cinnamon rolls on demand, I'd consider it."

As we reached the edge of the field, I spotted a cluster of trees silhouetted against the moonlight, their branches swaying gently. I felt a pull, a curiosity that nudged me forward. "Come on, let's see what's back there."

"Are you sure? It looks a bit ominous," Jake teased, his expression mock-serious. "I've read enough horror novels to know that's usually where things go wrong."

I chuckled, rolling my eyes. "You're not scared, are you? I promise I won't let any monsters get you."

"Right, because you're the resident monster slayer," he said, feigning bravery as he followed me into the shadows of the trees.

The air grew cooler as we stepped beneath the canopy, the world outside fading into a whisper. The leaves above rustled softly, creating an eerie melody that felt both magical and slightly unsettling. "What do you think is back here?" I whispered, my voice barely more than a breath.

"Probably a treasure map," Jake said, his voice dripping with sarcasm. "Or maybe a haunted swing set. I've always wanted to investigate creepy playgrounds."

I couldn't help but laugh at his antics, the tension from earlier moments dissipating like mist in the morning sun. "Okay, Mr. Adventure, lead the way. Just promise not to trip over your own feet."

As we ventured deeper into the grove, the moonlight barely filtered through the thick leaves above, casting intricate shadows that danced at our feet. Then, in the heart of the thicket, we stumbled upon a clearing bathed in silver light. The sight took my breath away.

At the center stood an ancient oak tree, its gnarled roots twisting dramatically around a large, weathered stone. Vines climbed its trunk like a lover's embrace, and small wildflowers peeked out from beneath the foliage, daring to bloom in the shadow of its magnificence. I felt an inexplicable pull toward it, as if the tree held secrets I was meant to uncover.

"Wow," Jake murmured, stepping closer, his hands tucked into his pockets as he took in the sight. "This is incredible. It feels... sacred."

"Exactly," I whispered, my heart racing as I approached the stone, tracing its rough surface with my fingers. "There's something special about it. Like it's been waiting for someone to find it."

"What do you think it is?" he asked, his curiosity piqued. "Some ancient relic? A magic stone?"

I shrugged, my gaze still fixed on the stone. "Could be anything. Maybe it's a wishing stone! We should test it out."

He raised an eyebrow, his expression a blend of skepticism and amusement. "And how do we do that? Just stand here and hope for the best?"

I laughed, suddenly feeling light-headed with the thrill of the moment. "Okay, okay. Let's make a wish. On three?"

He nodded, amusement dancing in his eyes. "All right, but I'm not wishing for anything ridiculous, like world peace or the ability to fly. I'm keeping it realistic."

"Fine, just keep it simple," I replied, grinning. "Ready? One, two, three!"

We both closed our eyes and silently spoke our wishes, my heart pounding in my chest. I wished for clarity, for a future that felt less daunting. I could feel the energy of the moment wrapping around us, almost tangible, as if the world held its breath.

"Did it work?" Jake asked, opening his eyes. "Should we feel different now?"

Before I could respond, a rustling sound broke the tranquility of the clearing. I turned, scanning the shadows, my heart racing again. "Did you hear that?"

Jake's expression shifted, and he stepped closer to me, a protective instinct kicking in. "Yeah. I did. It sounded like—"

Suddenly, from behind the tree, a figure emerged, cloaked in darkness, just beyond the reach of moonlight. My breath caught in my throat as the figure stepped forward, revealing a familiar face etched with worry.

"Willow! Jake! You need to get out of here, now!"

It was Kyle, my brother, his eyes wide with urgency. The urgency in his voice pierced through the tranquility of the night, and a chill raced down my spine.

"What's going on?" I asked, confusion and concern mixing in my gut.

"There's no time to explain! Just trust me, we have to leave!"

I exchanged a glance with Jake, a silent understanding passing between us. The world had shifted, and the sense of safety we'd just felt evaporated into the night. My heart thudded painfully in my chest, the question lingering on the tip of my tongue. What danger was waiting for us, and what would we have to face to find out?

Chapter 24: A New Dawn

The morning sun stretched lazily over the horizon, its golden fingers brushing away the remnants of night, illuminating the world in a warm embrace. I stood at the edge of our little sanctuary, the air thick with the scent of dew-kissed grass and blooming wildflowers, every blade glistening as if adorned with tiny jewels. This place—our place—had become a tapestry woven with the threads of our shared laughter, whispered dreams, and the occasional, clumsy bickering over what to watch on Netflix. It was more than just a house; it was a sanctuary where love had rooted itself deeply, growing stronger with each passing day.

As I took a deep breath, inhaling the freshness of the morning, the cool breeze whispered secrets of change, hinting at the untold stories that awaited us just beyond the horizon. My heart raced with the possibility of what lay ahead, the thrill of the unknown mingling with a touch of apprehension. How often had I stood on the precipice of a new beginning, only to shy away from the leap? But today was different. Today felt like a promise, an unspoken pact that together we could weather any storm, face any challenge, and emerge on the other side, hand in hand.

"Coffee?" A voice, deep and soothing, wrapped around me like a warm blanket, grounding me in this moment. I turned, finding him leaning against the doorframe, the morning light casting a halo around his tousled hair. There was something delightfully disheveled about him, a charming contrast to the crispness of the day. He held a steaming mug, the aroma wafting toward me, stirring memories of countless mornings spent together, often tangled in each other's arms, laughter bubbling over as we argued about who would brew the coffee.

"Only if you made it strong enough to wake the dead," I quipped, stepping closer. His eyes sparkled with mischief, the familiar gleam that sent butterflies fluttering in my stomach.

"Ah, but what if that would just wake up the neighbors too?" He raised an eyebrow, a smirk playing on his lips. "I can't have them thinking we're running a caffeine circus over here."

I laughed, a genuine sound that bounced off the walls of our kitchen, filling it with warmth. It was moments like this—so mundane yet so extraordinary—that stitched the fabric of our lives together. There was magic in the ordinary, a beauty that thrived in our shared rituals, no matter how small. As I accepted the mug from him, our fingers brushed together, a spark igniting between us, and I was reminded of the depth of what we had built.

"To new beginnings," I said, raising my cup in a toast, the steam curling toward the ceiling like tiny, eager spirits. He mirrored my gesture, and we clinked our mugs together with a soft chime that felt like a promise—an echo of our shared determination to embrace whatever the future held.

He took a sip, his brow furrowing slightly. "What do you think? Is it too strong?"

"Perfectly strong," I said, my smile teasing the corners of my lips. "Just like you."

"Flattery will get you everywhere, you know," he replied, his tone playful, yet there was an underlying sincerity that warmed my heart. I watched as he leaned back against the counter, a relaxed posture that belied the tension we had both felt in recent months. Life had thrown challenges our way, moments that could have torn us apart, but instead, they had forged a bond that was unbreakable.

Outside, the sun continued its ascent, casting long shadows that danced playfully across the floor. I turned my gaze to the window, watching as the world came to life—the chirping of birds, the rustle of leaves in the gentle breeze, and the distant laughter of children playing. It felt like the universe was aligning, encouraging us to take that leap into the unknown, to embrace the chaos and beauty of life together.

"What's on your mind?" he asked, his voice pulling me from my reverie.

I hesitated, contemplating the myriad of thoughts swirling in my head. "Just... wondering what's next for us. This feels like a turning point, doesn't it? Like everything is finally falling into place."

He nodded, his expression thoughtful. "It does. I can feel it, too. Whatever happens, we'll figure it out. Together."

His words wrapped around me, a soothing balm against the uncertainties that loomed. The world felt ripe with possibilities, and I was determined to explore them, not just for myself, but for us. I took a sip of my coffee, the warmth spreading through me, igniting a spark of courage.

"How about we start with a road trip?" I suggested, a mischievous grin spreading across my face. "Just us, the open road, and whatever adventure finds us along the way."

His eyes lit up, and I could see the wheels turning in his mind, imagining the places we could go, the memories we could create. "Are we talking spontaneous detours or a carefully plotted route?"

"Spontaneous," I replied, leaning closer, my heart racing at the thought of our wild escapades. "We could just see where the wind takes us. Get lost, find ourselves, maybe even discover a new favorite diner along the way."

"You know me too well," he chuckled, shaking his head in mock resignation. "Alright, I'm in. But only if you promise to take the wheel sometimes."

"Deal," I said, sealing our pact with another clink of our mugs, a quiet agreement binding us to the road ahead, whatever it may hold.

As we settled into the familiar rhythm of our conversation, the worries of yesterday began to fade, eclipsed by the promise of tomorrow. The dawn was breaking, not just outside, but within us as well, ushering in a new chapter filled with love, laughter, and the kind of adventure that made our hearts sing. And as the sun rose higher, painting the world in hues of hope, I knew deep down that this was just the beginning.

The kitchen was alive with our laughter, a rich symphony that danced through the open windows, mingling with the soft sounds of the waking world. We had just finished breakfast, remnants of toast crumbs and coffee rings scattered like remnants of a cozy battle. I leaned back in my chair, savoring the moment—a stolen slice of time wrapped in warmth and familiarity. His eyes, a deep blue that mirrored the ocean, sparkled with mischief as he leaned closer, the sun casting a golden hue over his features.

"Okay, Miss Spontaneous," he teased, crossing his arms over his chest, the gesture so familiar yet endearing. "Where exactly do you propose we go on this grand adventure? Last I checked, the only thing out there was the grocery store and my mother's house."

I rolled my eyes, feigning exasperation. "You're such a pessimist. Can't you dream a little? I'm talking about hidden beaches, roadside diners with the best pie, and maybe a quirky town where we can explore antique shops full of treasures and oddities."

"Pie and antiques? Now you're speaking my language." He chuckled, and I could see the gears turning in his head, the promise of adventure sparking like fireworks behind his eyes. "But are we really equipped for this? Do we even have a plan?"

"Ah, plans are overrated. It's about the journey, not the destination. You can always count on the universe to throw in a few unexpected detours." I leaned in, lowering my voice as if sharing a great secret. "And think about the stories we'll have to tell!"

"Stories? More like a series of unfortunate events." He raised an eyebrow, clearly recalling our past misadventures, the time we had gotten lost in the city or when we mistook a trail for a shortcut only to end up knee-deep in mud. "I don't know if my nerves can handle more of your brilliant navigation skills."

"Hey now, I'll have you know that my navigation skills have improved," I protested, feigning indignation. "Besides, you always end up loving it when we get lost. That's when the best memories are made."

"True," he conceded, his smile softening. "And I can't deny the magic of those moments. Alright, I'm in. Just don't expect me to rescue you from any swamp monsters this time."

I grinned, the lightness of our banter weaving through my heart like a comforting thread. "No promises, but I'll take my chances if it means pie is involved."

We decided to set off after a hasty round of packing. The car was soon filled with essentials—snacks, a couple of blankets, and an eclectic playlist that promised an auditory journey as vibrant as the one ahead of us. I felt a thrill surge through me as we climbed into the car, the engine purring to life like a contented cat basking in the sun.

"Where to first?" he asked, glancing over at me with an excited grin.

"Surprise me!" I replied, tapping my fingers against the steering wheel as I pulled out of the driveway. "Let's let fate take the wheel—figuratively, of course."

With the open road stretching ahead, we cruised past the familiar landmarks of our small town. The bakery with its fragrant pastries, the park where we had shared our first kiss, and the tiny bookstore that smelled of old paper and forgotten tales—all reminders of the life we had crafted together. As we crossed the town line, the scenery began to shift, a patchwork of fields and rolling hills unfolding before us, the trees whispering secrets in the wind.

"This is more like it," he said, leaning back in his seat, eyes fixed on the landscape as it changed like a painter's palette. "The wide-open spaces, the promise of adventure. It's invigorating."

I turned to him, catching the light in his eyes, a spark that mirrored my own excitement. "You know, this is what life is all about—embracing the chaos and letting it sweep us away."

"Or letting you sweep us into another misadventure," he quipped, the teasing lilt of his voice making me laugh.

Hours melted away as we traveled, the sun casting playful shadows over the road. We sang along to our favorite songs, our voices blending harmoniously, though neither of us was winning any awards for our vocal talents. With each mile, the weight of the past began to lift, the shadows that had loomed over us dissipating like morning mist.

Just as I was beginning to think about where we might stop for lunch, I spotted a sign—"Quaintville: Home of the World's Largest Potato."

"Stop!" I shouted, barely able to contain my glee. "We have to check this out. A giant potato? That's not something you see every day!"

He hesitated for a moment, but the corners of his mouth twitched in amusement. "You really have a talent for finding the most bizarre attractions, you know that?"

"Bizarre is what makes life interesting!" I argued, my enthusiasm contagious. "Imagine the pictures we could take! Besides, it could be a good story for our future grandkids—how we drove hours to see a potato and ended up discovering the town's best-kept secrets."

With a resigned sigh, he relented, and I veered off the highway, excitement bubbling within me. Quaintville was exactly as its name suggested: charmingly picturesque, with flower-filled window boxes and old-fashioned lampposts lining the streets. The air was filled with the sweet scent of homemade pies, and I could almost hear the cheerful banter of townsfolk as they greeted each other with warmth.

We parked and made our way toward the giant potato statue, which loomed over us like a colossal, starchy guardian. It was painted a cheerful yellow, with a smiling face that seemed to beckon us closer. We took turns posing next to it, the absurdity of the moment causing us to erupt into laughter, the joy spilling over as I attempted to imitate its goofy grin.

"I must say, you pull off potato chic quite well," he remarked, snapping a picture as I posed dramatically.

"Thank you! I've always wanted to be a trendsetter," I replied, winking.

After our impromptu photo shoot, we wandered through the town, stumbling upon a local café that promised the best pie in the county. The moment we stepped inside, the aroma of freshly baked goods enveloped us, wrapping us in a warm embrace. The walls were lined with quirky art, and the cheerful chatter of patrons filled the air.

"Let's get a slice of everything," I declared, unable to contain my excitement as I surveyed the extensive menu chalked up on the wall.

"Your wish is my command," he said, grinning as we made our way to the counter, where an elderly woman with twinkling eyes welcomed us like long-lost family.

"What'll it be, darlings?" she asked, her voice thick with the kind of warmth that comes from years of serving up comfort food.

"Everything," I replied, my enthusiasm spilling over as I pointed to pie after pie. "And maybe a side of your famous coffee?"

"Wise choice," she said with a wink, and I felt an instant bond form, as if we were conspirators in this delightful escapade.

As we settled at a small table adorned with a vibrant tablecloth, the anticipation of our pie bounty bubbling between us, I glanced around, taking in the essence of this little haven. Here, life moved at a slower pace, where the chaos of the outside world felt far away, and every moment was to be savored.

Our plates arrived piled high with slices of pie—apple, cherry, chocolate cream, and even a bizarre but intriguing lavender pie that the woman insisted we try.

"Alright, moment of truth," he said, picking up his fork as if preparing for battle. "Let's see if this lives up to the hype."

With the first bite, my taste buds danced, and I could barely contain my delight. "This is heavenly!" I exclaimed, savoring the rich, flaky crust and the burst of fresh fruit.

He nodded, eyes wide in surprise. "Okay, you win this round. I think we've found our new favorite spot."

The conversation flowed effortlessly as we indulged, sharing dreams of the future, teasing each other about our quirks, and laughing over childhood stories that seemed more like fairy tales with each telling. Time slipped away, the sun moving steadily across the sky as we devoured slice after slice, our laughter ringing out like music.

But just as I thought we were settled into this slice of paradise, a commotion near the door caught my attention. A couple burst in, their faces flushed and animated, as if they'd just returned from an adventure of their own.

"Did you hear?" the woman exclaimed, her eyes alight with excitement. "There's a festival in town tonight! Music, dancing, and food trucks! We have to go!"

My heart skipped at the thought of the festival—a spontaneous gathering of laughter and celebration, a perfect addition to our impromptu day. I turned to him, my eyes wide with possibility.

"What do you think? Should we check it out?"

His expression mirrored my own enthusiasm, a thrill sparking between us. "Absolutely! This is exactly the kind of detour I live for."

We quickly paid our bill, the kind-hearted woman behind the counter waving us off with a smile, as if she knew we were about to embark on another adventure. As we stepped back into the sunlight, I could feel the pulse of excitement in the air, a prelude to the festivities awaiting us. The festival would be a kaleidoscope of sights, sounds

The moment we stepped into the bustling festival, it was as if the air transformed, thick with the scent of fried dough, barbecued meats, and the unmistakable sweetness of cotton candy. The atmosphere hummed with laughter, the chatter of festival-goers blending into an exhilarating symphony. Colorful banners fluttered above us, vibrant splashes of fabric that danced in the gentle breeze, inviting everyone to join in the celebration.

I felt an electric thrill pulse through me, the energy of the crowd igniting a fire within my soul. The sun dipped low in the sky, casting a golden hue over everything, and I could see the excitement mirrored in his eyes as he surveyed the scene.

"Where do we start?" he asked, a wide grin spreading across his face, the contagious joy wrapping around us like a warm hug.

"Let's check out the food trucks first," I suggested, the thought of sampling culinary delights making my mouth water. "Then we can find a spot for the music. I heard there's a local band playing tonight!"

As we navigated through the throngs of people, we exchanged playful banter, dodging children darting after balloons and couples holding hands, their smiles radiant. A group of teenagers juggled flaming torches nearby, drawing gasps of awe from the audience.

"Are we certain that juggling fire is a good idea?" he remarked, raising an eyebrow as we passed by.

"Only if you're not planning to join them. I can't afford to lose my partner in mischief to spontaneous combustion," I teased, nudging him playfully.

"Oh, please," he replied with mock indignation. "I was practically born for the circus. Can't you see my natural flair for drama?"

I laughed, the sound blending into the cheerful chaos around us. We finally reached a food truck that promised gourmet grilled cheese sandwiches, the tantalizing aroma wafting through the air. After ordering a couple of sandwiches and a side of garlic fries, we settled at a small picnic table adorned with checkered cloth.

"I can't believe we're eating grilled cheese at a festival," he said, taking a giant bite, the cheese gooey and perfect. "Life really knows how to surprise us."

"Just think of it as our gourmet experience," I replied, grinning. "This is the kind of luxury I aspire to."

As the evening unfolded, the sun began to set, painting the sky in hues of pink and orange. The music started, a local band strumming their guitars, the rhythms beckoning people to the makeshift dance floor that had formed in front of the stage.

"Come on! We can't sit here all night!" I exclaimed, abandoning the remnants of our meal and pulling him toward the crowd, my heart racing with the beat of the music.

"I'm not a dancer, you know," he protested, but his eyes sparkled with anticipation, and I could tell he was more than willing to join in on the fun.

"Since when have we ever let that stop us?" I shot back, my enthusiasm uncontainable as I dragged him into the throng.

Once surrounded by the music and the thrumming energy of the crowd, the world around us blurred into a vibrant haze. We swayed, laughed, and spun, losing ourselves in the rhythm, each beat reverberating in our chests. As the music enveloped us, the worries that had lingered like shadows melted away.

After a particularly energetic song, we collapsed onto a nearby bench, breathless and giddy. "Okay, I'll admit it," he said, wiping sweat from his brow. "That was actually fun."

"Fun? Just fun?" I teased, nudging him with my shoulder. "I thought we were living our best lives out here!"

"Fine, it was exhilarating," he conceded, a genuine smile lighting up his face. "But only because I had you by my side."

"Now you're just buttering me up," I replied, feigning annoyance. "What's your angle?"

"Honestly? I just want to dance again." He winked, the playful glint in his eyes causing my heart to flutter.

As we sat there, lost in our playful repartee, I caught sight of a booth on the edge of the festival grounds, brightly colored and festooned with lights. "What's that?" I asked, pointing with curiosity.

"Only one way to find out," he said, standing up and offering me his hand. I took it, the warmth of his grip sending an unexpected shiver down my spine.

The booth turned out to be a fortune teller's tent, a deep crimson fabric draping down to the ground, giving it an air of mystery. A small sign read, "Curious? Find out what the future holds!"

"Should we?" I asked, half-laughing, half-intrigued.

He hesitated for a moment, then shrugged. "Why not? What's life without a little mystery?"

Inside, the air was heavy with the scent of incense, and dim lights flickered like distant stars. An older woman sat at a table adorned with crystals and tarot cards, her gaze penetrating yet inviting.

"Welcome, my dears," she said, her voice smooth like velvet. "What brings you to seek the whispers of fate?"

I exchanged a glance with him, excitement bubbling within me. "We're just curious," I admitted, my tone lighthearted. "What do the stars have in store for us?"

"Ah, the stars," she said, a knowing smile curling her lips. "They tell stories, you know. Each moment weaves a tapestry of possibilities. Sit."

We took our seats at her table, and she shuffled the tarot cards with a deftness that was mesmerizing. "Let me read your energies," she murmured, laying out three cards in front of us.

As she flipped the first card, the image of a sun blossomed into view, radiant and bright. "A sign of joy and success. You are on the right path," she stated, her eyes glinting with something deeper.

I beamed at him. "See? I told you today was a good idea."

The second card was more subdued, featuring a tower struck by lightning. "A warning. Change is coming, and it may be tumultuous. Prepare yourselves."

I felt my heart skip a beat, the lightness of the moment faltering. "What does that mean?" I asked, my voice barely a whisper.

"Only that the unexpected is often the catalyst for growth," she replied cryptically, her gaze locking onto mine with an intensity that sent a shiver down my spine. "And the third card..."

She flipped it over, and my breath caught in my throat. The image was dark, a figure cloaked in shadows standing at a crossroads. "Ah, choices," she said, a knowing smile playing at her lips. "Your path is not set in stone, and the decisions you make will shape your destiny."

Before I could respond, a loud crash erupted from outside the tent, reverberating through the air. The atmosphere shifted instantly, a tension tightening around us like a vise.

"Stay here," he whispered urgently, his expression morphing from playful to serious. "I'll check it out."

I nodded, my heart racing as he stepped outside. The fortune teller's eyes met mine, a flicker of concern dancing behind her calm demeanor. "Be careful," she murmured, her voice low.

Moments felt like hours as I waited, the air thick with uncertainty. Then, a loud shout rang out, followed by the unmistakable sound of chaos—a mix of startled gasps and hurried footsteps. My heart raced, and a sense of dread began to creep in.

"Everything okay?" I called out, but my voice was drowned out by the commotion outside.

Suddenly, he burst back into the tent, his expression grim. "We need to go. Now."

"Why? What happened?" I pressed, rising to my feet, my heart pounding.

"There's been an accident. A truck overturned nearby, and it's causing a panic. People are running everywhere."

My stomach churned at the thought of chaos spilling into our perfect day. "What do we do?"

"Follow me. We can get out through the back and find a safer spot," he urged, grabbing my hand tightly.

As we stepped into the thickening shadows of the tent, the echoes of panic grew louder, and the ground beneath us seemed to shift. Just as we reached the back exit, a piercing scream sliced through the air.

And then everything changed.